THE SILENT BRIGADE

The True Story of How One Woman
Outwitted the Night Riders

RON ELLIOTT

TURNER PUBLISHING COMPANY

TURNER PUBLISHING COMPANY

Turner Publishing Company Staff:
Publishing Consultant: Douglas W. Sikes
Designer: Herbert C. Banks II

Library of Congress Catalog Card Number:
95-62026
ISBN: 978-1-68162-227-9
Limited Edition.

The Silent Brigade is a nonfiction novel.

TABLE OF CONTENTS

DEDICATION

To My Mother
Eudelle Dawson Elliott
Who is a little like Mary Lou Hollowell

PREFACE

Politically and economically, the Silent Brigade made an impact which covered a wide area of the United States and touched thousands of lives, including such notable personages as President Theodore Roosevelt, Kentucky Congressman A. O. Stanley, and, of course, tobacco magnate James B. Duke. The tumult from the flat-lands of western Kentucky and Tennessee was heard by tobacco farmers all the way to North Carolina, politicians in Washington, and financial brokers on Wall Street in New York City. Those events have been copiously researched and recorded in the years since they occurred.

Overlooked in such works, however, are the emotions of the ordinary populace who were forced to bear the brunt of the night rider activities. This book details the activities and emotions of a few such people, some fictional and some real, including the Hollowell family who proved to be not quite ordinary. The reader is entitled to who and what is real and fictional.

Jimmy Singleton and Lorena Leeson are fictional characters, so all of their activities and relationships did not exist. They were created, however, to convey events that actually happened to someone. The incident of a boy being captured under the Nabb school and forcibly inducted into the Silent Brigade, for example, actually did happen. Adam Smoot, Josh Deaton, Norvell Hanks, and Mrs. Haynes are all products of my imagination. Robert, Mary Lou, and Price Hollowell were real people who did act (and react) as described. Mary Lou Hollowell did operate a boarding house in Princeton and I suppose she had boarders, but all presented here are imaginary. Every other character named in this book was an actual person who played the role depicted. Milt Oliver and Sanford Hall were Silent Brigade "traitors;" Wiley Jones was a former sheriff who operated the stable in Princeton; John Hollowell was Bob's brother; his wife, Lula, despised Mary Lou; and John Miller was the Hollowells' lawyer. All the persons named as defendants, attorneys, witnesses and the judge in the Hollowells' suits are the actual participants.

As for the events and places, the Association rally at Guthrie, the night rider raids on Princeton and Hopkinsville, the attack on the Hollowells and their ensuing odyssey, and the trials in federal court at Paducah all happened just as described. Jimmy's life in Caldwell County, Paducah and Princeton is, of course, fabricated.

The goal of this book is not only to entertain, but to present the factual history of the Silent Brigade in an accessible fashion. I am able to assure the reader that the events are described accurately because some of the people involved — most notably John G. Miller —did us the kindness of writing books to pass along their experiences, the courts kept records, and the newspapers reported the activities. From these sources, plus the scholarly works on the topic, I was able to gather an accurate picture of the events.

A frequently heard comment, "I hate history" leads me to agree that memorization of names and dates is one of the dullest of endeavors. When history is presented in that fashion it is, indeed, boring. On the other hand, when historical events are considered as the product of human emotions, history fascinates us because it makes us what we are and it causes us to wonder how we ourselves would react to a situation. The most fascinating aspect of any historical tale, I think, is the discovery that it happened to real, live, flesh-and-blood people. Bob and Mary Lou Hollowell were certainly that. I hope you enjoy their story.

Most books that published are the result of several people's efforts, and this one is no exception. Among those who participated with me in this project recognition is due to Jason Williams, John Snell, Harold McLaren, Bonnie Birkman, and Allan Elliot. My special thanks to Dr. Thomas D. Clark, who is, indeed, the fine gentleman that reputation has him.

Chapter 1

Tuesday, September 10, 1906

Panting from the long run up the dusty lane, I tried to yell, but no words came out of my mouth. All I could manage was the strength to pound on the screen door with both fists.

I heard someone rushing for the door from inside the house. "What's the matter?" Concern was etched on the man's face.

"Your barn's afire!" I managed to gasp between gulps of air.

A wide grin quickly replaced the look of concern. He opened the door and stepped out on the porch. "You ain't from around these parts, are you, son?"

I swallowed hard and inhaled deeply. "No sir, I ain't from hereabouts. But what's that got to do with all that smoke pourin' out of the barn yonder?"

His smile widened. "Catch your breath, boy." He waved me to a cane bottomed rocker. He sat beside me and placed a hand on the narrow board porch floor as he twisted to yell through the screen door. "Mary Lou, bring us some ice water out here." As he leaned away, the collar of his blue work shirt dropped to expose a shoulder the whiteness of which starkly contrasted with his neck. Likewise, the deep copper pigment of his forearms identified him as a man who spent many hours in the summer sun. Here in western Kentucky, he'd be a tobacco farmer.

My breathing had calmed to the point that I felt I might live after all. "You mean to tell me that your barn ain't burnin' to the ground?"

He smiled again. "No, son, it ain't. You don't know much about how we cure 'baccer here in the Black Patch, do you?"

"I reckon not. Up in Lincoln County, where I'm from, smoke means fire. When I seen all that smoke pourin' out of ever' crack in the barn, I thought sure it was afire. I run all the way up to the house here to tell you."

"Well, I 'preciate your tryin' to help," he said. "By the way, my name's Bob Hollowell." He extended his hand.

"I'm Jimmy Singleton," I said. "Happy to make your acquaintance."

The weakness in his grip surprised me as we shook hands. Although he was a big, strapping man, his hand felt like a three-days-dead fish. My pa always said that you could tell a lot about a man by his handshake. Despite the hard calluses on Bob's palm, this handshake conveyed some kind of weakness that I did not understand.

My heart had stopped drumming my ribs. The screen door swung open to reveal a sight that started it pounding afresh. A woman emerged from the house carrying a pitcher of ice water and three glasses on a tray. When she looked at me and smiled, I wondered that the ice in the pitcher didn't melt. She sat in the rocker beside Bob and placed the tray on a table.

"Jimmy," Bob said, "this here is my wife. Mary Lou, say hello to Jimmy Singleton."

"Hello, Jimmy." Her voice would have made an angel choir envious. She glanced up at me as she poured water into the glasses. The glow from her liquid gray eyes caused a burning sensation under my collar. "You look like you could use this," she purred, extending a full glass. The glass was covered with beads of perspiration and my neck was, too. I hoped her conclusion on my looks was due to the run up the lane rather than what her presence was causing inside me.

I accepted the glass with my left hand, using my right to tug at my shirt collar in an attempt to admit some fresh air to my burning chest. As I reached for the glass, my hand brushed hers. She smiled, seeming not to notice. As I could think of nothing to say, I gulped the water.

"Jimmy says he's from up around Stanford," Bob commented. "He run all the way up here from the big road just to tell us that the barn's on fire." He tried to contain a giggle, but failed. I was surprised that he'd know the name of my county seat town as Lincoln County was a good 200 miles northeast of here.

"Now, Bob," Mary Lou chided. "Don't be laughin' at the boy. He simply tried to do us a good turn." She tossed her head so that the sunlight filtered through her deep auburn hair, giving it a touch of red-dish-gold at the edge.

Bob assumed an apologetic pose. "I'm sorry, Jimmy. It's just that smoke pourin' from a 'baccer barn is such a common sight in these parts that we don't even notice it. Never fails, though, ever' fall, some stranger does the same thing you just did." He took a sip of water while his grin faded.

"We don't get many visitors 'way out here, though," Mary Lou said. "What are you doin' so far off the beaten path?" She was rock-ing slowly, her eyes focused on some faraway object.

"Well, to tell you the truth," I began hesitantly, "I kinda lost my way." I felt the flush of embarrassment creeping up my neck. They both burst into laughter, pushing my level of discomfort up another notch. Seeing the redness of my face, Mary Lou explained, "It'd pretty much go without sayin' that anybody that didn't come here on purpose was lost. This place ain't exactly on the way to anywhere." She paused for a moment, then asked the question I'd been dreading. "What in the world are you doin' out here all alone, anyway?" For the first time, her full attention was on my face. Her gaze imparted the same glow as the sun late on a fall afternoon.

In the three weeks since my parents had died, I'd managed to avoid telling the story, and I didn't want to tell it now. I suppose that a boy of my age, out wandering on his own, would have to answer some ques-tions, but still, the expectant silence hit me like a ton of bricks. As I hesitated, the stillness deepened. Fighting back my tears for the mil-lionth time, I began my tale. The words came slowly at first, but once the gates were open, the story poured out in a flood. As quickly as I could, I told the Hollowells about waking up in the middle of the night with the house on fire and how I'd watched my pa run back into the inferno trying to save Ma. Neither of them ever came out. I left out the part about how I'd run away from that damned orphanage, and slipped in a few lies where I thought it made the story sound better. I felt better once I'd said the words aloud.

When the words ran out, I rocked forward in my chair and let my head droop forward. The crickets chirping in the field enhanced the silence.

"Why you poor child!" Mary Lou arose and bent over to hug me. I realized that it was an act of Christian charity. Still, I could not help noticing how her breasts strained the fabric at the front of her dress as she leaned over me. I felt just a little guilty over such thoughts, but only just a little. Sixteen-year-old boys are like that.

"You'll stay to supper, then." Bob shot an approval-seeking glance at his wife.

"He'll spend the night, at least." She spoke matter-of-factly as she released me. The jasmine smell lingered even after she had moved away and the spots where her hands had touched me grew warmer rather than cooler. "I'll start supper," she said, moving quickly into the house.

For the next half hour Bob tried to entertain me to help dispel the gloom that had settled in. When he finally got back to farming, I remembered about the smoke pouring out of the barn.

"So, Bob, just how do you folks raise tobacco in this part of the world?"

Bob crossed his left leg over his right and gave a push to start the rocker. "Well," he began, "the growin' part ain't any different from what they do up in the Bluegrass region. You helped raise any 'baccer up there?"

"Sure have. What else can a man grow on no more land than most folks got?"

"Well, sir, I see that you understand the economics of 'baccer farmin'," he said. "Whenever it comes to a crop to put money in a man's pocket, 'baccer can't be beat, per acre of ground."

His use of "whenever" sounded a little strange to me, but I wasn't about to pass up a chance to display my knowledge of how to raise tobacco. "Yeah, and I know all about burnin' the ground to sterilize the plant beds before you sow the seeds in it, coverin' the bed with canvas to protect the plants, and then transplantin' them out into the field right after a rain, but what's all that got to do with the barn bein' afire?"

"All right." He smiled indulgently. "We'll skip the hoein' and suckerin' and toppin' and cuttin' and housin' for now." He gave a push with his foot to refresh the rocker's momentum. "Once the 'baccer's been cut and hung up in the barn — 'bout this time of year — that's where the smoke part comes in.

"What we grow hereabout is dark 'baccer. We call that stuff they grow up in the central part of the state 'white burly.' The soil and climate here in western Kentucky and Tennessee are better suited to the dark variety. That's why this area is called the Black Patch. Anyway, after it's cut and placed on sticks and hung up in the barn to cure, we build fires in trenches on the barn floor. All fall, we keep them fires goin' just enough to put out plenty of smoke. All that smoke filterin' up through the 'baccer gives it a flavor just right for snuff and cigars. 'Cause it's dark to begin with and 'cause of the smoking process, it's called 'dark fired 'baccer.'" Bob rocked contentedly.

"I never heard of no such. Sounds like they'd be a real art to that firin' business."

"You can bet there is." He allowed himself a self-satisfied smile. "Knowin' when to add more wood and when to cover the flames with sawdust and dirt is a trick of the trade. A man's got to use extry special care to keep the smoke level just right."

"I reckon I understand all that," I said. "And I guess I ought to feel a mite foolish for thinkin' the barn was burnin', but ain't there a fire hazard, really?"

"Yes, there is. It's not too dangerous at first while the 'baccer's still full of gum, but after it dries out some, somebody has to sit up all night in the barn to keep an eye on things. If a stick, or even one plant, falls, a man could lose a barn and a whole year's work right quick." He gave the rocker a fresh start.

"Sit up all night in the barn," I marveled. "Don't it get hot in there?"

Bob stopped in mid-rock. "Hot? I'll tell you 'bout hot. You see that mule lot yonder?" he asked pointing to a fenced plot a hundred yards south of the house. " Well, now, last summer, it was hot. I'd raised me a good crop of popcorn, and put it up in the crib there. Long 'bout, oh mid-September, I allow, that tin roof got so hot that the corn got to poppin' all by itself. It just kept poppin' 'til it filled the crib and then started overflowin'. Kept right on poppin' 'til the corn'd covered the whole lot three inches deep. That stupid mule I had in there thought it was snow and just naturally laid down and froze to death. Dumbest damn mule I ever owned."

Even though his face showed only a trace of a grin, I burst into laughter. Watching me, he laughed out, too. We laughed at each other laughing until tears streamed down both our cheeks. I didn't realize it at the time, but his story served its purpose. My sorrow was washed away on a wave of laughter, and we were both still chuckling when Mary Lou yelled that supper was ready.

Chapter 2

Monday, September 16, 1906

I stayed, all right. The morning after I got there, Bob told me that Mary Lou had decided that he needed some more help around the place, and that the job was mine if I wanted it. I'd started out with some vague idea about working my way down to the Mississippi to take up a life on the river. Now, I'd been offered a choice. The pick between river-boat gambler and hard work on a tobacco farm gave me some trouble, but stability won out. When I added in the opportunity of hanging around where a beautiful woman lived, the choice wasn't hard.

It might have been harder, though, if I had known what was going to happen. I didn't count on that beautiful woman moving out. That's right. Two days after I threw in with them, she and their eleven-year-old son, Price, packed up and moved to town. Their going didn't seem to upset Bob any. He said that Mary Lou wanted Price to get the best education he could, and if that meant he had to live a few miles away in Princeton, then that was the place for him. I guess the fact that the Nabb schoolhouse was a ten-minute walk up the lane didn't matter. Bob said they'd come back all right, next spring when school let out. To hear him talk, you'd think that a man living out on a farm while his wife ran a boarding house in town was the most natural thing in the world.

Another thing I didn't count on was that damned dark fired tobacco being so much hard work. Sure, I'd helped my pa raise burley up on the home place, but I didn't have to work so hard at it every day.

Only later did it occur to me that maybe Pa did. Anyway, the day after Mary Lou and Price left, Bob's two tenants, Steve Choate and Ned Pettit, showed up, and we went to work. We hitched up the mule and plowed the field where last year's crop had grown. The next day, we sowed it in wheat to cover it for the winter. Then, for the rest of the week, we cut hardwood trees to get wood to keep the firing process going and to heat the house. Bob, Steve, Ned, and I took turn-about sitting up all night in the barn. There wasn't much to do out there, just stay awake to make sure the barn didn't catch fire. Aside from that, a man could study on whatever he was a mind to. I studied on how beautiful Mary Lou was for a few nights, but I soon began to forget what she looked like. Then, I took to listening to the birds. This time of year, they were moving south for the winter, and I could hear them calling to one another at night.

On this particular Monday night, I hadn't been out there long enough to get real bored before I heard a lot of commotion up at the house. I ran out of the barn to see what it was all about. About 30 mounted men were gathering in the yard. I stuck to the shadows lining the lane until I got close enough to hear.

"Robert Hollowell! Come on out here. We want to talk to you," one of the men shouted. A light came on upstairs. Long minutes went by with no movement inside the house.

"Let's go in and drag his ass out here," a man yelled.

The leader of the group leaned back in his saddle. "No, he'll come out of his own accord." Then he yelled, "Bob, come on out here now."

The door opened a crack. "What do you want?" Bob's voice sounded weak.

The group's leader swung his leg over the saddle, dropped to the ground, and walked to the porch steps. "You know damn well what we want. Come on out here where we can see you."

The crack in the door widened a little. "I thought you called your-selves 'the Silent Brigade,'" Bob said. "You made enough noise to wake the dead."

"How the hell did he know that?" one of the men near me said. "I thought that name was one of our secrets."

"It's that damn woman of his," another answered. "She sticks her nose into everything."

The door opened wide, and Bob stepped out onto the porch. "John, why in hell do you boys have to come around roustin' a man out in the middle of the night?"

"It ain't the middle of the night, only a little past 10. Anyway, you know that we farm all day and can only visit at night." Most of the other men dismounted and formed a semicircle about the steps. Bob retreated a step toward the door as they approached the porch. "Bob, don't you think it's about time you joined the Association?"

"Now, John, you're my brother, and you know as well as I do how Mary Lou feels about your Farmer's Protective Association."

"Yeah, I do. But the fact is, we don't much care how Mary Lou feels about it." There were shouts of approval from the crowd. "You're aware that James B. Duke and his tobacco trust will starve us out if we don't stick together. Poolin' our 'baccer and holdin' out for a fair price is the only way we can fight him."

"I did all right for myself last year," Bob said with pride in his voice. He had his hand on the door knob as he spoke. "I got 12 cents a pound."

"And that's just, by God, why we're here," someone shouted.

John Hollowell turned and patted the air with a palm. "Calm down, boys," he said. Turning back to Bob, he went on. "Those of us in the Association averaged almost $7 a hundred pounds last year. Now, that's only a mite more than it costs to raise it, but that ain't the point. You know that Duke's Trust is in control of all the markets. If we don't hold out, they can make us take whatever they want to pay for our crops." Several voices in the crowd shouted agreement.

I thought about running down to the tenant houses and getting Ned or Steve. Ned's place was so far away that I figured that whatever was going to happen would probably be over before I could get there and back. Steve was simply too stupid to be of any help. I'd just have to do what I could by myself.

"If you and the rest of the hillbilly hold-outs will just throw in with the Association and put your 'baccer in our warehouse, we can put the shoe on the other foot — Duke'll have to pay us whatever we demand. He's got to buy 'baccer, and if we all stick together, there ain't no place else for him to get it." John's voice was almost pleading.

Bob paused a minute. "Well, I'll talk to Mary Lou about it."

John moved forward and placed one foot on the porch step. "Bob, you do that. You tell her that if you don't join, things is likely to get a mite rough. You tell her that we'd hate to see your barn catch fire some night. You tell her that we're having our annual rally over at Guthrie next week and that it'd be a good idea for y'all to come hear what the other growers have to say."

I heard one of the men nearest me say, "Most hen-pecked son of a bitch I ever saw."

"I wouldn't mind that hen of his peckin' around some on me," another laughed.

Bob's head wobbled on his neck, and I thought he was going to fall. I dashed out of the shadows and ran through the group of men. I bounded up on the porch to catch Bob. As I lit, he saw the movement and ducked inside the house. I don't think he knew it was me. I turned to face the group of men.

"All right now," I said as bravely as I could. "You've made your point. Go on and let us alone."

"You that waif what wandered up here to sponge off my brother's good nature?" John's voice was more gruff now.

"I'm workin' for ever' mouthful of food," I said, stepping toward him. He was a lot bigger than me, but with him on the ground and me on the porch, I towered over him. I tried to glare down into his face. "At least I ain't out threatenin' folks in the middle of the night."

John Hollowell glared at me for a long moment before he spun on his heel and mounted his horse. Wordlessly, the other men mounted and turned as a group. When they'd cleared the yard, I turned back to the door. "Bob," I whispered, "are you all right?"

The door opened slowly, and Bob poked his head out. He wasn't looking at me, but over my shoulder at the departing horsemen. His eyes were wide. "Jimmy, them night riders is gonna cause trouble. You mark my words. We'd best go talk to Mary Lou." He was shivering. Finally, when his gaze shifted to me, I guess the look on my face told him what I was thinking. He wrapped his arms about his chest and said, "Damn, it's cold out here." I thought he'd go on, but he just stood there, shivering although he was fully dressed.

It was only mid-September, and while the air was cool, it was far from cold. "Come on back to the barn with me," I said, taking his arm. "It'll be plenty warm in there, and you can help me keep an eye on things." I was thinking that the night riders might come back to carry out their threat, but I didn't say that. Bob allowed me to lead him to the barn.

"Jimmy, you think Mary Lou'd be up if we was to go to town?"

"No," I replied as we entered the barn. The heat did feel good. Maybe there was a little fear in me, too. "I'd allow it's pert nigh 11 o'clock by now — too late to go to town tonight." Despite the heat, he was still shivering as he sat, his back to a support pole.

"What was that all about?" I asked as I settled in beside him.

His eyes reflected the fire's glow as a dull red glare. He began to speak as if he were only partly aware of my presence. "It's a long story, son. 'Baccer prices have been fallin' for the last several years. They've tried to blame it on the bad economy, but the plain fact is it's the Duke trust that's forced prices down."

"I heard somebody mention that. What's the Duke trust?"

"There's only three buyers for dark fired 'baccer. The American Tobacco Company, the Regie, which buys for continental Europe, and the Imperial, which buys for Great Britain. A man by the name of James B. Duke has got control of all three of 'em, so he can just offer any price he wants. A man only gets one offer, and it's take that or eat the 'baccer.

"In response, the farmers started something they call the Association — it's got a big long name, but we just call it the Association — to fight back. Their idea is to pool all the 'baccer to force Duke's trust to pay a fair price. It's a good idea."

"Is it workin'?"

Bob turned to stare at me as if I'd spoken Greek. "It would if ever' grower'd join, but they's some who won't. They're called hillbillies. I'd sign right up if it was up to me, but Mary Lou don't think it's a good thing."

"We're only talkin' about a difference of a few cents a pound. Is that really worth the trouble?"

He seemed to relax a little. "You ain't used to payin' the bills, son. 'Baccer controls the entire economy in the Black Patch. It's the only cash crop we can grow, and if a man ain't got some cash money, then he can't pay the bank or the store or the doctor or the lawyer. Out on the farm, a man can grow corn to feed the cows and eat the beef and get vegetables out of the garden, but cash depends on 'baccer.

"I've seen figures that say it costs about 3 cents a pound to grow 'baccer, so you got to get more than that. The Duke trust offered 2 or 3 cents a pound before they started the Association. A man's got to have at least 7 or 8 cents a pound or else he's in a hell of a fix. And if the farmer is in a fix, then so's ever'body else." He sighed as if exhausted from the effort of speaking so long.

I thought on all that for a few minutes. He was right. Never having had to pay the bills, I'd never realized how even the lawyers and doctors depended on tobacco prices. Thinking over what the night riders had said, I asked, "How's not joinin' the Association worked out?"

Bob rotated his eyes to stare into the fire. "Good, for me. The Trust vowed they wouldn't buy no Association 'baccer, so they're willin' to pay a premium to us hillbillies. I got $12 a hundred pounds last year."

"Didn't I hear them say that the Association averaged $7 a hundred?"

"That's a fact, but only because Mr. Ewing — he's the Association's general manager — found an independent buyer in New York. The Association had set a goal of 8 cents a pound. They didn't get that, but 7 cents was a hell of a lot better than the 2 or 3 the Trust wanted to pay. It was a kind of victory for the Association."

"If the hillbillies got 12 and the Association got 7, it seems to me that the Association's done more good for the hillbillies than its members," I commented.

When Bob didn't answer, I turned to see if he was all right. He was sound asleep leaning against the pole. The twitching of his muscles betrayed the fear raging within.

I spent the rest of the night thinking about the Association and the Trust and the night riders. It became clear why they wanted to influence all farmers to join the Association. My pa taught me to always consider both sides of a question before I made up my mind. In this situation, it was easy to see that the farmers had a right to get the best price they could for their crops, but I could also see that if they didn't stick together, the Trust would starve them out. It was what my pa would have called "a puzzlement."

Chapter 3

Saturday, September 22, 1906

G uthrie, Kentucky, isn't the grandest place I've ever been. I don't
mean to say that I've ever been to any grand places, but Guthrie
is no more than a wide spot in the road right on the Tennessee border.
And not a very wide spot, at that.

However, on this particular day, Guthrie was transformed into the
center of activity for the universe. Well, for the Black Patch, anyway.
It was chosen as the site for the Association's rally because of its central location among the Kentucky and Tennessee counties concerned,
and because two lines of the Louisville & Nashville Railroad intersect
there. Considering all the folks that came on foot, in wagons, and on
the L & N, I'd guess there were upwards of 25,000 people in Guthrie
today.

People of all possible descriptions were in town. Barefoot farmers
in homespun garments rubbed elbows with ladies and gentlemen dressed
in the finest the stores had to offer. I reckon that the claim that the
Association saw every person as equal must have some truth to it.

"Where's the parade gonna start?" Price whined as we reached
town. Price wasn't too bad for an eleven-year-old, but I think he saw
me as a rival for his mother's attention, so we didn't hit it right off. He
was a little on the whiny side, but, like I said, not too bad for an eleven-
year-old.

"It'll go from the L & N depot to the fairgrounds," Mary Lou answered him. Then to Bob, "Let's find a nice spot about half way, where
we'll get a good view of all the doin's."

Bob drove the buggy on for a few minutes and then pulled up in the shade of a huge sugar maple tree growing along the road. "How's this look?" He sought Mary Lou's approval.

"It'll do, I guess." She looked up and down the road to see if anyone was too close to suit. Although the entire parade route was lined with spectators, this particular patch of shade was vacant.

We all got out of the buggy and Price and I stood aside while Bob and Mary Lou spread a blanket on the ground. A cloud of the fine brown powder that the late summer sun had made of the road swirled around a wagon slowly approaching from the direction of the depot. As it neared where we sat, a package headed toward me materialized out of the dust. "Enjoy that and the day," a voice from beyond the cloud shouted. I caught the package and unwrapped the paper to find a plug of Brown's Mule chewing tobacco and two packages of Duke's Best ready-made cigarettes. I quickly dropped one package of cigarettes into my lap and handed the rest to Bob. I hoped Mary Lou didn't see what I'd done.

Bob laughed as I handed him the tobacco products. "What's the joke?" I asked.

"Bitter irony, son," he chuckled. "Both of these products here are put out by the American Tobacco Company, the heart of the very Duke trust all these folks are here to protest against."

I didn't know what "irony" was, but I laughed just like I thought it was funny, too.

"Well, not ever'body," Mary Lou chimed in. "I'll bet there's plenty of hillbilly spies here, too."

By the time we got settled in good, the head of the parade had reached us. The Grand Marshall strutted by mounted on a magnificent white stallion. Next in the procession were a group of Association dignitaries riding in a Victoria carriage. A short, round faced man with a bushy red mustache was the center of attention.

"Who's that man?" I asked.

"That's Doc Amoss," Mary Lou answered, shooting a knowing glance at her husband.

"A doctor, is he?"

"Yes," she answered. "In fact, he delivered Price here." She patted the boy's head. In a moment, she added, "He's also the 'General' of the Silent Brigade."

"Mary Lou!" Bob snapped. He glanced quickly at the group of men who had stopped just to our left. "You'd best watch your mouth."

She tossed her head flippantly causing the sun to highlight the red in her hair. "Well, ever'body knows it."

"That don't matter," he chided. "Knowin' is one thing, talkin' is another."

"Bob Hollowell, you know good and well that I'll say whatever I please to say to whoever I please to say it." The set of her shoulders added an air of finality to her words.

Bob studied his shoes for a moment. Before he could speak, Price jumped to his feet and squealed with glee at the sight of the Association members coming into view. Formed into ranks, four abreast, were not only farmers, but merchants, lawyers, and men from all walks of life. They marched down the dusty road with a military precision unknown in the Black Patch since General Grant's army went east back in '64.

A total of ten groups of men marched by, each in perfect formation and preceded by a brass band. Price bounced up and down and clapped his hands to the tune of *Dixie* or *My Old Kentucky Home* as each group stirred the dust afresh.

"Who woulda thunk them boys could march like that?" one of the men on our left commented.

"Doc Amoss is one of Ferrell's boys, you know," another said. "Major Ferrell passed along all the trainin' he got in the Rebel army to all the boys that attended his school. From the way these shopkeepers and farmers march, it looks like Doc learned his lessons pretty good."

I had surreptitiously slipped the package of cigarettes into my pocket. The only tobacco I'd ever smoked was straight out of the barn, and to say the least, I didn't enjoy that. I was eager to give the ready-rolled ones a try. "I think I'll walk around a bit," I announced, standing.

"Well, don't get lost," Mary Lou smiled. "We'll be moving on to the fairgrounds in a few minutes."

I walked around the group of men to get to where the Hollowells could not see me. Pulling the package of cigarettes out of my pocket, I asked one of the men if he had a match.

"Sure," he replied fishing a box out of his shirt pocket. "Mind givin' me one of those?"

I handed him a cigarette. He struck a match, lit my cigarette, then his. I sucked the smoke into my lungs and started coughing. "Been smokin' long?" he laughed.

"I just ain't used to these ready-rolled things," I replied as casually as possible.

"Well, they do take some gettin' used to." He smiled and extended his hand. "I'm Milt Oliver."

"Glad to know you, Milt. I'm Jimmy Singleton." I took another puff on the cigarette, being more careful this time. As I blew out the smoke, Milt smiled at me.

"Have you been there?"

I didn't know what he meant. "Been where?"

His smile faded, and he wordlessly turned on his heel and walked away. I started to yell after him, but I saw Bob coming around the group. I quickly threw my cigarette away. "Come on, Jimmy. We're going up to the fairgrounds to eat."

* * * * *

The fairgrounds were crowded. All the Association members who had marched in the parade, as well as all the spectators, had gathered to partake of the vast array of food. There was barbecue pork, beef, and mutton along with all kinds of vegetables. Barrels of lemonade and ice water provided drinks for those who did not arrive better prepared. After we had eaten all we could hold, Mary Lou suggested that we move on down to the speakers' platform to get a good seat.

As much as everyone in attendance had enjoyed the parade and the meal, the speaking was the main event of the day. The first speaker was Governor Bob Taylor of Tennessee. He stepped to the front of the platform looking exactly as you'd expect a southern governor to look. The rumpled white linen suit and black string tie were the uniform of a gentleman. Before he opened his mouth, the graying hair and silver mustache said that here was a man in his natural element. He looked over the crowd with an air of confidence for a few moments. When he began to speak, his voice dripped with a southern drawl. "My friends, y'all know that I'm a politician. We're not gathered here today to discuss politics, but I've been asked by the Dark Tobacco District Planters' Protective Association of Kentucky and Tennessee to make a few appropriate remarks. While it may be difficult to determine just what is 'appropriate,' I do have a few little stories I'd like to share with you.

"On the way up here today, I thought I'd take the opportunity to visit a friend. Not being entirely sure where he lived, I stopped in a country store and inquired of the proprietor for directions.

"The old gentleman rocked back and said, 'You go on down the road here about three-quarters of a mile and then turn left up into the holler. You go up the holler just as far as you can go, and then turn around. It's the first house on the right on the way out.'"

Governor Taylor paused for the expected laughter and launched into another story. The cigarettes were burning a hole in my pocket. "Bob, I'm going to walk around a little."

As usual, Mary Lou answered for him, "We'll be right here for some time. Have fun." She turned that smile of hers on me as I walked away. I worked my way between clumps of people sitting on blankets on the ground until I reached the back edge of the crowd. To my left I saw a group of men standing in the shade of a tree. Pulling the package of Duke's Best out of my pocket, I approached them to ask for a light.

"I'm telling you, boys, destroying Trust 'baccer is the best way to fight 'em. After all, ain't ruinin' the goods the same idea as the Boston Tea Party?" The speaker had his back to me. On the other side of the circle, facing me, was Milt Oliver. Milt saw me and said something to the others.

"Howdy, men. Anybody got a match?" I sensed an atmosphere of slight hostility although I couldn't imagine why.

"Hello, Jimmy," Milt greeted me. He handed me a box of matches. I lit a cigarette and offered the pack to the group. Milt took one and passed the pack on. "Jimmy, let me introduce you. This here is Bill Larkins, Richard Pool, and the ugly one there is Buck Tandy." Each of the men smiled and shook hands.

"You enjoyin' the speeches?" Buck asked.

"Well," I said, "I ain't much on politics and even less on speeches. What's goin' on back here?"

Bill Larkins started to say something, but Milt cut him off. "Oh, just standin' around tellin' lies is about all." After an awkward pause, he went on,"We was just gettin' ready to go back up front. Doc Amoss is speakin' next." The men started to move away.

I stood under the tree and finished my cigarette. Being careful and not inhaling too deeply made it much more enjoyable. Just as I was ready to go back, another man approached me. "Howdy. Got one of them to spare?" he asked, indicating my smoke.

"Sure," I replied, handing him the package. I handed him my cigarette, and he lit his from it. "Thanks," he smiled. "Have you been there?"

It was the second time I'd heard that question, and I still didn't know what it meant. I did know the wrong answer, though. "I guess not," was all I could think of to say.

"Well, thanks for the smoke." He hurried away.

I weaved my way back through the crowd and sat down between

Mary Lou and Price. Price stuck out his tongue at me and whined a little. Doc Amoss was already speaking. "... and so, my friends, it is the duty of every farmer and friend of the farmer, to stand by the Tobacco Grower's Association; and those business and professional men who fail to encourage the tobacco growers in their struggle for better prices are not worthy of their patronage." The crowd roared its approval.

"What's he mean, Mom?" Price inquired.

"He means that we should not buy anything from anyone who's not a member of the Association."

"But, we don't belong," he whined. "Does that mean that nobody will stay at our boarding house?"

"Don't worry about it." She smiled indulgently.

The next speaker was Kentucky congressman A. O. Stanley. Even I knew that Stanley was the best friend the tobacco farmers had in Washington. I didn't know until he was introduced that he was the Association's lawyer. He began speaking in much the same tone and style as Governor Taylor had before. "This is not a political rally — the Association owes no loyalty to any political party." He droned on for the next hour about the evils of the Duke Trust and the virtues of the Association.

When the speaking at last ended and the rally was over, we gathered up our stuff and started out. As we walked by a group of men, I heard one of them sum up the Association's stance: "If the Trust wants to renew the fight, let it come. We are not going to ask any quarter, and we are not going to give much. They have got to march through a slaughter house into an open grave, or we will do it. Which shall it be?"

Chapter 4

Saturday, November 17, 1906

I awoke to the sound of Bob's pounding on the bedroom door. "Up and at 'em, Jimmy," he yelled. "'Baccer's in case!"

The ache in my back started spreading down to my toes . "In case" meant that the weather was such that it was a good day to get the to-bacco down from where it had cured in the barn and strip the leaves from the stalk. And that meant another long day in the little lean-to on the side of the barn. As I dressed, I remembered that it was Saturday, so it figured to be an extra long day in the stripping room.

After I had eaten breakfast, I headed for the barn. As I came out of the house, the late fall nip in the air hit me with full force. I could see smoke trailing from the stovepipe sticking out of the tin roof of the stripping room. I hoped Bob had a good fire going — by the time I got some tobacco down from the barn, I'd be chilled. Inside the barn, Ned Pettit was waiting for me. Ned was a huge, old black man whose leg was mangled from a long-ago accident with some farm machinery. The constant smile on his face was evidence that his good nature had not been handicapped.

"Mornin', young Jim," he greeted me with a smile that showed even white teeth in contrast to the color of his face. I liked Ned. Not only did he always have a smile for me, he was the only person who called me "Jim."

"Mornin', Ned. You ready to strip some 'baccer?"

"I is. You'll have to do the climbin'. This old leg of mine ain't gonna 'llow me up in them tiers."

I climbed to the first tier. The sticks stretched horizontally across the rails in front of me contained the split tobacco stalks hanging upside down like so many russet-colored horsemen in precise formation. As I moved into position to hand the first stick down to Ned, the warm, pungent odor of the cured leaves permeated the stagnant air. We only had a few sticks in the basket when I heard Bob enter the barn.

"Handle that stuff gentle, boys," he yelled. "That's money in the bank you're throwin' down and we'll need ever' penny. We've got a mortgage payment due at the bank come the first of the year."

I handed sticks down until we'd filled the basket. Then I dropped to the ground and helped Bob carry the basket into the stripping room. The fire was roaring in the stove, but a slight chill clung to the fringes of the tiny room. Steve Choate was stacking more firewood by the stove.

"Wipe your hands on that meat skin there," he directed, pointing to a strip of translucent grease tacked near the door. "It'll keep the 'baccer gum from stickin' to you so bad." I held my breath against the foul odor as I slid my palms down the slimy surface.

I'd helped strip burley before up home, and I thought I knew what I was doing. After I'd pulled about two dozen leaves of what I graded to be tips from the ends of the stalks, I was ready to wrap another leaf around the ends to tie it off into a "hand" when Bob noticed what I was doing.

"Hold on here, son. What's that you got there?"

"A hand of tips."

He smiled indulgently. "This ain't white burley we're dealin' with here, Jimmy. You just sort dark 'baccer leaves into three grades, leaf, lugs, and trash. Here. I'll show you."

Bob spent the rest of the morning explaining the difference in the grades to me, while Steve and Ned did most of the work. Before I knew it, it was dinner time.

* * * * *

The afternoon hours slipped by without a lot of conversation. Since it was getting on toward Christmas, Bob was eager to get the crop stripped and ready for market, so we worked steadily. I was just starting to wonder if it wasn't about supper time when I heard someone open the door. A blast of frigid air accompanied a man into the room.

"Well, how you doin' there, Archer?" Bob smiled at the new arrival.

"Fair to middlin', I allow," Archer answered, moving to the stove and rubbing his outstretched palms. "Howdy, boys," he said to Ned and Steve. Then to Bob, "I got all my 'baccer stripped and in the press. I thought I'd stop in and see how you're gettin' on."

Bob finished tying off the hand of trash he'd stripped and joined Archer at the stove. "Don't think you've met Jimmy here have you? Jimmy, this is my brother, Archer."

Archer smiled at me and extended his hand. I started to take it, but noticed the dirt and tobacco gum made my hand look pretty nasty. Archer perceived my hesitation and dropped his hand as he pulled up a stool.

"Well, Archer, you say you're all through strippin'?" Bob asked.

"Yep," he grinned toothlessly. "Pert nigh ready to sell."

"Are you still amongst us hillbillies or have you decided to go with the Association?"

Archer shot an anxious glance around the tiny room. Ned and Steve seemed to be paying no attention.. I made a show of gathering up loose leaves off the floor. "These boys are all right," Bob said. "No need to worry about them."

Archer shifted uneasily on the stool. "Well," he began slowly, "to tell you the truth, them night riders scared the hell out of me, and you know I ain't afeared of nothin'." His gaze was fixed on his boots.

"What's happened?"

Archer's eyes did not waver, but an expression of fear mixed with dread spread over his face. "'Bout 25 or 30 of 'em come by my house night afore last. I was fast asleep whenever they started shootin' into the house."

"Shootin' into the house?" Bob was incredulous.

"Shot out ever' one of my window lights." Archer seemed to shiver as he spoke. "I had my shotgun handy, 'course, but whenever I seen how many of them they was — well, what could a man do? Ain't you heard the tales 'bout them bastards beatin' the hell out of some of the hillbillies?"

I knew I should stay out of the conversation, but "What did you do?" came out of my mouth before I thought about it.

He tilted his head slightly to turn as sad a pair of eyes as I ever saw on me. "I laid my shotgun down and went out like they demanded. They quit shootin' once I's out on the porch. I'm here to tell you, I was mighty surprised to see that our own brother, John, was with 'em. Anyway, I guess they just come to give me a talkin'. I don't mind sayin' that I was mighty relieved."

"What'd they say?" Bob insisted.

"Well, you know. You've heard the same yourself. They pointed out that joinin' the Association might be pretty good life and fire insurance."

"They didn't shoot up nothin' here, though."

"Aw, they didn't do no harm. Just like I said, scared hell out of me. But it does seem like they're gettin' rougher in their ways. I was right glad, before it was over, that John was there. Thing is, though that a Regie buyer was by my place early this mornin'."

"Did he make you an offer?" Archer had Bob's full attention now.

"Yep, if you want to call it that. Offered me 2 cents a pound."

"You ain't gonna take that, are you?"

"I told him I'd just wait for the next buyer, and he told me there ain't gonna be no next buyer. Said that my farm was in his territory and he was the only buyer I was gonna see. Also said that if I didn't want his 2 cents today, he'd give a penny a pound in town tomorrow, and that if I didn't want that, I could just eat that 'baccer."

"You mean to tell me that the Trust buyers have divided the country into territories?" Again, Bob was incredulous.

Archer managed a wry laugh. "The man told me that my neighbor's farm split betwixt two buyers. He said that he was only authorized to buy half of that crop."

Bob looked as if he had no idea what to say. "Well," I interjected, "even the Trust is got to buy 'baccer someplace. They ain't gonna buy no Association leaf, or so they say, so what choice have they got?"

Archer shook his head. "The buyer claimed that they had a surplus left over from last year and didn't really want to buy none anyway."

"Hell," I spat. "I heard 'em tellin' that the reason prices was so low last year was 'cause of poor quality. And now they've got too much of it? It don't make no sense."

"You're right, Jimmy, it don't," Bob said. Turning back to Archer, "What do you plan to do?"

"That's what I come to talk about, Bob. Do you think us hillbillies could form up some kind of organization? You know, to fight 'em back."

A look of terror crossed Bob's face. "I don't know about that," he managed to say. After a few moments, he turned to me. "'Bout quittin' time, Jimmy. What say you boys take the rest of the day off?"

I figured that he wanted to say something to Archer, but it didn't matter to me. I was always ready to stop work. "Won't get an argument from me." I put on my coat and walked with Steve and Ned out into the late afternoon sun.

* * * * *

After we'd eaten supper, I decided to take a little walk up the lane. Although it was late in November and most of the day had been chilly, the afternoon had warmed somewhat, and the evening retained a hint of the sun's radiance mixed with the nip of late autumn. I strolled slowly up the packed earth road in the gathering dusk, lost in thoughts about what condition Christmas would find me in this year. As I neared a bend in the road, I heard a snicker of picketed horses. Wondering why horses would be tied out here, I moved to the side of the lane and peered cautiously through the trees. From this angle, I could see a pack of 25 or 30 horses standing a hundred yards or so from the Nabb schoolhouse. I walked as quietly as possible through the trees until I was close enough to see the building. Burlap bags covered the windows, allowing only a faint glimmer of light to penetrate. I could see dim figures moving around inside. This must be one of the night rider meetings! I circled to approach the building from the back side that had no windows. When I reached the back wall undetected, I silently crawled under the floor. Sounds of chairs scraping on the boards covered any noise I made getting into position.

"All right now, quiet down ," someone shouted. "Doc Amoss is here tonight, and we'll all want to hear what he has to say." The only sound I heard for a moment was my heart pounding against my chest. When someone I assumed to be Doc Amoss started speaking, the sound seemed directly over my head.

"Good evening, men." The voice was so low I had to strain to hear. "I'm glad you all could make it here this evening. As all of you know, we're engaged in a dire struggle with the Duke Trust. The time has arrived that you'll be selling your crops for this year, and we've got to ensure that you get a fair price.

"To gain that assurance, we're going to be forced to get the Trust's attention. It's time for action! To burn the warehouses and factories of the Trust, and its agents, who have robbed you of the fruits of your labor, is taking no more from them than they have taken from you. The law has enabled them to rob you, and you have no recourse. To burn, or otherwise destroy, the property of growers, and to whip them, and other persons who refuse to co-operate with you in winning your fight against the Trust is no more than they deserve." His voice got louder as he spoke, and I had no trouble hearing the last part.

"To burn 'em out is a noble act," someone shouted.

"You're right, Doc. It's the same as the Boston Tea Party."

I could envision Doc Amoss raising his hand for quiet. "There is no reason why a few persons should continue to make the masses suffer," he continued, "when their co-operation would not only *not* be to their detriment but would increase the earnings and thus improve the conditions of all equally."

I was feeling a little cramped. Shifting my position, I accidentally bumped the floor above me. My blood froze as dead silence seeped through the flooring. "Lieutenant, take your men and see if that's a spy or a hog."

"I'd better get the hell out of here," was the only thought in my mind. I scrambled from under the floor and was running as fast as I could when a bullet whistled over my head. I stopped in my tracks. "Get back up here!" burned in my ears.

I turned to see five rifles pointed at me. The leader of the men walked toward me. When he was close enough for me to see his face in the dim light, I realized that it was Bob's brother, John Hollowell. "What the hell do you think you're doing?" He grabbed my shoulder and squeezed hard.

Now my heart was really pounding. The excitement, aided by the exertion of the running, accelerated my breathing. "Nothing," I managed to stammer.

"That's that kid that's living with Bob Hollowell," one of the men said.

"I see it is," John mused. "Don't you know what happens to spies, son?" The concerned look on his face worried me.

"I'm no spy," I said. My mind raced to think of something else, but since I could think of nothing, I decided to keep quiet.

"Well," John sighed, relaxing his grip slightly. "I don't know what the hell is to be done with you."

"Let's kill 'im!" The man wasn't joking.

John Hollowell stood gripping my shoulder silently for a moment. Turning me over to another man, he said, "Hold on to him for a minute. I'll be back directly." With that, he disappeared into the darkness.

I stood feeling like a calf in a stockyard pen. There was no glow of the sun left in the air now. A trickle of icy sweat ran down the back of my neck. No one spoke for what seemed an eternity. At last, John reappeared. "We've got a choice for you, son," he announced. "Either you can join us, or else we'll have to make damn sure that you never tell anybody what you've heard here." His demeanor made it a pretty easy choice.

"I believe I'll join up."

John smiled, but there was no warmth in it. He simply nodded and turned back to the building. Two of the men took my arms and led me toward the school building. Most of the men went inside while my guards held me at the steps. They weren't holding me tightly; it was more like an escort now. In a minute the door opened and someone said, "Come in."

Inside the door, a lantern focused a brilliant light directly into my eyes. I could see nothing of the interior, only the bright light. I sensed bodies on each side of me, so I assumed I was being led down the center aisle. After a few paces toward the front of the room, my escort stopped and forced me to my knees before the light. I saw nothing, still, but a voice behind the light commanded, "Repeat after me." So, I repeated the oath a few words at a time:

"I, Jimmy Singleton, in the presence of Almighty God and these witnesses, take upon myself these solemn pledges and obligations: That I will never reveal any of the secrets, signs, or passwords of this order, either by word or writing, to any person or persons who are not entitled to the same in accordance with the rules and regulations of this order. I furthermore promise and swear that I will never reveal, or cause to be revealed by word or act, to any person or persons any of the transactions of this order in the lodge room or out of the lodge room, unless after due trial and examination, I find him or them justly entitled to the same, and not then unless I believe the welfare and business of the order will be benefited by such information given. I furthermore promise and swear that I will obey all orders or summons coming from my lodge, either day or night, unless prevented by sickness of self or family. I furthermore promise and swear that I will not use this order, or under cover of this order, to do anything to a personal enemy for personal revenge. To all of this I most solemnly promise myself under no less penalty than may be put upon me by order of this lodge."

I stood as the light was extinguished. Although I still could see nothing, many men came up and shook my hand and pounded me on the back, each with some kind of welcome to the order. Through this means, I learned that the penalty for breaking the oath was death by violence with secret burial in an unmarked grave and that in the absence of a specific password, the members greeted each other with "Silent Brigade." I also learned that the next time someone asked me if I'd been there, I should say, "Yes, on my bended knees," to indicate that I was a member.

* * * * *

Walking back to the house later, I had a very strange feeling inside me. I couldn't identify the emotion — it wasn't exactly fear or elation, but kind of a mix. I thought over what I could remember of the oath I'd sworn never to reveal anything to anybody. I'd thought the name they called themselves meant that they made very little noise sneaking up on people when they went night riding, but as I entered the Hollowell's yard, I started to realize the full meaning of the name "Silent Brigade".

Chapter 5

Friday, November 30, 1906

I had a problem. In the two weeks since my induction into the Silent Brigade, not only had I learned all the secret codes and passwords and such, I'd learned their plans, too. Knowing the plans was the problem.

In the meetings I'd attended, they'd explained the organization and make-up of the night riders. Although the officers insisted that they were not a part of the Association, that was hard to swallow in view of the fact that some men were officers in both organizations. They boasted that they "feared no judge or jury," and with the county judge, the chief of police, and even the local Commonwealth's attorney all in our lodge, it was easy to see why they felt that way.

I'd also learned how serious these men were. At one of the meetings, Doc Amoss said, "I want all those who will pledge themselves to take up arms and shed blood for the Association to stand up." Most of the men present stood up, and I did too. I wasn't sure I was ready to shed blood, but I didn't want to look like a coward either. Those that didn't stand were thrown out of the meeting.

The plan that was causing me a problem was a raid on Princeton. Tonight. Now that most of the hillbillies had sold their crops, the tobacco was stored in two huge Trust warehouses in Princeton. The Silent Brigade had plans to take over the town and burn the warehouses with the tobacco in them. That would hit the Trust where it'd hurt the most. Not only would the Trust be out the money they'd paid the hillbillies, but they'd lose the tobacco as well. Doc Amoss said that this action would sure as hell get somebody's attention. I didn't care about the warehouses or the tobacco, but I did care about Mary Lou being right there in the middle of it all.

Our lodge, as it was the local chapter, was in charge of the whole operation. We'd been divided into squads of six men, and each squad had a specific assignment. My squad, led by J. T. Jackson, was to take over the telephone office and cut the wire so nobody could call in or out. J. T. had said he'd be around to check on me this afternoon. I'd no more than walked out on the porch when I saw him riding down the lane.

"Howdy, J. T.," I hailed him at the gate.

J. T. Jackson was a bantam rooster of a man. Compact and brown, he gave the impression of being as tough as a green hickory nut. The fact that he'd served in the Spanish-American War carried a lot of weight with us younger members of our lodge. His wry sense of humor showed through when he was relaxed, but when Silent Brigade business was at hand, he was as focused as a dog after a rabbit. When J. T. gave an order, we obeyed.

"Anybody around?" He glanced right and left.

"Nope," I replied. "Bob's gone to Hobson's store. We've got the place to ourselves."

"All right, then," he said. "Let's go over it one more time. We'll meet up at the fairgrounds at midnight. All six of us will go on up to the telephone office and capture whoever's on duty. You, bein' young and spry, climb the pole and cut the wire. After that, the town's ours. Whenever you hear Doc Amoss blow three times on his gun barrel, it's over. We'll go back out the same way we came in."

"I ain't never heard anybody blow a gun barrel. What's it sound like?"

"It don't sound like nothin'. Kind of a cross betwixt a whistle and a horn. You'll know what it is whenever you hear it. Speakin' of hearin', remember to bring some gunny sacks to tie on your feet."

That made about the hundredth time I heard somebody say "whenever" when I would have said "when." I guess I still hadn't adjusted to the western Kentucky idiom. Or should I say they said "whenever" when*ever* I would have said "when?" J. T. was waiting for an answer about the sacks. "What for?" I asked.

"So's you won't make noise on the board sidewalks. Hell, boy, ain't you never been to town?"

I didn't care much for his teasing, so I changed the subject. "What will the other squads be doing?"

J. T. gave me a puzzled look. "Well, not that it's any concern of yours, but we'll have squads takin' over the police station, the telegraph office, the courthouse, and the fire station." He smiled smugly. "We will be in control of the town."

"Why do we want the fire station?"

"Why, hell, son. You don't want 'em puttin' out the fires we're goin' to so much trouble to start, do you?" His grin became more smug. "Oh, yeah, have you got something to make a mask out of?"

"I need a mask?"

"Yep, you'll need a mask. We don't want to take no chances on anyone bein' recognized. You got a feed sack or somethin'?"

"I'll find somethin'," I said.

"One other thing. The password for tonight is 'big smoke.'" He broke into a wide grin and poked an elbow into my ribs. "It's a joke, son. Get it? Big smoke!"

I caught the double meaning. All that burning tobacco would make a mighty big smoke indeed.

"Can you get out all right?"

"Yeah. Bob goes to bed early. I'll just slip out after he goes to sleep." I wasn't worried about it.

* * * * *

I should have been. As soon as J. T. left, I searched the house for something to use as a mask. I finally found a strip of black cotton cloth in Mary Lou's sewing basket. I was practicing wrapping it around my head when I heard Bob at the door. I hid the cloth in my room and dashed downstairs. He soon gave me something to worry about.

"Guess what!" He was all smiles as he bounded in the front door.

"What's that?" I couldn't help returning his smile.

"Mary Lou wants you and me to come to supper at the boarding house tonight. She called up the store on the telephone while I just happened to be there. I talked to her myself — on the telephone. His words tumbled out so fast they ran together. "Yes sir, she sure wants us to come to supper." He rubbed his hands together in gleeful anticipation.

"Are we comin' back tonight?" As soon as I asked that, I wished I'd said something else.

Bob looked at me as if I'd spoken in an alien tongue. Slowly, the look changed to a sly grin. "I surely do hope not," he said.

* * * * *

Princeton, county seat of Caldwell County, was home to about 1,000 people, 1,002 when Mary Lou and Price were in town. We came into town from the south on the Cadiz road. Across the Illinois Central railroad tracks, we rolled right past the fairgrounds where my squad was to assemble later tonight. A slight angle to the left brought us to Main Street. Bob guided the mare to a stable behind a sturdy brick house about a block from the courthouse. We were just getting out when Mary Lou came out through the screened-in porch on the back of the house.

"Well, hello men," she purred in that voice that gave me shivers. I tried not to make too much of the idea that she'd called me a man.

Bob rushed to hug her. "Hello, honey. How're you and Price gettin' on?"

"Tolerable." She turned a smile on me as she freed herself from Bob's grasp. "How are you, Jimmy?"

"Doin' fine," I lied. I was worried sick about getting out and then back in tonight. Although I was somewhat relieved about being in town where I could keep an eye on Mary Lou, I figured that the chances of getting caught sneaking in or out were much greater here than out in the country.

"Where's Price?" Bob asked.

"Doin' his homework," Mary Lou replied distractedly. "Come on inside, Jimmy. Bob, put OGM away and get on in. Supper's 'bout ready." OGM was their pet name for the Old Gray Mare. The authoritative tone of her voice left no doubt that she was in charge here.

* * * * *

Inside, all the boarders were gathered in what I took to be the dining room. Seated around the oblong cherry table were three men —I guessed that they were traveling salesmen, drummers, they were called, Price, and two ladies. Well, one lady and one girl who looked to be about 18. Mary Lou introduced me around. The names? The girl's name was Lorena, and she was a beauty. Her long black hair was pulled into a bun at the back of her head exposing a graceful white neck. She knew how to fix her hair. With it pulled away from her face like that, her high cheek bones were displayed to full advantage. She was wearing a blue print dress that complemented her skin tone perfectly. I wanted to see her standing up.

The supper table conversation was about as insipid as expected — Who was doing what with whom around town, the weather, and the evils of the Duke Trust were the major topics of discussion. As if I didn't have enough things on my mind, I had to divide my attention between Mary Lou and Lorena. Fortunately, Mary Lou and the drummers did most of the talking. Lorena caught me giving her the eye twice. Or did I catch her looking at me?

When the meal was finished and the dishes cleared, Mary Lou excused herself and went into the kitchen, In a moment she reappeared bearing a cake with lighted candles. The whole group burst into "Happy Birthday" as she placed the cake in front of me. "Surprise!" she exclaimed.

It was a surprise, all right. My birthday is in April. "But, ..." I sputtered.

"Cut the cake, son. We've all been looking forward to it." The familiar tone of command in her voice said that protest was futile. I blew out the candles, sliced into the cake and passed plates around the table. Mary Lou left the room again and came back with her arms loaded with gift-wrapped packages. "Time to open your presents," she announced.

Thoroughly embarrassed, I tore the colored wrapping paper from the boxes. Inside was a complete new outfit of clothes — new coat, new shirt, and new corduroy pants. "You certainly needed these," Mary Lou said.

"Thank you very much," I muttered, "but you shouldn't have done this."

"Son," Bob said, kindness in his voice, "We know it's probably not your birthday. But since we didn't know whenever it actually is and you needed some new duds, Mary Lou decided now is as good a time as any." For the first time in a while, I felt like I had a family. They were right, I needed the clothes. Tears filled my eyes as Bob shook my hand and Mary Lou hugged me. Price glared at me across the table.

* * * * *

When Lorena arose from the table, I got my chance to see her full figure. I was disappointed, and I wasn't, too. The long blue dress had a full skirt that left the bottom half of her to my imagination. The bodice, however, was form fitting and she filled it out very nicely. She was tall and relatively thin and "elegant" was the only word that came to mind. The ladies adjourned to the parlor while the men lit up cigars around the table. As Lorena and I didn't fit into either group, we wandered out onto the front porch. The weather was really too cold to be standing around outside, but I'd had enough of the company inside. I guess the same was true of Lorena.

"Beautiful night out, ain't it?" I said for lack of anything better.

"Sure is," she agreed. "It's one of those cold, clear winter nights when you can see a million stars." I followed her gaze up to the sky.

"You can't see nearly as many in town as out in the country," I observed.

She moved a little closer to me. "You live out in the country, do you?"

I'd just assumed she knew all about it. "Yeah," I said. "I'm living out with the Hollowells."

"You mean Mr. Hollowell," she laughed. "Mrs. Hollowell holds court here with us." She was quiet for a moment, then said, "Yes, I know about you and the Hollowells. She told me all about you and your calamity. It's so sad — just like a romance novel."

"I don't feel much like a character in a book."

Lorena clasped her hands in front of her breast, fingers laced as if in prayer. "Oh, but you have the chance to wander through the panorama of life, be a seeker of truth, a champion of justice who owes allegiance to no man."

I'd heard tales about these young girls that live in boarding houses. I had even fantasized about meeting one, even one as beautiful as Lorena, but this scene was not directly from my dreams. I had absolutely no idea of what to say to her. I guess she tired of waiting for me to speak. "I wish I had somewhere to live," she sighed.

"Don't you live here?"

"Yes, but I mean something of my own. Living here is all right, I guess, but I get so tired of all the drummers trying — well, I want something worthwhile." She turned to face me and lifted her chin so that she was looking right up into my face. She was almost as tall as me, and her lips were only inches away from mine. "You know, something that I could hold on to."

That moment made me realize that I had nothing of my own either. She was so close and so inviting. I was thinking that maybe here was something I could hold on to.

I was trying to work up the nerve to kiss her upturned lips when Mary Lou stuck her head out the door. "You two better get inside. You'll catch your death out there."

Lorena continued to look into my eyes for a long moment before she sighed and turned to go inside. Her hand brushed mine as we passed through the doorway. I wished I knew whether she did it purposely.

Everyone was gathered in the parlor now. Lorena went to one side of the room, and I went to the other. I settled in for a boring evening of listening to Mary Lou tell more town gossip and the drummers off-color jokes. Every time my eyes wandered to Lorena, which was pretty often, she was looking at me. When she'd see me looking at her, she'd flash that ice-melting smile on me. I had some kind of strange hollow feeling going on deep in my stomach.

I stretched my arms in the air, yawned, and did everything I could think of to indicate that I thought it was bedtime. No one seemed to take any notice of my actions. At long last, as the grandfather clock in the hall chimed 10, Mary Lou arose.

"Good night, all." It was an announcement. She ushered the others out of the parlor and took my arm as I came to the door. "Come along, Jimmy. I'll show you to your room."

We walked down the hall, then up the back stairs. At the top of the stairs, another clock ticked away against the wall. She opened the door to a room on the left of the hall. "It's all made up for you," she said. She kissed me quickly on the cheek and closed the door.

At last I was in a room alone. I never considered myself antisocial, but I'd had enough of people for one night. I'd enjoyed seeing Mary Lou and the time I'd spent with Lorena, but with all that was on my mind, enough was enough. Trying to be pleasant all evening had been hard on me. I was tired, and the bed beckoned, but I was afraid to get in it. I figured it'd take me twenty minutes or so to get to the fairgrounds from here, so I only had an hour and a half to wait. Knowing that if I laid on the bed, I'd be a goner, I sat in a chair and listened to the house grow quiet. In a little while, the ticking of the clock outside my door was the only sound I could hear. I was vaguely aware of my eyelids growing heavy while visions of that scene on the porch danced in my head. I guess I must have dozed off because the next thing I heard was the clock chiming.

Chapter 6

Friday, November 30, 1906

I nstantly, I was wide awake, my heart pounding. No one knew better than I how seriously the Silent Brigade took their obligations. I really didn't even want to think about what they'd do to me if I was late. Despite that dread, when the sound of the chimes faded, I sat still for a minute, listening. When I heard nothing, I crept to the door and opened it a crack. Everything was still. A peek at the clock revealed that it was 11:30 — perfect timing. I had just enough time to get to the fairgrounds by midnight.

I felt very lucky that the old clock chimed the half-hour. Actually, I was doubly lucky. Moving to the window on the right hand wall, I saw that it was only a few feet above the roof of the screened in porch. I tried to open the window only to find that it was stuck. Where did my luck go? I tugged at the sash and it suddenly broke free and shot up, banging at the top loud enough to wake the dead. The cold night air pouring through the opening did not arrest the sweat pouring off my body. The curtains swayed in and out with the cold breeze. Straining my ears, I still heard nothing. Maybe my luck was still running — the glass didn't break and apparently no one had heard. I thought about peeking into the hall again but decided that I'd wasted enough time. Swinging my legs through the open window, I dropped to the roof of the porch. There was a little scraping noise when I hit and I was tempted to lie still to make sure no one had heard. Deciding it was too late to worry about it now, I dropped to the ground and was off to join the squad.

The town was perfectly still as I walked along Main Street and turned south on the Cadiz pike. An occasional dog bark was the only sound I heard, but I kept to the shadows just to be safe. My estimate must have been a little off; I think it was a few minutes past midnight when I arrived at the fairgrounds. There was no sign of anyone as I entered through the gate. Suddenly, a voice to my right demanded, "What's the password?"

Startled, I jumped about four feet in the air, panic setting in as I descended. I couldn't remember the damned password. "Fat cigar, ... no, ... uh, ...I don't remember." The clicks of two pistols being cocked improved my memory. "Big smoke, big smoke!" I shouted.

J. T. Jackson, Steve Choate, and Milt Oliver stepped out of the shadows. "Keep your voice down," J. T. whispered. "You don't have to tell everybody in Princeton what it is."

A wave of relief swept over me. "Sorry, J. T., I couldn't think of the password."

Milt Oliver was one of the men I'd met at the Guthrie rally. While he was several years older than me, he wasn't very mature and related well to the younger members. He'd taken me under his wing in the lodge. Milt was just another tobacco farmer, but compared to me, he had a world of experience. I considered him my best friend, partly because he usually tried to interpose himself between my inexperience and J. T.'s gruffness. He knew I needed that now.

"Well, you thunk of it just in time," Milt flashed a snaggle-toothed grin. "The hair trigger on this old Navy Colt was 'bout halfway back whenever you yelled it out."

I looked from J. T. to Steve to Milt. J.T. was as serious as a heart attack. Steve was a quiet type and none too bright. His face was impassive. Only Milt was smiling.

"You wouldn't of shot me, would you?"

Milt started to answer, but J. T. cut him off. "Damn right we'd of shot you and at this range, we couldn't miss, either."

I caught the significance of the "we" in J. T.'s comment. Knowing him as I did, I was certain he wasn't joking. "Glad to see you made it, son," J. T.'s voice softened some.

"I'm not late am I?"

"A little. It's just that whenever we come by the Hollowell house earlier and didn't see you there, we begin to wonder what'd become of you."

I started to explain about Bob and me coming to town, but J. T.

stopped me with an upraised palm. "No time now, Jimmy. Doc's got this whole thing timed right down to a gnat's whisker and we ain't gonna be the ones to foul up the schedule. You boys get them sacks tied on your feet. This here squad of the Silent Brigade is gonna live up to its name tonight. Ever'body got some kind of a mask?"

"I got the standard night rider equipment," Milt chortled. "A mask, a gun, and an alibi."

Needing an alibi hadn't occurred to me. "If anybody was to ask, where are you right now?" I asked Milt.

"Cut the chatter, boys," J. T. growled. "We got serious work to do."

We all tied gunny sacks to our feet and I wrapped the black cloth around my head. I couldn't see too well and the thing interfered with my breathing, but I didn't want to hear what J. T. would have to say if I didn't have it on. When everyone was ready, we started back toward town in the reverse of how I'd just come out. The sacks worked; the six of us moved along without a sound.

After we'd walked a few minutes, Milt stepped aside and waited for me to come even with him. He fell in step with me along the sidewalk. "If anything comes up, you and me'll both swear that we was 'possum huntin' tonight, OK?" he whispered.

"That won't work," I replied in a low voice. "There's a bunch of folks who know that I was at Mary Lou's boarding ...." A hand around my throat stopped my explanation.

"Shut up, damn it!" J. T. was not pleased.

When we reached Main Street, we turned left and stopped in front of the gray stone courthouse. Two other squads were already waiting there. When the clock in the tower hit 12:30, I was startled by the firing of many guns.

"That's it boys," J. T. yelled. "Let's go to work."

One squad headed into the courthouse, and another dashed for the police station around behind. Following J. T., my squad ran a block on down Main to the telephone company's office. J. T. motioned us to a halt.

The town was awake now. Every dog in town was sending up a howl. Lights started to show in windows all around us. Just across from where we were standing, a man in a night shirt appeared in a doorway.

Milt pointed him out to J. T. who whirled and fired his pistol into the transom over the doorway. "Get back inside," he shouted. "The night riders are here!" The man disappeared.

J. T. moved to my side and whispered, "There's the pole, son. Whoever's inside the office don't know what's goin' on yet. We'll give you a minute to get up there before we go in and capture the operator. Soon's you get to the top, cut the wire. You can stay up there if you want — should be some show." He slapped me on the back and moved away. Steve Choate handed me a pair of pliers. He and the other men were standing in the office entrance doorway as I started for the pole.

I'd never climbed a telephone pole before, but it wasn't much different from a tall skinny tree. I jumped as high as I could and wrapped both arms and both legs around the pole when I hit. The wood was rough and saturated with some kind of sticky, foul smelling tar. I guessed the adhesive quality of the tar would help me. With my ankles crossed on the opposite side of the pole, I slid my legs as high as I could, then moved my hands and body, inching my way up. Somewhere along the way, it occurred to me that I probably would have been smart to remove the sacks from my feet as they didn't make the chore any easier. By the time I got to the top of the pole, I must have had a dozen splinters in my hands, and my mask had come unwrapped. With the pliers in one hand and a death grip on the pole with the other, there was nothing I could do about it. I was just as glad, anyway. The exertion of climbing the pole was causing me to breathe hard, although the absence of the cloth around my mouth made it easier to get air into my lungs. As I leaned out to reach for the wire, the black cloth let go of my neck and fluttered to the ground.

My hand shook a little as the pliers contacted the wire. I was afraid it'd shock me. I gripped the pole tightly with my legs and left arm, closed my eyes, and squeezed the metal jaws of the pliers with my right hand. I heard a slight snap and opened my eyes just in time to see the wire swing away. The wire didn't shock me — there weren't even any sparks. When I saw the end of the wire touch the ground, I knew that the town of Princeton was out of touch with the outside world. Come what may, no help for the town would be coming tonight.

I had a great view of the town. It wasn't a real bright night, but I was above the level of the roof tops, and the trees were bare. I could see all the way to Hogan's Hill to the north and the Illinois Central depot to the south. As I looked south, I saw the most awesome sight of my life. A company of at least 200 horsemen was moving north on the Cadiz road, not making a sound. The flickering light given off by the pine tar torches many of the men carried added to the strangeness of

the sight. Four abreast and in perfect order, they glided like an appari-
tion. The phantom riders turned west onto Main, then north at the
courthouse and glided up North Jefferson until they turned in front of
the J. G. Orr tobacco warehouse. I suppose that the night riders had
forced everyone back indoors — the town was perfectly quiet once
again. A few of the riders dismounted and entered the building. From
my perch, I could even observe that these men carried cans of coal oil.
In a few moments, the men ran out of the building followed by a great
roaring sound as a ball of flame shot skyward from the Orr warehouse.
I could even feel the heat of the blaze.

"Big smoke" was an aptly chosen term for the event. The windows made popping sounds as the glass shattered from the frames.
Fingers of orange flame licked up the sides of the building from the
openings the glass vacated. Overhead, a tall column of thick black
smoke marked the conflagration.

The ghostlike riders started moving again. They went on in front
of the inferno that was the Orr building and turned south on Seminary
Street. As they rode by below my roost, I observed the method of their
silence — the horses' hooves were wrapped with gunny sacks. Doc
Amoss didn't miss a trick.

The light and snapping noises of the fire brought the town awake
again. Whenever a light appeared in a house, I'd hear a shouted, "Get
back," or "Lights out." If the demand was not promptly complied with,
a shot through the window drove home the meaning. The specter troops
stopped opposite the Illinois Central Depot at the Stegar & Dollar warehouse. Here the same scene was repeated and in a moment, it too
erupted in noise and flame. A plume of thick black smoke from each
of the two flaming buildings rose to a terrific height and merged into
an umbrella-like overcast. Reflected light from the fires lit the entire
town. Clinging to my perch, I took in the awesome scene. Then I
heard it.

Three shrill blasts of the weirdest sound that had ever entered my
ears. J. T. was right — it didn't sound like anything I'd ever heard
before, but I knew it was Doc Amoss's recall signal. I slid down the
pole, reaching the ground just as J. T. and the squad exited the telephone office. "Time to get the hell out of here," he shouted. I guess he
saw no need to be silent now.

"J. T.," I said as we ran down the street, "what's the plan from
here?"

"Where the hell's your mask?"

I hadn't given it a thought. "Came off while I was up on the pole," I replied.

"Well, you better make damn sure nobody sees you. There's liable to be hell to pay for the property that's been destroyed here tonight."

We were passing the courthouse. I gripped J. T.'s arm to stop him. "I'm stayin' in town," I puffed.

He stared as if he did not comprehend what I'd said. After a moment, he said, "Do as you please. I'm gettin' as far as fast as I can." With that he was off down the Cadiz road. I tore the gunny sacks from my feet. I could see that the residents of each house were gathered at the front windows. Taking my cue from that, I ran through the side yard of the nearest house and rounded the corner in the back. I figured Mary Lou's boarding house was about a dozen houses away.

I didn't figure that every yard would be fenced. Climbing each one made for slow progress. I'd scrambled through five or six yards when I decided to take a rest. I leaned against a tree to catch my breath. Suddenly the back door of the house flew open. Against the dim glow of light from within, I could see the outline of a man with a shotgun. "Who the hell's in my yard?" a gruff voice demanded as he advanced toward me.

From a standing start, I cleared the fence with room to spare. The man may have seen my face, but I wasn't staying around to find out. He didn't fire the shotgun, and I don't think he followed me. I eventually reached the boarding house. I crept along the side to get a glance at the front. Sure enough, Bob, Mary Lou, Price, and all the boarders were watching the parade of horsemen. I ran to the porch around back. On the side was a rose trellis. I was up it in a flash and sprang through the open window into my room. I was happy to discover that the window went down easier than it had gone up. Turning into the room, I caught my reflection in the mirror on the back of the door. I was a mess. The tar from the telephone pole covered the front of my coat, the inside of my pants, and my hands and face. I tore off my clothes and pulled on the red wool night shirt I'd brought along. Quickly, I poured some water into the dry sink and scrubbed my hands and face. Some of the tar came off. I put my pants back on under the night shirt and headed downstairs.

"What's all the racket?" I tried to sound casual and stand aside so they wouldn't see my face too well.

The whole group turned to stare at me. I was sure someone would say something about how I looked. Fortunately, they were more interested in the scenes outside. Turning back to the window, Mary Lou said, "You must be a sound sleeper, Jimmy. You've missed all the excitement."

"Yeah, I'm a sound sleeper, all right. What's happened?"

"Looks like the night riders have burned half the town," Mary Lou said without looking around.

Outside, the riders flowed down the street as leisurely as if headed for a Sunday picnic. As we stood in awe, the strains of their singing *My Old Kentucky Home* wafted into the house. Listening closely, I determined that their version differed slightly from the original. They were singing "The fire shines bright ...".

"Did any of you folks recognize any of the riders?" Mary Lou asked.

"I did," one of the drummers—his name was Brice — answered. "I saw B. Malone out there."

"How could you tell?" the lady boarder asked. "They were all wearing masks."

"Recognized his horse," the man replied. "I was out at his place yesterday. Sold him a new plow and got a good look at that horse. That was Malone all right, no doubt about it."

I thought I detected a note of hesitation in Brice's voice. "Have you been there?" I asked him.

"Malone's place?" he replied. "I just told you I was there yesterday." He didn't belong to the Silent Brigade.

Mary Lou turned to look at the drummer. "You're right, Mr. Brice. I saw Malone's horse, too. I saw Richard Pool, Buck Tandy, Bill Larkins, and the Murphy boys, Teedy and Joe, as well."

"Mary Lou!" Bob puffed. "You'd best keep your mouth closed. You know that the night riders wouldn't take kindly to anyone talking about who was involved in this."

"Pshaw!" she exploded. "Those rascals come in here terrorizing decent folks and destroying their property, why ..." She began to sputter with anger. "Why, bein' talked about is the least they deserve."

"Now, honey," Bob pleaded, "these men mean business. We'd all best keep quiet about anything we might know."

"Well, they're gone." Mr. Brice observed. "Guess the show's over."

"I suppose so," Mary Lou said turning from the window. "Let's all get back to sleep. We'll ride out and view the damage in the morning." All present knew we'd been dismissed.

Walking down the hall, I realized that Lorena was not out. Maybe she was a sound sleeper, too. After I entered my room and closed the door, I pulled my pants off. They were filthy. I simply pitched the garment into a corner. I needed the birthday gifts more than I had realized. Although I was dead tired, I took the time to scrub more of the tar from my hands and face before I slid between the sheets. The bed was cold and hard, but it felt good. What a night it had been! I thought a few seconds of listening to the steady ticking of the clock would put me to sleep, and I guess it wasn't more than a few minutes before I was totally relaxed and beginning to drift off when I heard the bedroom door open. My heart froze as footsteps crossed the room. Had the man followed me? Was it the police coming after me?

"Jimmy," a tender voice said in a whisper. "Are you awake?" I turned to see a woman standing there in a white night gown. As I rubbed the sleep from my eyes, I realized that it was Lorena. In the pale light, she was exquisite. "Yes," I whispered, "I'm awake. What do you want?"

She did not answer. Instead, she glided across the room and crawled into the bed beside me. The bed no longer seemed cold or hard as she ran her toes up the inside of my calf. "Ready for my birthday present?" she whispered.

What a night indeed!

Chapter 7

Saturday, January 19, 1907

How ridiculous! Mary Lou exploded from behind the newspaper. For someone who had come for a peaceful weekend in the country, she was quite agitated.

Startled, Bob looked up from the farm books. It was unusual for her to raise her voice. "What's that?" he asked.

"'Whereas, the city of Princeton has been recently visited by a calamity which we very much regret and for which we are in no wise responsible,'" she quoted from the paper, "'and we deplore the public sentiment excited by the press which has cast reflection upon our organization.

"'Be it resolved by this meeting of tobacco growers that we condemn all lawlessness, riot and destruction of property.' How ridiculous," she repeated.

"What's wrong with the Association making that announcement?" Bob asked. "It seems to me that they are just being right-minded citizens."

"What's wrong with it is that the ones who signed this silly resolution are the very same men who planned and executed the raid. How stupid do they think we are? Look here," she thumped the page. "Doc Amoss, Guy Dunning, why your brother, John, even signed this thing!"

"Now, honey, you don't know who planned the raid." His voice was pleading.

"I most certainly do! Don't you think for a minute that I don't know what goes on in Princeton."

"How do you know, Mom?" Price looked up from the Christmas present puzzle he was working on the floor.

"The men talk around the table, darling." Her voice was much softer when speaking to her son. "I know all about it. I know who planned it, who participated — not all of them, of course — but most of them." At that point in her narrative she shot a cryptic glance in my direction. "I know that 400,000 pounds of Trust tobacco worth nearly $100,000 was destroyed, and I know that it got the Association the attention they wanted."

I was uncomfortable with the look she'd given me. "You also know that they pulled the whole thing off without anybody being hurt, don't you?" I asked, attempting to deflect her direction.

"I'm not saying it wasn't well planned and well executed. It is remarkable that no one was killed or injured, and I'm sure Doc Amoss is proud of himself. I'm simply saying that it's ludicrous for these men to unlawfully destroy private property and then expect us to applaud them for condemning the act. The whole bunch ought to be arrested and tried."

"After all," I said, "the only harm done was to the Trust."

"That's the night rider line, Jimmy, but it's simply not true." She gave me that peculiar look again. I was beginning to wonder just how much she really did know. "The night riders had warned the insurance companies in advance, so they canceled the policies on both Orr's and Stegar & Dollar's. So, you tell me, who pays the bill?"

"The Trust?" I offered.

"Of all the things you've impressed me with, young man, stupidity is not among them. Do you actually think that Mr. James B. Duke, sitting in his office on Wall Street in New York City, cares a fig about what happens in Princeton, Kentucky?"

"He will if it affects the bottom line of his financial statements," Bob said.

"Yes, he'll notice that," she conceded. "But it wasn't that big a deal. What's a little old $100,000 to him?"

"Well, it got the state government's attention. The fire marshal sent an investigator, didn't he?" Bob was interested in the discussion now.

"And a fat lot of good he did, too," she said, her voice laced with sarcasm. "Called in all those men to testify — Association members, Orr's employees, and the city officials — night riders, ever' last one of 'em. They might as well have asked the Easter Bunny to provide evidence."

"Caldwell County brought in two indictments," I reminded her.

"A farce! I've heard the night riders say that they 'fear no judge or jury.' Bill Winters and J. T. Jackson were in absolutely no danger of being convicted. All they were trying to do is pacify the state fire marshal."

I decided to give her a test. "Do you think J. T. was involved?"

"I know very well that he was," she declared.

"Now, Mary Lou," Bob said. "It's okay for us to discuss anything here, but you should tone it down a bit before you go back to town."

"I'll do no such thing!" She glared defiantly at Bob. "When a secret organization thinks they're so powerful that they don't have to be secret anymore, something needs to be done. I say that the guilty should be brought to justice ,and I'll say that to anybody in the county."

* * * * *

Despite how beautiful she was and how I enjoyed her affection and company, I wished Mary Lou had picked another day to come for a visit. There was a Silent Brigade meeting at the Nabb school this evening. Her being here would provide difficulty in getting out of the house. Little did I suspect that she herself would give me an excuse to be out. About dusk, I was in the barn loft throwing down hay for OGM when Mary Lou came through the door.

"Jimmy, you in here?"

"Yeah, I'm up here," I said peeking over the edge of the loft floor.

"Well, come on down. I've got an errand for you."

She met me at the foot of the ladder and held my arm as I stepped to the dirt floor. It seemed to me that she never passed up an occasion to put her hands on me, but that might just be my imagination. "What's on your mind?" I asked.

"I brought some coffee and sugar from town that I want you to deliver," she said handing me four brown paper sacks. "Take a sack of coffee and a sack of sugar to Bob's mother and the rest to his brother's house."

I wasn't sure I'd have time before the meeting. Despite her tone of command, I said, "Wouldn't you rather do it yourself and visit a little?"

She gave me a brief look of impatience. "I've got to get supper," she said. "Actually, I wouldn't mind seeing Bob's mother, but wild horses couldn't drag me to John's house."

"Don't you like John?" It was the first I'd heard of any disagreement between them.

"Well, he's big on the Association and active in the night riders, but I don't hold that against him. It's that wife of his that I can't abide. That Lula is a witch with a capital 'B.' The only redeeming quality I can find in her is that she doesn't like me either." She chuckled at her last comment.

"What's the matter with her?" I asked. I'd never met Lula Hollowell.

"Well," she drew out the word, "she seems to think that I .... Oh, never mind. Just get yourself on over there. I won't hold supper for you. Momma Hollowell or John will feed you. Now get." I found it interesting that she said that John, not Lula, would feed me.

Mrs. Hollowell's place was just across the pasture from Bob's house. I'd been there several times before, and she was glad to get the coffee and sugar. She did invite me to eat, but I told her that I had to get on up to John's house and got away as quickly as I could. A few minutes walk up the lane brought me to John Hollowell's farm.

"Hello in there, anybody home?" I shouted as I knocked on the door. John appeared in the doorway.

"Hello, Jimmy," he said with a puzzled look on his face. "What are you doing up here?" He motioned me into the house.

"Brought you some gifts," I answered, handing him the sacks. "Mary Lou sent you some coffee and sugar from town." Lula Hollowell walked into the room. She was a plain woman. Short and plump with long sandy red hair cascading down her back, she was dressed in a faded house dress. Everything about her appearance, including the red and callused hands, signaled that she was a farm woman.

"Well, you just take it right back. I won't have anything that woman's touched in this house," she declared.

John smiled as he took the goods. "Thanks for the delivery, son. We're just sitting down to supper. Come on in." Lula whirled on her heel and left the room. "I thought something might be wrong about the meeting," he said when she was gone.

"No," I replied. "As a matter of fact this made it easier for me to get out of the house."

"Let's eat a bite, then we'll get on down to the school." He ushered me into the kitchen. Lula hardly looked up as we entered. She wordlessly took another plate from the cupboard and set it on the table. With a glare at John, she took her place as John and I sat.

"How's things down at Bob's?" John asked, passing me a platter of ham.

"It's been pretty quiet for the last two weeks," I replied. "We've got plenty of wood cut and piled up on the tobacco plant beds. It won't be long now before we'll burn the ground."

"You're right," he agreed. "Spring'll be here before you know it, and we can start all over again with a new crop. Pass me the biscuits."

I handed the plate over to him. "Mary Lou and Price came out for the weekend," I said thinking he'd want to know.

Lula slammed her fork down on the table. "I won't have that name mentioned in this house," she shouted, her green eyes blazing.

"Calm down, Lula," John said. "The boy means no disrespect."

"I don't care what he means or don't mean," she said. "I don't even care that she is your brother's wife — in fact, I wish she wasn't. She's a trollop. Any woman who'd forsake her family and be seen in the company of ever' man in town is no fit topic for supper table discussion."

"Then stop discussing her," John declared. "Everybody knows how you feel about her. There's no need to make Jimmy suffer for it."

"She's the one who ought to be made to suffer." Her chagrin was evident. "She ought to be took out and whipped."

John pushed his chair back from the table. "Me and Jimmy got an errand to run," he announced, standing. "I'll be back later." With that, he motioned me to the door.

I wasn't through eating, but I was just as glad to get out of Lula Hollowell's presence. The basis of the conflict between the two women apparently was Mary Lou's living in town part of the time, but I suspected that jealousy on Lula's part was a factor, too. I wondered if Lula's attitude was typical of the other wives.

John and I walked out the front door and started down the lane toward the Nabb school. After a few minutes in silence, he said, "I'm sorry about that, son. I should have warned you against talking about Mary Lou."

"I'm sorry I brought it up. Your wife doesn't care much for Mary Lou, I take it." My comment contained a question I hoped he'd answer.

"That's puttin' it mildly," he chuckled. "Lula seems to think that Mary Lou pays a little too much attention to men who ain't her own husband, especially me. I guess you might say that the two of 'em ain't got much in common."

Just as I started to ask him to explain that, a figure leapt out of the trees along the road. "What's the password?" he demanded.

"Swinging bridge," we answered in unison. The challenger stepped closer and I could see that it was J. T. Jackson.

"Howdy, boys," he said. "Happy to see the women let you out tonight."

"Yeah, and I'm glad to see that the jailer let you out," John said with a laugh.

J. T. laughed too. "We 'fear no judge or jury,' you know. How you doin', Jimmy?"

"I'm fine. What are we doin' tonight?"

"You'll find out inside. You two better get on in. Meetin's about ready to start."

We walked up the path as J. T. retreated to his post behind a sycamore tree. As usual, the windows of the school building were covered with burlap and the lights within were dim. We could hear a hot debate going on as we entered.

"I'm sayin' that we got to put the son of a bitch out of business," Denny Smith was shouting as I found a seat between Milt Oliver and Steve Choate. Smith was the district's Commonwealth's Attorney.

"Let's think this thing through," Guy Dunning said. As second in command, Guy often presided at the meetings when Doc Amoss wasn't present. "We ought to give Wallis a chance to join us. A lot of folks are changing their minds since the Princeton raid. Our membership is steadily rising. Maybe he'll take the oath, too."

"Hell, Guy," B. Malone said, "Wallis has done been warned two months ago. Even after that, he continued to buy up hillbilly 'baccer for the Trust."

"And," Buck added, "he's refused to join the Association. I say we go over there, whip his ass, and burn him out." Shouts of approval followed.

N. E. Nabb rose to speak. Mr. Nabb was a magistrate in Trigg County and a highly respected man. When he spoke, men listened. The room went quiet. "Men," he began in a soft voice, "we've already agreed to lay low for a little while. It is the dead of winter and there's no growing or buying activity right now. I agree with Mr. Dunning. Let's wait and see what happens." Nabb returned to his seat.

"I'd think you, above all, would be in favor of teaching the son of a bitch that we mean business," Malone insisted. He was referring to the fact that Wallis had managed to identify Mr. Nabb as the author of the threatening warning letter he'd received and attempted to have a Trigg County grand jury indict Nabb because of it

"I bear him no malice on that score," Mr. Nabb said quietly. "Nothing came of his efforts."

"That's only because Denny here headed it off," Buck Tandy said. "I think it's high time that we give these Trust buyers to understand that we don't aim to let 'em starve us another year!" Again, the majority of those present shouted agreement.

"All right, men," Dunning called for quiet. "We've got a new year coming up. There'll be plenty of time to conduct our business when spring comes. If Wallis and the other Trust buyers don't see the error of their ways, we'll see to it that there isn't any hillbilly tobacco for them to buy. So, we'll table that issue for now. For the present, I want everyone to continue their efforts to attract new members. If we can get most of the growers to join up with us, the problem will take care of itself." I wondered if his use of the word "us" meant the Association or the Silent Brigade.

* * * * *

The house was dark when I returned to Bob's. I eased the door open carefully and removed my shoes just inside. I was tiptoeing down the hall toward the stairs when I heard Mary Lou's soft voice. "Good night, Jimmy." Putting anything over on that woman is tougher than sneaking daylight by a rooster.

Chapter 8

Thursday, February 28, 1907

L et's go, son. We got work to do this afternoon,Bob yelled up the
stairs. I'd been anticipating that the rain would halt the farm activities for the day. I had plans to get into Princeton to see Lorena this
evening, and Silent Brigade business was afoot, too.

"Are you sure it ain't still too wet to burn the beds?" I asked, bound-
ing down the stairs.

"Mother Nature waits for no man," Bob replied. "It'll be spring
before you know it. If we don't get the ground sterilized, the weeds'll
take the place, and we won't have no 'baccer plants to set out."

"I was hoping to go to town this evenin'," I murmured as we walked
out of the house. The rain had given way to bright sunshine, and the
temperature was unseasonably warm. We walked to the edge of the
woods north of the tobacco patch where we had brush and logs piled
up on a site about 10 yards wide and perhaps 100 yards long. Ned
Pettit was waiting with a stack of newspapers.

"Well, let's get a fire goin'," Bob said. "Maybe you can get away
early. What's goin' on in town?" Ned handed me a stack of newspapers.

"Oh, nothin' in particular," I said, stuffing the wadded papers into
the brush pile. "Maybe Milt and me'll shoot a little pool." I moved
down one side of the pile, stuffing in paper, while Ned did the same on
the other side. When we met at the end of the bed, Bob struck a match,
lit a roll of paper, and handed it to me. Ned and I moved back up the

bed in the opposite direction lighting the paper inside the pile. By the time we reached the beginning point, fire was blazing throughout the length of the heap of wood. We stepped back to escape the heat.

"Nothin' don't never come to no good in that pool hall," Ned commented with a smile.

"He's right, son. Besides, Mary Lou don't hold much with hangin' around a pool hall, you know," Bob added.

"I didn't aim to tell her." I didn't plan on going to the pool hall, either.

"You don't have to tell her much that goes on in town," Bob laughed.

"That's for a fact," Ned smiled. "Miz Mary Lou, she do seem to have her ways of findin' out 'bout things."

"Yeah, I know." I was a little worried about what she'd say about Lorena and me although I was pretty sure she didn't know about that. I was a lot more worried about whether she knew I was in the Silent Brigade, and if so, what she'd do about it.

In silence, we watched the fire burn for a while, occasionally shifting the wood around some to keep the flames going. Late in the afternoon, the blaze died down and the ashes imparted a glow to the waning sunshine. Overhead, a flock of purple martins chattered to each other about a roosting site. Bob stared at the birds intently for a few seconds, then said, "The birds say there ain't gonna be no rain tonight. Go on into town if you want. Ned and me'll keep an eye on the fire. Tomorrow'll be soon enough to turn these ashes under and smooth out the bed."

"Thanks, Bob," I said, heading for the road. "Don't wait up. I might be late."

Over my shoulder, I heard, "Don't let Mary Lou catch you in that pool hall or there'll be hell to pay." It was much later than I'd hoped to get away. There was plenty of time before the squad was to meet, but as going by the boarding house would add an hour to the trip to the fairgrounds, I wouldn't have much time with Lorena.

* * * * *

All seemed quiet as I slipped behind Mary Lou's boarding house. Although it was suppertime, I hoped they'd finished eating by now. Moving quietly down the side of the house, I saw the light come on in Lorena's room. I snatched up a handful of pebbles and tossed them at her window. In a moment, the curtains parted, and she appeared behind the glass, peering intently into the gathering dusk. I waved to get her attention, and she opened the window.

"Jimmy!" she shouted. "Come on up here!"

"Keep your voice down," I said as loudly as I dared. "Can you come out?" She nodded and started to lower the sash. "Don't let anyone see you," I added.

I ran around to the back porch and stood at the side of the steps. When she came out, I touched the hem of her skirt as she descended so she'd know where I was. She rounded the foot of the stairs and threw her arms around my neck. "Where have you been?" she sighed. "I've missed you so."

"Keep it quiet," I tried to say through the kisses she was showering on my face.

She let her hands slide to my shoulders and backed away, holding me at arms length. "What's the big secret?" Her eyes were questioning.

I was pretty sure that she knew nothing about my Silent Brigade activities. Lorena had her assets, but power of observation wasn't on the top of the list. "We wouldn't want Mary Lou or the boarders to catch us," I answered. "I can't stay long anyway, but I did want to see you."

The warmth of the afternoon had faded with the sunset and a chill was in the air. She hadn't bothered to get her coat and was shivering. Apparently satisfied with my answer, she slid her hands to the back of my neck and moved her body against me. "I'm so cold. I'm glad you're here."

With her voluptuous form pressed against me, I remembered why I'd taken time I could not afford to see her. I hugged her tightly and brushed her hair aside to kiss the side of her neck. She smelled heavenly. "I can only stay a minute," were all the words I could manage.

"Have you made any progress on our plans?" she said, her mouth near my ear.

I was unaware that we had any plans. Fact is, we had not shared a lot of conversation the night of the raid, and I hadn't seen her since. Maybe females had their fantasies, too. "I've been thinking about it," seemed like a good answer.

"Come on up to my room and we'll talk about it," she whispered. I wouldn't have thought it possible for her to press even closer, but she found a way.

"I'd really like to," I said, knowing she'd believe that. "But I just don't have the time. I'm supposed to be someplace in just a few minutes." I made a feeble attempt to escape her embrace.

"Can't it wait?" She wiggled around a little in my arms. Her grasp on me loosened slightly.

"No, I'm really sorry. I have to go."

"Can you come by later?" Her arms fell to her sides, disappointment covering her face.

"Maybe — I doubt it, though. I'm really sorry, but I have to go." I made a stronger effort to escape.

Lorena screwed her face up into a pouty-mouthed frown. "Well, maybe I'll just have to find a new playmate," she said as she started up the porch steps.

As much as I wanted to stay and as much as I wanted to retort to that remark, I knew that J. T., Steve, Milt, and the rest of the squad were waiting for me at the fairgrounds. I was late enough already. "I'll be back when I can," I said to her back as she entered the house.

I slipped around the house and started toward the fairgrounds. Milt had agreed to supply a horse for me. He and Steve were waiting when I arrived. "Where the hell have you been?" was Milt's greeting.

Milt knew, of course, about Lorena, but I'd said nothing to Steve. I smiled, a bit coyly, I thought. "Sometimes things come up, you know."

"Sometimes things come up that ought to stay down," Steve commented. I don't think even he knew what he meant.

"You ought to do your thinkin' with your head," Milt said, handing me the reins of a beautiful black gelding.

J. T. appeared out of the darkness. "Let's get. We got a long way to go." As usual, he was all business.

We mounted and rode away from Princeton to the southwest . At Hobson's store crossroads, we were to meet another group of night riders before heading on to the town of Rockcastle, a hamlet on the Cumberland River in Trigg County. When we arrived at Hobson's, I expected to be challenged for the password, but there was not a soul in sight. "Are we late?" I asked J. T.

"I don't think so," he replied, looking around. "Let's get back in the trees over here where we can keep an eye on the road." We moved a short distance off the side of the road into a grove of cedars. "Colder'n a witch's tit out here, ain't it?" Steve said as he dismounted.

My horse was lathered and ready for a rest. As I climbed to the ground, the animal and I both heaved a sigh of relief. "Do you know what we're gonna do at Rockcastle?" I asked as I patted the horse's neck.

"Yeah," Milt replied. "We're gonna finish payin' off old man Wallis for defyin' the night riders."

"Why, hell, we destroyed his tobacco two weeks ago."

"The son of a bitch got out there and put the fire out after we left. He's packed what he managed to save up in hogsheads and hauled 'em to the river for shipment. We're gonna hold our own version of the Boston Tea Party," Milt laughed.

Before I could reply, we heard the clip-clop of horses approaching. J. T. cocked his rifle and crept near the roadside. A group of 15 or so horsemen slowed as they neared. "What's the password?" J. T. challenged.

"Silent Brigade," the leader answered.

"We'll be right with you," J. T. said. Turning to us, he ordered, "Get your masks on, and let's ride."

I had a mask made from a flour sack. I'd cut holes for my mouth and eyes and I figured that I'd have less trouble keeping it on. I pulled it over my head and mounted. Our party moved out into the road to join the other group. Our 10 made a total of about 25 masked riders. The group rode out, more to the west now, headed for the river.

* * * * *

Six hogsheads of tobacco sat basking in the moonlight on the wharf . With a whoop that would have made the Boston Tea Party "Indians" envious, we descended on the landing. Without spoken command, four or five men rolled each great cask to the edge of the dock. A mighty heave sent each splashing into the muddy water. Milt and I were pushing the last of the lot off the dock when some old man came running down the bank.

"Damn it," he was screaming, "Why are you dumping my 'baccer?" He ran up to J. T. and pushed him back from the wharf. Much to my surprise, J. T. did not shoot him on the spot.

"What are you talkin' about?" I could hear a note of confusion in J. T.'s voice.

"I'm talkin' about that's my 'baccer you pitched in the river, damn it," he cried. "Why in hell are you doin' that to me?"

J. T. assumed an apologetic stance. "I'm sorry, Mr. Holland," he said. "These hogsheads belong to Wallis. Maybe he'll listen to us now."

"You damn fool, three of 'em belong to Wallis. The other three are mine. Damn it!"

"Well, it was a mistake," J. T. said. "I know that you belong to the Association, Mr. Holland. We didn't know you had 'baccer here — we don't mean you no harm."

"Damn it to hell!" Holland exploded. "Makes no difference whether you meant it or not. My 'baccer'll be ruined if we don't get it out of the water!"

J. T. whirled around. "Let's go, boys," he shouted. With one last whoop, we rode away up the river bank. I looked over my shoulder as we reached the top of the ridge. Holland was shaking his fist in the air. He was shouting something I was just as glad I couldn't hear.

Chapter 9

Thursday, April 18, 1907

W here the hell are you? Bob was yelling from the back yard. He'd been like a newly adopted kid at Christmas all morning. The cause of his excitement was the fact that we were going to Princeton this morning to bring Mary Lou and Price home for the summer.

I had OGM hitched to the wagon and had just started to drive out when he came running into the barn. Seeing the wagon comin out, he presented a comical sight by digging his heels into the dirt in an effort to reverse direction. That accomplished, he turned around and leapt onto the seat beside me.

"Pretty spry for an old codger like you," I joked.

He tried to fake a menacing look. "I ain't so old as a whippersnapper like you might think," he said. "In fact, if you was to pay a little attention, you might just learn somethin' today." The attempted sinister countenance gave way to a beaming smile. Bob was in a good mood today.

"I checked the beds this morning," I said, not wanting to get into any discussion about women with him. "The plants are peeking out of the ground. When do you think they'll be ready to transplant?"

His eyes wandered to the sky. "If this warm weather holds, we'll be settin' 'em out in another three weeks or so. Did you get the canvas covering back over the plants?"

"Of course." I was a little insulted that he'd question my competence.

"That's good. We don't want the frost gettin' them plants. We'd be in a hell of a fix if anything happened to the beds."

"How's that?" I'd never considered what might happen if something got the plant beds.

"Hell, son, if a man didn't have 'baccer plants, he'd be out of business. No plants means no crop which means no money."

"Couldn't he fix up another bed?"

Bob smiled indulgently. "If it was early enough, he could. But if it was late in the season, there'd be no time to start all over again."

I thought on that for a minute. We approached a pot-hole in the road and I had to steer to the left side to avoid it. "Couldn't a man borrow some plants from his neighbors if he needed to?"

Bob's face turned somber as all trace of his happiness disappeared for a moment. He brightened before he answered me, but he was still serious. "Ordinarily, yes. That is if the neighbors had any plants to spare. They'd look after their own crops first, of course. But the situation bein' what it is right now, me bein' a hillbilly and all, I'd have about as much chance as a snowball in hell." We rode along in silence for a few minutes before he spoke again. "No sir, if anything happened to them beds, we'd be in a hell of a fix."

"Are you worried about it?"

"There's been quite a few instances of the night riders destroyin' hillbilly beds," he replied. "They've been known to scrape 'em with a hoe. One of the worst tricks is to sow grass seed in the bed. By the time a man discovers that, he ain't got nothin; but grass and it's too late to start another bed. There's even a few cases where they've forced a man to scrape his own bed. It's bad business."

"Didn't I hear that there's a new state law against scrapin' beds?"

Bob turned to stare at me. "Yes, the Legislature did set up a prison term for it," he said. "But you know as well as I do that they ain't gonna convict — or even indict — none of the night riders, no matter what they do." His voice was gloomy.

I felt a little badly about spoiling his jovial humor. In an attempt to repair the damage, I said, "Bob, did I ever tell you about the time that smart alec come in the blacksmith shop?"

"No." He didn't seem very interested.

"Well, he come in there while the blacksmith was working on a horseshoe. You know how hot they have to get those things to work on 'em. The blacksmith put the horseshoe on the anvil and the smart alec picked it up. Of course, he threw it down right quick. Ever'body in the place laughed at him. The blacksmith said, 'Burned yourself, didn't you?' The smart alec says, 'No, it just don't take me long to look at a horseshoe.'"

It worked. He laughed and I laughed along with him. By the time it wore off, we were past the fairgrounds. We were at the boarding house in a few minutes. Lorena was sitting in a rocker on the porch. As we pulled in beside the house, she jumped up and waved.

"What does a big smile from a pretty girl that like mean ?" Bob asked.

"If you pay attention to me, you might learn something," I answered, pulling OGM to a halt.

Bob was off the wagon and into the house like a shot. I stepped up on the porch into Lorena's arms. She gave me a big hug and kiss before I had a chance to say a word. She was wearing a pink dress and had her hair pulled away from her face. She looked good. In a moment, she became aware that the whole neighborhood might be watching and released me. She resumed her seat and assumed a demure pose in the rocker. "We've got a few problems," she announced.

"I thought things were going pretty good. What's wrong?" I pulled up another rocker and sat beside her.

"For one thing, Mrs. Hollowell is closing the boarding house for the summer. That means I'll have to go elsewhere." She sat with her back braced in the rocker, not looking at me. The thought that Mary Lou's coming to the country for the summer meant closing the boarding house had not occurred to me.

"What'll you do?" It dawned on me that I didn't know much about Lorena.

"I've been through this before," she sighed, relaxing a little. "Usually, I spend the summers with my aunt and uncle in Louisville." She turned to look at me with soulful eyes. "But, I don't think I want to leave you." She placed her hand over mine on the rocker's arm.

"Lorena," I said, not really knowing what to say, "I don't want you to leave, either." My brain was racing, but, try as I might, I couldn't really understand what she considered the problem. Given that, I was not likely to produce a solution. We rocked in silence while I contemplated the best way to learn what I needed to know. "Is money the problem?"

She continued to sway in the rocker until I wondered if she'd heard. "No," she said at length. "You don't know the background on me, do you?" That was just as I'd hoped she'd say.

"Please tell me all about it." I shifted my weight in the chair so that I faced her.

She looked into my eyes for a minute before she spoke. Transferring her gaze to a tree across the way, she swallowed hard. "I'm an orphan, too." She hesitated, unable to find the words she wanted.

I knew what she was feeling. Taking advantage of her pause, I said, "You don't have to tell me about it if you don't want to."

She managed a weak smile and looked at me briefly. "You're sweet. My father went to Cuba with the army and didn't come back. The government provided a pension for Mom and me, but she... I don't want to give you chapter and verse. I'm sure you understand."

I simply nodded that I did. Tears rolled down her cheeks and I fought mine.

She placed her hand on mine on the arm of the chair. "The thing is, I get enough money from the trust, so that's not a problem."

"The Trust? What the hell do you have to do with the Trust?"

She looked quizzically at me. Slowly, a full smile crept across her face. "Not the Duke Trust, silly. My Mom put up the pension money in trust for me at the bank."

"Oh," I said, embarrassed.

"You see, when I'm 21, all the money will be mine. In the meantime, they give me an allowance each year. 'Maintenance,' they call it. As I said, I have some relatives in Louisville, but I don't like the city much and I don't want to leave you for the summer, either." She laced her fingers in mine.

"Well, then, there's no problem. There's other boarding houses right here in town, you know."

"Yes, I know," she said with a sigh. "I've looked into two of them. I like it here with Mrs. Hollowell — for all the talk there is about her, she takes good care of me." After another deep sigh, she went on, "I guess Mrs. Haynes' place down the way would be all right for the summer."

"Just move down the street here and I'll be happy to take care of you this summer." She smiled brightly as I squeezed her hand.

"That'll be nice," she said, still smiling. "There's one other thing. I usually do my yearly shopping when I go to Louisville for the summer. If I'm not going to stay this year, I was thinking of going on a shopping trip for a few days. How'd you like to come along?"

The grin on my face answered her question. "I'll have to think of something to tell the Hollowells," I thought aloud.

"I've already taken care of that. I talked to Mrs. Hollowell about it this morning. We have tickets for the train on May first." Her smile revealed sublime pleasure at the prospect. I felt the same.

Lorena started to lean toward me, her lips inviting, when a roar rolled out the front door of the house. "What in the world ever possessed you to do a thing like that?" It was the first time I'd ever heard Bob Hollowell raise his voice. I jumped up and started for the door. Lorena tightened her grip on my hand.

"Come on back here," she said, tugging my arm.

"What's goin' on in there?" I asked.

"I told you we had a couple of problems. That's the other one. Mrs. Hollowell saw fit to give the Caldwell County grand jury the details of the night rider raid on Princeton. We knew that Mr. Hollowell wouldn't like it."

"She did what?" I was dumbfounded.

"She told the grand jury all she knew about the raid. And she knew plenty. I tried to talk her out of it. We thought that since half the jurymen were night riders anyway, her testimony wouldn't tell them anything they didn't already know. She suspects the county judge is one of 'em, too. She told them, anyway."

I understood why Bob was roaring. Knowing the members of the Silent Brigade as I did, it was clear to me that they would not take kindly to any such action. In fact, they'd seriously frown on it. I repeated Bob's question, "What would posses her to do a thing like that?"

"I'm not entirely sure. Between you and me and the gate post, I think her dislike for Mr. Hollowell's family had something to do with it. At any rate, she had to know that it wouldn't do any good — and it didn't, either. Despite the fact that she named names and places, the grand jury did not hand down a single indictment. That's clear evidence that she was right about the jury members all being in on it."

I already knew that they were. My first worry was whether she'd implicated me. I'd been told, "we fear no judge or jury" many times since I'd joined the Silent Brigade, but if she supplied accurate information — and I was sure she did —it seemed to me that the grand jury would have to take some kind of legal action.

Lorena seemed to read the concern on my face. "There's nothing to worry about, Jimmy," she soothed. "In the first place, nothing happened. In the second place, she's going to the country for the summer. Out of sight, out of mind. It's all over now."

As much as I wanted to find comfort in Lorena's words, I knew damned well that this wouldn't be the end of it. The powerful men who comprised the membership of the Silent Brigade weren't about to tolerate such defiance, especially not from Mary Lou Hollowell.

* * * * *

Bob was reserved as we drove back to the country. He and Mary Lou rode on the seat while Price and I occupied the wagon bed along with the grips and trunks. She tried to carry on a light conversation, but neither Bob or I were in a bantering mood. Price was unaware, I guess, but I was sure that the thoughts going through Bob's mind were about the same as mine.

Eventually, she gave up the effort. We bounced along in sullen silence, the creaking of the wheels providing the only relief. Finally, just as we turned toward the Nabb school, Bob broke the morose atmosphere. "Just tell me one thing," he asked Mary Lou. "What did you hope to accomplish by talking to the grand jury?"

"To bring that lawless bunch to justice," she rejoined. "If no one else has the courage to stand up to those ruffians, I'll just have to do it myself." The usual tone of sensual softness was totally absent from her voice.

"But, honey," Bob said, a plea in his voice, "You had to know that it was a waste of time. The law ain't gonna do nothin'. All you've done is make the night riders mad."

Her jaw tightened. "Then we're even," she spat, "they made me angry."

We'd reached the house. Bob drove through the gate and stopped in front of the porch. He looked as if he had more to say, but he realized, just as I did, that Mary Lou was determined to have the last word. He dismounted and helped her down. Price sprang to the ground and ran off in the direction of the creek. As Mary Lou dusted off her clothing, I saw Bob heave a sigh of resignation. "Go on in, sugar," he said, "I'll bring the goods in."

She shot a grin at me and disappeared inside the house. I picked up a trunk and handed it to Bob on the porch. "She's stubborn as Job's mule, ain't she?" I tried to make it sound like a joke.

"She's a good woman, Jimmy," Bob replied. "I know that folks talk about her somethin' awful, and I guess ..." His voice trailed off as he assumed the weight of the trunk. Lowering it to the floor, he straightened and looked at me. "She's as fine a wife as a man could hope for. It's just that I just don't understand her, sometimes."

I lifted a grip and pitched it to him. "I never heard any man claim that he understood women. That is, none but some pool room know-it-alls."

Bob smiled for the first time all afternoon. "You're right about that son." He dropped the grip and took the cardboard box I handed him. When he set it down, he pulled a red bandanna from his pocket and mopped his brow. "Jimmy, do you know what she's done?"

I was surprised that he'd ask. "Yeah, Lorena told me."

He nodded. "I just can't imagine what got into her."

I was at a loss for what to say. I thought about telling him that Lorena had suggested that perhaps she was taking a slap at Lula, but decided that was best let alone. Likewise I didn't want to mention that I knew she was smart enough to know that she was asking for trouble. "You want me to put OGM away?" was the safest thing I could come up with.

"No," he sighed. "I'll do that. A little time alone in the barn might do me some good. You carry this stuff in." He jumped from the porch into the wagon and climbed over the seat. I dropped to the ground and watched him pull around the house.

"Where do you want this trunk?" I yelled through the door. Mary Lou appeared from the kitchen. "Where's Bob?" she asked.

"He's putting OGM away. "Where do you want this thing? It's heavy."

"Just sit it down." She flashed that smile of hers on me. "I want to talk to you a minute."

I eased the trunk to the floor with a dreadful feeling. She either was going to mention the Princeton raid or Lorena. I wasn't eager to discuss either topic with her. "What's on your mind?" I asked, sitting on the trunk. I tried to look as innocent as possible.

She fixed a stern gaze on me for a moment. "I want you to know that Lorena is a fine girl. Her parents were some of the most respected folks in the county. I'll not have you spoiling her reputation."

It seemed to me that if she'd started worrying about reputations, she ought to think about her own. Knowing that she'd have to have her say before I got a word in, I kept quiet.

"I insist that all my young ladies maintain an air of decorum. I tried to talk her out of taking you to Louisville. But she is 18 years old, and I'm not her guardian or even trustee, so I really don't have any authority in the matter, but I can talk to you. I suppose that what you and she do is between the two of you, ..."

She paused in her monologue as if deep in thought. I sat quietly until she resumed.

"Well," she heaved a deep sigh, "nobody understands better than I how people talk. You'll be seen at the depot. Just try not to give the local gossips any more ammunition." She smiled at me, then added, "Please."

Even though I didn't know what "decorum" meant, I did realize that I'd gotten off lightly. Relief in my heart, I said, "I know Lorena's a fine woman. Please believe me, I wouldn't dare do anything to damage her in any way." I returned her smile. After I'd said it, I hoped she wouldn't pick up that I'd called Lorena a "woman" while she'd referred to her as a "girl."

Her eyes seemed to flash as we heard Bob coming in the back door. "Take that stuff to the bedroom," she snapped. "Supper'll be ready soon." Turning to Bob, she commanded, "Go find Price. By the time you get him in and get cleaned up, we'll be ready to eat."

It took several trips to get all the baggage upstairs. By the time I finished and washed up, Mary Lou was calling us to supper.

The atmosphere in the house was somber through the meal and late into the evening. I sat out on the porch for quite a while, thoughts of Lorena and Louisville dominating my mind. I finally decided that the sooner I went to bed, the sooner it'd be tomorrow. With her on my mind, I had some trouble getting to sleep, but slept like a dead man.

* * * * *

At breakfast, Bob and Mary Lou seemed to have patched up their difficulties. They were both in a much better frame of mind. His usual light-heartedness had returned and the tone of sweetness was back in her voice. He had a twinkle in his eye that I hadn't seen since last September.

When we'd finished eating, Bob arose and slapped me on the back. "Let's go check the 'baccer beds, son. The weather was a little nippy last night ..." He slid a sly grin at his wife. "..I want to make sure that the frost didn't wilt the plants."

"Can I go, too, Daddy?" Price whined. I just didn't like that kid.

"No, darling, you stay here with me," Mary Lou answered. Then to Bob and me, "Get out of my kitchen now." She made shooing motions with her hands, a broad smile on her face. "Go on, there's woman's work to be done."

We walked out the back door and around the house. Moving south along the path, we entered the field where this year's crop was to be grown. The minute I saw the canvas, I knew what had happened. The wispy white covering of the tobacco beds was in shreds. The Silent Brigade's "hoe toters" had made a call during the night. As we approached through the dew soaked weeds edging the bed, Bob's face went ashen.

"Well," he said slowly, "we're ruined."

Indignation swelled within me as we inspected the damage. The ground within the bed showed the effects of the hoe. The fledgling plants lay on top of the dirt, torn and dead. How could the Silent Brigade do this to one of its own?

"Did you hear anything?" Bob asked, digging at the ground with a toe.

"No. I had some trouble going to sleep, but slept soundly."

His chin sank to his chest. "We'd best go tell Mary Lou." He turned and started back for the house.

I was not eager to hear what Mary Lou would have to say. Thoughts of how I might approach J. T. Jackson about this filled my mind as I trailed along behind Bob. J. T. and John Hollowell must have organized this outrage, but neither hated Bob. Political differences aside, John was his brother. How could they do this?

Mary Lou was seated in the parlor when we entered. Observing the pallor on Bob's face, she laid the newspaper aside. "What's wrong?"

Bob merely crossed the room and sank into an upholstered chair. Mary Lou turned her questioning gaze to me. "What's wrong?" she repeated.

"The night riders destroyed our plant bed," I said as calmly as possible.

She exploded from the sofa. Nearly leaping into the air, she sprang to her feet and started for the door. "What? Who?" She stopped at the door and turned to face her husband. Taking a deep breath, she said, "Bob, tell me about it."

Bob seemed in a daze. Staring straight ahead, he said, "There's nothing to tell. The night riders' hoe toters crept in last night and scraped the 'baccer bed. They destroyed the canvas and laid waste to the plants. We're ruined." His lips were the only part of his body that moved.

"Somebody will pay for this," she screamed. "It's your brother and 'B' Malone that did this. I'm going to talk to the sheriff right now." She started for the bedroom.

Bob snapped out of his stupor. He bounded across the room and grabbed her arm. "Hold on, now," he said. "You know the law will be of no help." In my mind, it was her talking to the law that brought it on. Anyway, Bob was right — the law would do nothing.

Mary Lou jerked her arm free of Bob's grasp. His crestfallen look seemed to calm her a little. "Well," she said with a sigh, "I guess you're right." She re-crossed the room and resumed her seat on the sofa. In a moment, she went on, "You are right, the law will look the other way, just like they did when I told about the raid. That simply means that we're on our own. Somebody will pay for this!"

* * * * *

The days seemed to crawl by. It was glorious springtime, the lilies and dogwoods were in full bloom and the gentle breeze carried the full perfume of their flowers. The robins frolicked in the budding trees while the grass greened underfoot. Yet, the atmosphere at the Hollowells carried no hint of gladness.

At church that Sunday, Mary Lou spotted Lula and John Hollowell as we were leaving. Detaching herself from Bob's hold, she made a bee-line for Lula. Everybody in the congregation knew what was coming and gathered around in anticipation. John, in an effort to avoid the confrontation, picked up Lula and deposited her in the buggy. He ran for the other side, but didn't make it before Mary Lou was on them.

"Hold it right there," Mary Lou shouted. "I want to talk to you." She seized the horse's reins to prevent John and Lula's get away.

"We got nothin' to say to you, you harlot." Lula's face was black with rage.

"I thank you for your Christian attitude this fine Sunday morning," Mary Lou fixed Lula with a counterfeit smile, "but it's your husband I want to speak with." The contrast between the two women was never more obvious: Mary Lou looked fabulous, calm and composed, while Lula was plain-looking and seething with rage.

"He's got nothin' to say to you, either. Why don't you just go on back to town and operate your brothel and leave decent folks be?" Lula's voice was high pitched with passion. A mummer went through the crowd as the ladies whispered to each other behind their hands and the men laughed openly.

"I've got a few words to say to the decent folks who scraped my plant bed. John Hollowell, I know that you and Malone are responsible. I just want you to know that you're going to pay for it."

Bob had reached her side. "Now, honey," he pleaded, "let's just go on home." He forcefully removed her hand from the reins. It was the most manly display I'd ever seen from him. John shot Bob a look of relief as he snatched up the reins. As John whipped the reins, the buggy tore out of the church yard as if the very devil was chasing it.

Mary Lou jerked away from Bob, contempt on her face. "Look at that coward run," she cried. The semicircle of people around her recoiled from the heat of her wrath. Bob took her in hand and guided her toward the buggy. When she was seated, still sputtering with anger, he motioned to me to get in. "I think I'll walk," I shouted. He nodded, the look on his face conveying that he wished he had such an option. I waited in the shade of the huge maple tree until the buggy was out of sight before I set out for the walk back to the Hollowells. I was in hopes that she'd cool off by the time I got there.

Since I was in no hurry to get there, I took my time on the walk. It was a beautiful sunny Sunday. As I crossed the creek, the water looked inviting; I decided to take my first swim of the year. I stripped off my clothes and dashed for the bank, leaping high into the air. Pulling my legs up, I wrapped my arms around my knees as I fell toward the water with a whoop. I yelled even louder when I hit the water — it was ice cold. I guess I'd pushed springtime a bit. I scrambled out so fast that I thought that any observer would have thought that the water threw me back out. I lay on the bank in the sun and out of the wind until I was dry, then got dressed. Wanting to give Mary Lou plenty of time to cool off, I loafed along on the road, kicked dirt clods, and threw rocks at birds. I guess it must have been about 2:30 in the afternoon by the time I passed the Nabb school. Another couple of minutes brought me to Steve Choate's shack. It appeared deserted. Finally, I reached Bob's house. Just to be on the safe side, I decided to go around and enter through the back door. As I rounded the corner of the house, I spotted Mary Lou engaged in animated conversation with Ned and Steve in front of the barn. She had her back to me, but Ned saw me and waved. Mary Lou spun around to see the cause of Ned's wave. Spotting me, she frowned and turned back to the conversation.

Chapter 10

Wednesday, May 1, 1907

A t long last, the day Lorena and I were to leave for Louisville had arrived. Although I did like and admire Mary Lou Hollowell, her railings against the Silent Brigade in general and John Hollowell and B. Malone in particular were wearing a little thin. Every minute of every day at every location was consumed by her declaration that "somebody would pay" for the destruction of our plant beds.

Although the train wasn't scheduled to leave the Princeton depot until 10 AM, I did not plan to be late, so I left the house at 6:30. Keyed up with excitement, I'd been totally unable to sleep, anyway. Bob and Mary Lou got a lot of laughs out of my leaving so early, giving me all the more reason to be on my way.

The sky was beginning to lighten in the east as I set off up the lane. The birds were chirping their early morning roll call as I passed Steve Choate's shack. I noted with only casual interest that there was no light inside. I would have thought that he'd be up preparing to set out tobacco plants. Past the Nabb school, I thought I saw a shadow moving along the side of the lane. I stopped and listened, but heard nothing. Maybe it was a deer.

Sunrise burst over the horizon in the full glory of a spring morning as I walked along. A few low-hanging clouds in the east imparted a spectrum of pink and blue hues to the golden rays streaming toward earth. The wind carried a slight chill, but the sun's rays promised a warm day. All thoughts of the Silent Brigade and tobacco beds were far from my mind as I neared the Princeton depot.

The clock inside the waiting room read 8:30. I was plenty early and, as I had the place to myself, I guess no other passenger trains were scheduled this morning . I thought about walking on down to the widow Haynes' boarding house to pick up Lorena, but decided against it. We'd agreed to meet at the depot, and she wouldn't be ready yet anyway. After a few minutes, I wandered outside to enjoy the sunshine.

Seating myself on a bench against the wall of the depot, I leaned against the backrest and stretched out my legs. The town was peaceful and quiet in the morning air. Basking in the sunshine, my eyes became heavy and I closed them against the bright light.

In what seemed only a moment, I became aware of someone shaking my shoulder. "Wake up, Jimmy, you're burning daylight." I opened my eyes to find Milt Oliver standing beside me.

"Where'd you come from?" I had not heard a sound.

"Don't you know I'm a member of the Silent Brigade?" His smile looked a little pained.

"Yeah," I said unenthusiastically, "me too, although I'm not too proud of it anymore."

Milt looked seriously into my face for a moment. Then he looked away before he spoke. "What are you doin' in town?"

"I'm goin' on a little trip," I said. "What are you doin' here?"

"Oh, I had a little business to take care of." Milt studied the ruins of the Trust warehouse across the street as if deep in thought. At length, he said, "Jimmy, you're my friend. I want you to know that I had nothin' to do with the scraping of Bob Hollowell's 'baccer bed." His facial expression begged understanding.

"I never thought you did."

Milt turned to look into my eyes. "What you said about not bein' proud ..." He hesitated, searching for the right words. He was about to go on when the tranquillity of the morning was shattered by the sound of horses galloping down the street. The county sheriff flashed by, two deputies in hot pursuit, whipping their horses hell bent for leather.

"What's goin' on?" I wondered aloud.

"More night rider business," Milt said matter of factly. He paused to adjust the military style blue cap that topped his dusty clothes. Brushing his sandy hair back under the cap, he added, "Seems like they had a little ruckus out in the country last night."

What now? I thought. Whatever it was, it would probably involve Mary Lou. I'd noticed that J. T. and John had been pretty scarce around me since before our plant beds were destroyed. That had to mean that they were up to something that didn't involve me and they didn't want me to know about. Before I could ask Milt to go on, the town hackney pulled up containing Lorena and three huge grips. The bulk of her luggage made me feel a little self-conscious with just my grubby knapsack. I walked to the edge of the platform to greet her.

She was wearing a linen duster that covered her green silk dress. Her hair was tucked up under a triangular hat of matching color. As she lifted her eyes to me, the expected happiness was absent from her appearance. "Have you heard?" Her face was pallid.

"Heard what? What's happening?"

She offered me her hand to help her down. She turned to face me as the driver placed her grips on the plank flooring beside us. She silently eyed Milt Oliver who was busily making an in-depth study of the platform at his feet.

"I'm sorry," I said realizing that they had not met. "Milt, this is my friend Lorena."

She smiled briefly and said hello. Milt's face turned beet red. He rocked back on his heels and mumbled something inaudible. After an awkward moment, he announced, "Well, I got to get," and walked away toward town.

The hackney driver was standing beside Lorena looking bored. "Oh," she said fishing around in her bag. The driver smiled as she handed him a bill. "You young folks have a good trip," he said as he turned away.

Alone on the platform, I asked, "Now, what's all the excitement about?"

"Somebody scraped John Hollowell's and B. Malone's plant beds last night," she said. All color was now gone from her face.

"Is that why the sheriff tore out of here like a house afire?"

"Yes. He's going out to investigate."

"The law didn't seem to care much when our bed was destroyed," I snorted.

"No, they didn't," she agreed. "I don't understand this." Everybody in town is upset this time."

The same outrage I felt when we discovered our bed destroyed welled up within me. This foolishness was getting totally out of hand. "Well, apparently there's a difference between the destruction of a hillbilly bed and those of fine upstanding citizens like John and Malone." Even I could hear the indignation in my voice.

"Apparently so." Her voice was very soft.

The loud whistle of the approaching train suspended our conversation. We stood back from the edge of the platform as the locomotive pulled into the station amid a cloud of black smoke and the screech of brakes. The locomotive slid slowly by and ground to a halt with a passenger car directly in front of where we were standing. As soon as the car stopped, a conductor appeared on the steps and dropped a stepstool to the ground at the base of the car's entrance.

I'd never ridden a train before, but I'd seen plenty of them load and unload passengers. The conductor's faded blue wool uniform and even the man it contained always looked just the same. My Pa used to joke that it was a "puzzlement" how that same fellow could appear on so many different runs.

A couple of drummers exited the car, giving Lorena a lustful eye as they passed. "Gettin' aboard, Miss?" the conductor asked.

"Yes, we both are," Lorena answered. A faint hint of a smile crossed her face.

The conductor motioned to the baggage boy to get her grips as he stood aside to give us access to the steps. "Shall I take your, uh, luggage, uh, sir?"

The idea of turning over the knapsack containing most of my worldly possessions to a stranger did not appeal to me. Before I could answer, Lorena came to the rescue. "No, we'll keep that with us," she told the conductor as she started up the steps. I followed her into the car.

The interior of the car was pretty much what I'd expected. The cloth upholstery of the seats, showing the original deep blue in the seams, was now faded to an indiscriminate shade of gray. The floor had not seen the benefit of a broom for some time, and the light fixtures hanging from the ceiling were covered with dust. Only a few people occupied the seats. A group of four men — drummers, probably — was chattering away at the opposite end of the long aisle, while a couple of other men and a few women with children were scattered among the seats. Lorena glided smoothly halfway down the aisle and selected a seat facing one of the women. The lady appeared to be about thirty, was fairly attractive and smiled faintly as Lorena sat opposite her. "Hello," Lorena said with her best smile as I stowed my knapsack in the overhead rack.

The woman smiled weakly but did not speak, turning her attention to the baby in her arms. I was just as glad — I didn't want to talk to her anyway. Lorena slid across the seat to make room for me next to the aisle. The train rolled slightly backward as the brakes were released, then lurched forward sending me first toward the woman and then re-coiling back into my seat.

Lorena eyed the woman across from us for a moment as the steady clackety-clack rhythm rocked us and the car. As the lady busied her-self making cooing sounds to the baby, Lorena said, "Jimmy, are you happy?"

That's one of those questions a man has to answer carefully. Nei-ther "yes" nor "no" would convey how I felt. I wanted her to under-stand that I was happy to be here with her, but I didn't want her to think that just being on the train was all I needed to be content. After consid-ering a moment, I said, "Well, I'm happy to be out of all that foolish-ness goin' on and I am happy to be here with you, but a little worried, too."

She smiled that beautiful smile and wiggled her fingers into mine. "What are you worried about?"

"I'm worried about Mary Lou, for one thing," I admitted. "And about bein' in the big city for another."

She laughed. "Mrs. Hollowell can take care of herself, I assure you. As far as the big city goes, I'll take care of you."

"I was in hopes that you would." That sounded more casual than I had intended.

The lady seated across from me frowned and looked away. In a moment, her eyes returned to me. "If you'll excuse us, it's the baby's feeding time," she announced, undoing the button at the top of her shirtwaist.

I removed my hand from Lorena's grasp and stood, slightly em-barrassed. "Why don't you go out to the landing between the cars?" Lorena suggested.

"Good idea," I said. "The fresh air will do me good." Everyone in the car ignored me as I made my way down the aisle. Outside, the air rushing by was warm, but full of coal smoke from the engine. The country rushing by was bursting into spring. The grass was turning green and the trees were budding into life. Although I could not hear them, I felt sure that the robins were chirping. I had no idea how long it took to feed a baby, but I stayed about twice as long as I thought it would take, just to make sure.

When I came back to our seat, Lorena and the baby were asleep. The lady was looking out the window and although I'm sure that she heard me, did not acknowledge my return. I sat and my lack of sleep overtook me.

* * * * * *

I awoke with a start as the train screeched to a stop, nearly flinging me into the aisle. The lady and the baby were gone. Lorena was holding my arm, pulling me back into the seat. "We're here," she announced.

"Louisville?" I asked, rubbing my burning eyes.

"The Falls City," she said. "We're in for a big adventure."

I retrieved my knapsack from the overhead rack and we exited the car. The platform was a milling crowd containing more people than I'd ever seen in one place before. Men and women were hugging each other in embraces of welcome or good-bye while porters weaved carts of luggage through the throng. The noise of people shouting and the trains added to the confusion. Lorena glided through the confusion to somehow locate the cart bearing her grips.

"Take these out front and get us a cab," she directed the old black man who was managing the cart. He simply nodded diffidently and wheeled the cart around. We followed in the wake of the path he cleared to the exit of the station.

The scene on the street was little different from the depot. For a boy accustomed to being in the country, this seemed utter bedlam. Lorena, however, was perfectly at ease. She stood aside as the porter hailed a waiting hackney. A hansom cab pulled even with us. The driver, dressed to the nines, was seated high above us. As the porter loaded Lorena's grips into the boot, she attempted to get inside. The first step was 18 inches above the pavement and her skirts wouldn't allow her to climb up. After several tries, she looked at me in frustration. Seeing no other option, I place my hands on her rump, shoved her into the cab and followed her in. She was giggling as I sat beside her.

"Wow," I exclaimed, "this is nice." The interior was snug, made for two, and offered blinds for privacy. "Where to folks?" the driver asked through the opening in the roof.

"The Galt House," Lorena answered as the trap door in the roof fell shut. She snuggled against me as the vehicle began moving. "What do you want to do first?"

I restrained my impulsive reply. "Well, we are headed for a hotel, aren't we?"

She mirrored my smile, but moved slightly away. "You're checking in," she said. "I'm staying with my aunt and uncle."

"What?" My illusions were shattered.

"Not to worry," she patted my knee. "We'll have some time alone, but we also need to maintain some semblance of propriety." I had no idea of what she said but I understood what she meant.

The cab turned right off 2nd Street onto Main. A block later, we stopped in front of the Galt House Hotel. It was the biggest building I'd ever seen. "Jump out and help me down," Lorena directed. As I took her hand, a black man in a purple uniform pulled her grips from the boot of the cab. "No," she said, "leave those there." Lorena gave the driver some money and a smile and told him to wait. She hooked her arm through mine. "Allow me to escort you," she smiled.

In the lobby, she led me to a circular sofa. "Just sit and take it all in while I make the arrangements," she said leaving me in a swirl of skirts. The lobby of a hotel was something I'd never seen before. It was not busy — only a few people were sitting about. The carpet was plush and the light from the electric chandeliers overhead reflected from the surfaces of the highly polished tables. I was still soaking in the atmosphere when she returned, a key in her hand.

"You've got Room 14, right here on the first floor," she announced. "It'll be nice not to have to ride the elevator."

"I was kinda lookin' forward to that."

She handed me the key. "Just you wait. I'll give you something to look forward to." She extended her hand. I took it as I stood. She laced her fingers in mine as we walked down the hall. "I know you're a little uncomfortable," she said when we reached my door. "I must leave you to your own devices tonight, but we'll get my money business done at the bank in the morning, then we'll have some fun. I'll see you at nine." She kissed me lightly on the lips and walked away. It'd been quite a while since I felt so alone.

I'm not sure what I expected of a big city hotel, but this room in the Galt House exceeded my wildest dreams. From the plush carpeting to the elaborately figured wallpaper to the highly polished walnut furniture, every aspect of the interior was first class. I crossed the room and gingerly sat on the edge of the huge bed, feeling more than slightly out of place. As I turned to face the closet, I caught my reflection in the full length mirror attached to the door. Viewing the not so handsome lanky form in the mirror as a stranger, I found myself wondering what I was doing in this kind of surroundings. Clearly, I thought, I was only here because Lorena had invited me and was footing the bills. Twisting to rotate my likeness in the mirror, I heard my own voice asking the image aloud, "What in the world does that lovely girl see in you?"

* * * * * *

The soft knock on my door told me that Lorena was prompt. I opened the door and gasped at her beauty. She had spent more time with her hair and make-up than usual and she looked terrific. "Good morning," she smiled, moving into the room.

"It is a good morning," I replied. "As a matter of fact, I think it's about to get even better." I put my arms around her waist.

She kissed me on the lips, but pulled gently away. "Not now," she said taking my hands in hers. "We're due at the bank in a few minutes."

We walked out the front entrance of the Galt House and turned left on Main Street. Five blocks down, we found the Louisville National Bank on the corner of Market Street. Inside the bank, Lorena asked to see Mr. Weaver. The clerk showed us to an office. A tall gray-headed man came through the door, a huge smile on his face. "Miss Leeson," he exclaimed, "you're looking as lovely as ever!" It was the first time I'd heard Lorena's last name.

"You're too kind, sir." I thought I'd seen every kind of smile she had, but this was one I hadn't seen before. "Jimmy," she said, "I'd like you to meet Mr. Ben C. Weaver. Mr. Weaver, my friend Jimmy Singleton."

Mr. Weaver extended his hand. "How are you, young man?

"I'm doin' pretty good," I replied.

"Mr. Weaver is the vice president in charge of my trust fund," Lorena explained.

"Indeed," Weaver said, "and a pleasant chore it is. Come on in."

"Excuse us, Jimmy. This won't take long," Lorena said as she and Mr. Weaver went into his office.

In only a few minutes, she reappeared, a check in her hand and a smile on her face. "Let's take this over and get some money," she said. We walked across the lobby to the counter. The clerk was busily moving papers around behind the grill. He looked irritated by the interruption as Lorena slid the check across the counter.. "Deposit this in my account and give me $100 cash, please."

The clerk eyed Lorena in a way that made me proud and angry as he handed her a receipt and the money. With a glance at me, he immediately returned to his paper shuffling.

On the street, she hooked her arm in mine and steered me along Market Street. A short walk brought us to M. Cohen & Sons, Louisville's Largest Tailors, according to the sign. "Let's go in here," she declared.

"What for?"

"To get you some new clothes, silly." She led me through the door.

"Lorena, I don't need any clothes, and I don't want you spending your money on me." I was embarrassed.

"You most certainly do need clothes, and you're going to get them."

Before I could protest further, she had taken the clerk in hand and was telling him what I wanted.

* * * * * *

On the way back to the Galt House, she informed me that she'd purchased tickets for an excursion on the steamer *America* for tomorrow. "Fastest boat in the water," she said. "We'll make the round trip to Cincinnati in less than six hours."

"Sounds like fun." I was beginning to enjoy this trip.

I was sure that every eye in the place was on me carrying all the packages from Cohen's through the hotel lobby. I walked fast down the hall to my room, Lorena following in my wake. I unlocked the door and dropped the packages on a table. "My, you do look handsome in that new suit of clothes," she declared from the doorway.

I turned to face her. "How do you think I'd look out of it?" I was surprised at my boldness, but I'd waited long enough.

Smiling, she closed the door and threw the bolt. "Well, let's just see about that."

* * * * * *

Through this whirl of excitement, events in the Black Patch never entered my mind. The plight of the tobacco farmers in general and the Hollowells in particular was lost in the stimulation of new sights, sensations, and perfume. All too soon, the week was up and we were on the train headed back to Princeton.

Lorena seemed exhausted and slept most of the time, leaving me plenty of time to think. I was really glad to have gotten a break from all the trouble, but I felt a little guilty about it, too. In one of my more reflective moments, I realized that the trip had helped me grow up. I'd learned a lot about Kentucky, Louisville, shopping, people, the Ohio River, banking, and riverboats. Oh yeah, and women.

Chapter 11

Thursday, May 9, 1907

The Princeton depot was deserted when we arrived late in the evening. I was glad that there was no one around as it gave us the opportunity for a long, sensuous good-bye. A deep sense of sadness overtook me as I turned away from Lorena to begin the trek out to the Hollowell's. The sky was partly overcast, and although warm, the weather seemed to mirror my own melancholy mood.

Steve Choate's shack was dark as I passed. I wasn't sure what time it was, but it seemed a little early for lights out. Maybe Steve'd put in a hard day, I thought as I trudged along. Much to my surprise, the Hollowells' house was dark as well. As I mounted the porch, I wondered why everyone would have gone to bed so early . Instantly, I knew something was wrong. The front door was standing ajar, the jagged glass clinging to the edges of the frame reflecting the moon-light flitting through the scurrying clouds. My sense of foreboding increased as I stepped inside the silent house. Only the whistling of the wind accompanied me as I peeked through the open door of the Hollowell's bedroom. "Hello," I yelled to no answer. A gust of wind drew my attention to the fact that the window was open. I walked across the room to observe that the sash was down — the missing glass panel was admitting the wind. Something crunched beneath my shoes. Bending down, the glass shards told me that the window had been broken from the outside. A sense of terror went through me as I looked around the room. The front wall looked like Swiss cheese, each hole admitting a pencil thin shaft of moonlight. I checked the wardrobe; all the clothes were hanging in place. As I turned, a dark spot on the floor beside the bed drew my attention. In the darkened room, I could not tell what it was. Fearing that it might be blood, I touched the spot to find that it was dry.

The upstairs was deserted as well. All Price's clothes were hanging in his wardrobe. What had happened here? Where was everyone? I ran back down to Steve Choate's place, my heart pounding. I leapt up on the porch and beat on the door. It flew open under my blows. Inside, I yelled, but this place was as desolate as the Hollowell's. I ran across the fields to Ned Pettit's place. Same story. Had everyone in the county disappeared?

The muscles in my legs were screaming as I ran for Momma Hollowell's house. Topping the hill, I could see lights in the windows. At least there was somebody still alive. I paused inside the fence to catch my breath before walking up on the porch. I heard movement inside the house in response to my knock.

"Who is it?" Mrs. Hollowell asked through the door.

"It's me, Jimmy, Mrs. Hollowell." The door opened a crack and she peered at me through the narrow slit.

"What do you want?" I could hear the terror in her voice.

"There's nobody at Bob's house, there's nobody at Steve Choate's house, there's nobody anywhere. Where have they gone? What's happened?"

The door opened wide and a frail hand gripped my arm, pulling me inside. Mrs. Hollowell hurriedly closed the door behind me. "Lands sakes, child, where have you been?" She looked much older than when I'd last seen her.

"I've been away on a trip. Please tell me what's happened."

She looked deeply into my face for a moment. With a sigh of resignation, she crossed the room and sank onto the sofa. "It's bad, boy, it's real bad," she sobbed.

I sat beside her. "What is it? Please tell me."

She nodded, but continued to cry. Visions of all kinds of horrors filled my mind while I waited for her to compose herself. "The night riders visited Bob and Mary Lou," she finally managed to choke out. "They shot up the house, whipped Bob and shot Mary Lou." She dissolved into blubbering.

"Are the all right? Where are they?" I was fighting back my tears.

"It was his own brother that done it," she said between sobs. "My own natural son." She blew her nose on a handkerchief and recovered her composure slightly. "How could a boy I raised do that to his own flesh and blood?" She looked as if she actually thought I could answer that.

"You say Mary Lou was shot? Is she ... Is she all right?"

She looked disappointed that I hadn't answered her question. "I don't know child, I just don't know." In a moment, she went on. "It was me that first went to 'em. I heard the shootin', but I could do nothin'. I'm just an old woman you know. After that bunch of ruffians went away, I went over to do what I could for 'em."

"Please, Mrs. Hollowell, tell me about it."

"Ain't too much to tell, son. I done told you, I'm just an old woman. I done what I could to help 'em." She burst into tears again. "My own flesh and blood," she sobbed.

"Where are they? Please tell me where they are."

She made an effort to gather herself. "Bob and Price are over to his brother Archer's place. Lord only knows where Mary Lou is." She buried her face in the handkerchief. I felt that she needed help, but I wasn't sure there was anything I could do for her. I thought Bob might need my help more. I comforted Mrs. Hollowell for a few minutes and got out of there as quickly as possible.

Even though I'd never been to Archer's home before, my feet seemed guided by some unknown force. My only conscious thoughts were of the condition of Mary Lou and Bob. Light streaming from the windows of Archer's house illuminated the porch and yard. A gruff "Who is it?" answered my knock.

"Jimmy Singleton." I could see the figure of a man through the glass. He had one hand on the door knob, the other arm extended beyond the door frame. There was no question in my mind that a gun was propped beside the door.

"Who?" The voice was a little softer.

"You remember me, Archer. You met me the day we were strippin' tobacco at Bob's place."

The door swung open. Archer Hollowell stepped aside to allow me to enter, leaning the shotgun back against the wall. "Get in here quick," he said, peering into the darkness behind me. The interior of Archer's front room was just like all the others I'd been in. The typical sofa and wooden rocking chairs occupied the standard locations atop a threadbare carpet. He closed the door as soon as I was clear. "What do you want?"

"Mrs. Hollowell said that Bob was here." Archer's wife was lurking in the darkness of the hallway.

"What if he is? What's it to you?" He clearly meant to protect his brother.

"He's my friend, you know that," I pleaded. "Let me see him. I want to help."

"I doubt there's much you can do for 'im, but I reckon you can try if you've a mind to." There was a tone of resignation in his voice. "He's back yonder," he said pointing down the dim hall. The woman I thought I'd seen was nowhere in evidence as I walked toward the back bedroom. A weak light from a coal oil lantern marked the open door of the bedroom. I didn't want to startle Bob, so I knocked softly on the door frame. "Bob," I called.

"Who is it?" His voice was weak and tinged with alarm.

"It's me, Jimmy. I'm back from Louisville," I said entering the room. Bob was lying on the bed on his stomach. A sheet draped over chairs backed up to the bed was covering him. He had his hand on a rifle under the bed.

"Oh, Jimmy," he moaned. "Come on over, son. Sit here." He let go of the rifle and indicated a ladder-back wooden chair near his head.

Seated in the chair, I could see beneath the white tent covering Bob. His back was a swollen, oozing mass of scabs, welts and deep cuts and bruises. Repressing nausea, I gasped, "My God, Bob. What happened?"

"The night riders whipped me, son. Musta been forty of 'em. Caught us in the middle of the night, shot up the house — one shot got Mary Lou —and drug all three of us out in the yard. Two of 'em held my arms around a tree while two others beat me with buggy whips. Damn near killed me." He painfully turned his face to the wall so I wouldn't see his tears.

"Just because you refused to join the Association?" Indignation was raging within me.

He was silent for a moment. Finally, he turned to face me again. His face reflected his physical pain as well as internal anguish. "It ain't only that. They didn't like what Mary Lou'd done."

"You say she's shot? How is she?"

A faint grin showed through his pain. "She's OK, Jimmy. She's tough, you know." The grin faded. "She's a hell of a lot tougher'n I am. Part of a shotgun blast caught her in the neck. It bled a lot and she got some rough treatment outside, but she's fine."

"Where is she?" My heart ached as if I felt as much pain as Bob.

"Gone to Paducah. It was her talkin' to the grand jury that started all this. After they beat me and kicked her some, they told us to get out of the country or they'd kill us. I don't doubt that they meant just that, too. So, after Doc Amoss patched her up, she went on to Paducah. Me and Price'll join her there soon's I'm able."

A wave of relief covered me. At least they weren't seriously injured. A tinge of guilt had started to creep into my mind. If I hadn't gone off on a joy ride with Lorena, I'd have been there. That thought was followed by a worse one —if I'd been there, would they have whipped or shot me, too? I wasn't feeling too good about my Silent Brigade affiliations. Then I realized what Bob had said. "You mean to tell me that Doc Amoss fixed her up?" Strange that the head of the night riders would provide medical treatment to the victim.

"Well, aside from all else, he is our family doctor. I'm tired now, son. Get Archer to put you up for the night. We'll talk more in the mornin'."

"Do you know who it was?" I was ready to go hunt them down.

A look of terror crossed his face. He closed his eyes for a moment, then opened them, but avoided my glance. "They wore masks," he whispered.

"Is there anything I can do for you, Bob?" I placed my hand gently on his bare shoulder.

He winced in pain at my touch. "Well, there are a few things you can help me take care of. I'll be all right. I just need a few days to rest up. We'll talk tomorrow."

* * * * * *

Sunshine streaming through the window woke me early. The smell of sausage and eggs wafting into the room helped me get dressed and into the kitchen quickly. Archer Hollowell, his wife, Jean, and Price were seated around the table. "Good mornin'," I said as I sat opposite Price.

Price mumbled something: Archer and Jean merely stared at their plates. After an uncomfortable pause, Jean said, "Well, go on Archer, tell him."

Archer heaved a deep sigh. Slowly, his eyes moved up to mine. "It ain't that we don't like you, son," he began, speaking slowly. "You're perfectly welcome to eat breakfast with us, but ... well, the fact is that we just can't afford another mouth to feed around here." His eyes dropped to the plate in front of him.

"Here, let me get you some eggs," Jean offered.

The appetite I'd had when I awoke was gone. "No, thanks," I said, "I ain't hungry."

Archer looked up again. "Now, son, don't be too hard on us. Like I said, it ain't that we don't like you or nothin' like that." He glanced at his wife before continuing. "My 'baccer from last year is still in the Association's warehouse, and we got a bill due at the store ..."

"It's all right, I understand," I interrupted him.

"I hope you do," Archer mumbled. "I'd feel better if you'd eat some breakfast."

He offered me the plate of biscuits.

Price was stuffing his face. Jean and Archer both faced me with looks pleading for understanding. "Well, I could eat," I said. I really wasn't hungry, but I did feel that I should help ease these folks out of what had to be a difficult situation for them. Besides, it might be my last meal for a while. We ate in silence until Archer asked, "What did Bob tell you last night?"

"Not much," I replied with a side glance at Price. Although I realized that the boy had witnessed the whole horrible event, I figured that there was no point in making him relive it.

Jean took the hint. "Price, honey, would you go pump me some water for washing the dishes?"

I guess Price had more sense than I'd given him credit for. Or maybe he just wanted to go outside. Anyway, he jumped up, grabbed the wooden bucket resting by the sink, and went out, letting the screen door fly back with a resounding bang.

"Bob just told me that the Silent Brigade beat him and shot Mary Lou." As soon as I said that, I realized that I should have said "night riders" instead of "Silent Brigade."

Archer did not seem to notice my wording. "It's a bad business," he began. "I guess you heard about Ned Pettit and Steve Choate?"

Jean started to clear the dishes from the table. "No, all I know is that neither one of them was around last night," I said. "Where are they?"

"In the county jail, under indictment for scrapin' brother John's and B. Malone's plant beds."

"What? How'd anybody get the idea that Ned and Steve did that?"

Archer poured himself another cup of coffee, thinking as he stirred. "Well, there's a couple of things. First, the sheriff followed a trail through the weeds from John's plant bed right to Ned Pettit's front door."

"Anybody could have left that trail," I opined.

"You're right, son. But you know how Pettit drags that bad leg of his. The trail was made by a man dragging one foot."

"Yeah, I know Ned drags that leg, but that still don't mean somebody else couldn't have done it."

Archer looked at me over the rim of his cup. "As far as the law's concerned, Pettit's the man. Secondly, they found a notebook belongin' to Steve Choate at Malone's bed site."

"Mighty convenient of Steve to leave it there, wasn't it?" I couldn't believe that the evidence fell into place so neatly.

"I doubt he left it on purpose," Archer said, draining his coffee. "Anyway, that ain't the worst of it. It only took the law half a day to wrap up the whole case. And before that same day was over, Choate'd confessed that none other than Mary Lou Hollowell had paid him and Pettit $10 each to do the deed."

"What?" I was incredulous. "Do you believe that?" I said nothing about the dirty look Mary Lou had given me when I observed her conversation with Steve Choate the day of the church incident..

"It don't matter what I believe. The county officials believed it right enough. Mary Lou's under indictment, too."

"For what?"

Archer smiled grimly as he scratched his head. "Hell, son, beatin' and banishment weren't good enough for them boys. They've got the law again' scrapin' plant beds hanging over her head, too just to make sure that she ain't gonna cause no more trouble."

"That's why she had to get out of the country?" Even I heard the incredulity in my voice. This whole thing was getting ridiculous.

"She and Bob figured that if she didn't make herself mighty scarce, either the night riders would kill her or the law would put her away," Archer paused thoughtfully. "I'd say she's got less to fear from the law than from the night riders."

"Seems to me there ain't a hell of a lot of difference."

* * * * * *

Bob had explained that all they could do after the Silent Brigade left was pack a few things into trunks and get themselves to the doctor. They'd just left most of their belongings in the house, so he gave me some money to make arrangements to get their stuff to the depot for the trip to Paducah. He said that I should try to sell everything else. The sun was high on a warm spring day as I walked, headed for the Princeton depot. Farmers —Association members all —were busily tending their plants in the fields lining the road as I trudged along. I was nearing town when someone riding a mule waved and headed toward me. As he got closer, I saw that it was Milt Oliver.

"Jimmy! Where the hell have you been?" It seemed to me that he tried too hard to sound cheerful.

"You know damn well where I've been. What've you been up to?"

Milt read a lot more into the question than I actually meant. He climbed down from his mount and looked into my eyes. "I'll tell you the truth, Jimmy. Truth is a rare commodity hereabouts. I ain't proud of it, but I was there."

I started to say something, but Milt cut me off with an upraised palm. "Just hear me out. You're my friend, and friends that a man can trust are pretty scarce, too. I aim to save our friendship if I can. Like I said, I was there, but I swear to you, I didn't do nothin'. I didn't shoot and I didn't hold and I didn't beat nor kick. God, I'm sorry, Jimmy." Milt dropped his chin to his chest and pushed the dirt around with the toe of his boot.

Mixed emotions of outrage for the Hollowell's and sympathy for Milt filled me. As indignant as I was about the whole affair, deep in my heart, I knew that any individual could not control what the Silent Brigade did. My feelings for Milt won out. "I understand, Milt. If you're willin' to help me, maybe we can make amends."

Milt's head snapped up. "I'd love to do something, Jimmy, but what can you and I do up against the whole organization?"

"I don't know," I admitted. "Let's sit a spell. We can start by you tellin' me everything you know about the whole business." We walked a short distance off the road. While Milt tied his mule to a sapling, I found a shady spot beneath a huge maple tree.

Milt joined me and sank to the ground with a huge sigh. "I got word from J. T. Jackson the evening you went to Louisville," he began. "He just said to be at the Nabb school after it got good and dark. I swear, if I'd knowed what they were gonna do, I would've stayed home. The whole bunch was assembled when I got there. Musta been 30 of us, includin' — would you believe — John Hollowell's wife."

"Lula? I've never known the Silent Brigade to allow women."

"They sure allowed her. I have to say it, she had the time of her life, too." Milt fixed his eyes on the ridge above us and went silent.

"Well," I urged, "go on."

He continued to stare into the distance for a few moments, "Well, we started down the lane toward Bob's place. I still didn't know where we were goin'. The group hesitated at Steve Choate's house. After a little millin' around, they started shootin' into Steve's shack."

"Was Steve in there?"

"I don't reckon he was. I guess they done had him in jail by that time. I tell you, Jimmy, the lodge was out of hand. This wasn't like the raids we've been on before. They was out for vengeance, that's all.

"Anyway, I figure that the shootin' musta woke up the Hollowell's. If it didn't, ever' dog in the county barkin' its lungs out did. That's what give me the feeling that they was under cover inside the house by the time we got there. As we come up to the yard, somebody yelled out 'Close up.' They crowded up to the porch, Lula Hollowell right in the front. I hung to the back of the pack. Then somebody yelled, 'Mary Lou Hollowell, come on out.' Nobody answered, so they started shootin' into the house. Didn't take more than a minute before all the window-lights was shot out and the wall was full of holes. I figured that they musta been under the bed or else all three of 'em woulda been killed right off." Milt paused in his monologue to look at me. "I sure was glad that you wasn't in that house."

Milt was being sincere and open with me, so I decided to be honest with him. "I'm glad I wasn't in there, too." My guilt about being absent was lessening.

"Suddenly, Mary Lou screamed. It sounded like she was near the front door. She screamed, 'You people have shot me.' Somebody yelled back, 'That's what we meant to do.' In a minute, she yelled out, 'We're comin' out,' and ever'body left off shootin'.

"Bob and Mary Lou and Price come out onto the porch, all three of 'em in nightshirts. She was bleedin' like a stuck pig. Looked like a shotgun blast had hit her neck. Son, it was a sad sight. Price was sobbin' and Bob was scared to death. Mary Lou wasn't near as sassy as she usually is, but damn, she looked sexy in that nightshirt." Once again he paused and looked away. I think he was sorry he said that.

"Let it pass, Milt. Go on."

"Well," he sighed, "the first thing they did was read 'em the riot act. Mary Lou just stood there holdin' her neck. Bob was shakin' like a wet dog and Price cried the whole time. Then they grabbed Bob and drug him over to a tree. Two men held his arms around the tree while two others got buggy whips. Mary Lou started to run over there to help Bob. One of the boys knocked her down the steps. Then they knocked her to the ground and started kickin' her while she was down. Lula Hollowell said, 'This is sweet revenge for me,' while Mary Lou was squirmin' on the ground. All the while, Bob was screamin' under the whip and Price was crying." There was a sob in his voice.

"I woulda stopped it if I could, I swear I would. After they'd beat Bob half to death, we started to leave. Then the saddest part of it all happened. Somebody yelled at 'em, 'Get out of the country and never come back or you will be killed.' I was standin' near where Price was. 'What's she done?' he sobbed.

"George Brown answered him, 'We'll kill her if she don't quit talkin' so much.' I really felt sorry for the kid. It was a hell of a thing for me to witness, I can't imagine how the poor child musta felt. Bob and Mary Lou will get over their wounds, but I'd allow that kid is scared for life." Milt sank back against the bole of the tree, exhausted from the emotional effort of telling the tale.

The sun was sinking low to the top of the ridge. I don't know how long we'd been talking. I didn't have any better ideas about what to do than I had before, but at least I knew what there was to know about the whole affair.

"Milt," I said, "why'd you join the Silent Brigade in the first place?" When he didn't answer, I thought maybe it really was out of place for me to ask. "Never mind if it's none of my business."

"No, it ain't that." He hesitated with a sigh. "It's just that I'm embarrassed to admit the truth. It just sounded like a fun thing. I thought we'd go out and whoop and holler and generally raise a little hell."

"Kinda like we did throwin' old man Wallis' 'baccer in the river over at Rockcastle?"

"Yeah. I never dreamed that we'd get involved in destroyin' plain folk's property and 'specially all these beatings and things." His voice was weary.

"I really doubt that anybody envisioned those things," I empathized. "You was there when they made me join, I didn't have much choice. It does seem like things have got out of hand, don't it?"

We sat in silence for a while — each of us lost in our own thoughts. Finally, Milt broke the tranquillity of the moment. "You know, Jimmy, I seem to remember something in that oath we swore about not using the power of the Silent Brigade for personal reasons. Seems like ever'body's forgot about that."

"It does seem that way." That was an interesting thought Milt had had. I guess if you tried hard enough and swallowed the night rider line, you could make a case that the Hollowells deserved what the Silent Brigade gave them.   But I saw no way — from any point of view — to justify Lula Hollowell's being involved. That made the thing smell like personal vengeance, pure and simple.

"Well," I said, "I promised Bob that I'd help get some of his affairs straightened out. Want to help?"

"Yes, by God, I do. Lord knows, somebody ought to set things straight." The weariness in his voice had given way to resolve.

Chapter 12

Friday, May 10, 1907

W e spent the night at Milt's house in the country. After we'd
whipped up a breakfast of gravy and biscuits and I helped him
with his chores, he asked what I thought we should do.

"Bob said that they'd packed up some trunks before they left the
house. Who could we get to go out there and pick 'em up?"

'Let's go to the stable in town," he suggested. "We'll see if we can
get them to go out and get Bob's stuff."

"Good idea. When we get that taken care of, me and you'll go on
out to Bob's place and see what else there is to deal with."

On the way to Princeton, Milt filled me in on the stable owner.
"Wiley Jones is a hell of a man, Jimmy. He used to be the county sheriff and he don't take no guff off nobody. 'Most ever'body likes Wiley,
and he's well respected. If he'll agree to help us with this thing, he's a
good man to have on our side."

Wiley Jones turned out to be a burley, good-natured hulk of a man,
he was sitting with his chair leaned back against the front wall of the
stable building, a plaid flannel shirt topping his denim jeans. "Howdy,
Milt," he greeted us, "how's ever' little thing?"

"Tolerable," Milt smiled. "Wiley, do you know Jimmy Singleton?"

Wiley eyed me a moment. "Can't rightly say as I do." He leaned
forward, extending his hand.

"Jimmy's a friend of the Hollowell's," Milt said as I shook Wiley's
ham-like right hand. With his left, he scratched at a tuft of strawberry
blond hair protruding beneath his old felt hat.

Wiley chuckled. "There ain't many folks hereabouts that'd admit to that."

My fingers tingled from his firm handshake as my hand dropped. "I reckon that's all the more reason to be proud that I am," I said. I thought I'd better find out just where things stood with Mr. Wiley Jones. "Have you been there?" I asked.

A confused look covered his face. "The Hollowell place? Hell, son, I've been damn near ever' place in Caldwell County." Milt and I exchanged a knowing look — Wiley was not a member of the Silent Brigade.

Wiley looked as if he was going to say something to me but then thought better of it. He shifted his eyes to Milt. "What can I do for you boys?"

"Jimmy wants to have you go out to the Hollowells and bring some trunks to town," Milt answered. Then he added, "If you don't mind."

"Packin' folks stuff around is part of what I'm in business for, politics aside," Wiley said with a wide grin. Shifting his gaze to me, he asked, "You got money to pay fer it?"

Before I could answer, Milt said, "Wiley, you know what's happened out there, don't you?"

Wiley smiled. "I don't live in a cave, son. Of course I know."

"Just wanted to make sure you were aware of what you might be lettin' yourself in for," Milt said.

"Them boys don't scare me much," Wiley said. "I've dealt with most of 'em before and I found that they ain't too fearsome in daylight without a mask."

"I got money," I said, pulling Bob's crumbled bills from my pocket. "How much?"

"Oh, 'bout two dollars will cover it, I reckon. Put your money away, son. A man don't pay Wiley Jones 'til he's earned it." I was beginning to see why everyone liked Wiley. He leaned to his left, placing a hand on the flooring so he could yell through the open livery door. "James Louis! Get your lazy hide out here." Wiley pushed himself erect in the chair.

In a few moments, a lanky boy clad in dirty bib overalls ambled out the door. "What is it?" he mumbled.

Wiley shook his head in frustration. "How many times have I told you to show a little respect for the boss?" His tone was only slightly harder than before.

James Louis hung his head and thrust his hands deep into his pockets. "What is it, sir?" His voice was no more distinct than before.

"Get the wagon and go out to Bob Hollowell's place and pick up the trunks you'll find out there." Rotating his eyes to me, he asked "Where they at?"

"I don't know. Maybe on the porch, maybe in the bedroom."

"Don't matter," James Louis said, "I ain't gonna do it."

"What?" Milt and I said in unison.

James Louis ignored us and spoke to Wiley. "You know as well as I do that them night riders will frown on anybody helping Mary Lou. I like my job here right enough, Mr. Wiley, and I'd like to keep it, but I ain't gonna cross them bastards." The different tone of his voice told all three of us that he meant what he said.

Wiley heaved a deep sigh. "Well, git back to muckin' the stalls then." James Louis' look of concern gave way to relief. He turned and walked back inside. "Can't get good help nowadays, you know," Wiley joked.

"This mean you ain't gonna help us?" How would I get Bob's stuff to town? I was considering pleading when a nudge from Milt told me to be quiet.

Wiley tilted back his hat and rubbed the top of his head. "As the old sayin' goes, if you want somethin' done, you got to do it yourself," he said, standing. "Tell you what. If you two boys will ride along, the three of us will just promenade right on out there and pack that stuff right over to the depot. How 'bout it?"

"Sure," I said, "Let's go." I turned to walk inside.

"Hold on here, son. Mr. Oliver here ain't been heard from yet." I realized that Wiley was just making sure that Milt and I understood that we'd be flying in the face of the Silent Brigade. I turned to face Milt, ready to remind him that he'd said he wanted to help.

Milt hesitated only a moment, looking directly at me. His face broke into a grin. "I'm game."

* * * * * *

The trip out to the Hollowells' was uneventful. Milt and I nervously scanned the trees lining the road every step of the way but no threats appeared. Wiley seemed perfectly at ease, entertaining us with stories of his days as a lawman. "I ever tell you boys about the time old Norvell Hanks called me out to his store 'cause of some counterfeit money?"

"Old Norv's place is so far off the beaten path, I can't imagine counterfeiters out there," Milt said.

"That's just the thing," Wiley continued. "Some city slickers thought they'd pass it off on somebody ignorant. When I got there, I asked old Norv what made him think it was bogus money. He told me he knew right off, 'cause they was three-dollar bills."

"Three-dollar bills? I never heard of such as that," I laughed.

"Norv said that they handed him six of them three-dollar bills and wanted to know if he could make change."

"What'd old Norv do?" Milt asked, unknowingly playing the straight man for Wiley.

"Old Norv said he just asked 'em if they'd prefer three sixes or two nines."

Past Steve Choate's deserted shack we rounded a curve and ran smack into the trouble we'd been expecting. A group of fifteen or twenty men was lounging around a pile of fence posts and rails blocking the road. Wiley pulled the horses to the side of the road. "Howdy, boys," he said with a smile.

Buck Tandy stepped forward. "Wiley Jones, what the hell are you doin' out here?" His voice was gruff.

Wiley pushed his hat back and rubbed his head. Leaning against the back board, he said, "Oh, just doin' a little business." Readjusting his hat, he asked, "What are you doin' out here, Buck?"

Tandy placed one foot on the pile of posts. "Just makin' sure that nobody don't steal Bob's stuff," he said, glaring at me. I was amazed that Buck could say that with a straight face.

Wiley laughed. "Don't aim to steal nothin', Buck. I've been hired by Bob's agent here to haul some trunks to town," he said jerking a thumb at me.

Buck moved a step closer to the wagon peering at me. "Jimmy, I'd of thought you'd have sense enough to stay away from here."

A drop of icy sweat rolled down the back of my neck. "We don't want no trouble, Buck. Bob asked me to get his stuff to town, that's all." I hoped my voice did not crack.

Buck rubbed his chin as he studied the other men. "Well, sir, I just don't know about that."

Wiley dropped to the ground and approached Buck. He was a head taller than Buck and outweighed him by thirty pounds. Buck seemed to shrink even smaller as Wiley got right in his face. "Now look," Wiley growled, "I ain't got all day to stand around here. You fools can do whatever you like out here, but this boy is payin' me to haul some trunks away, and I aim to do it. You got any questions?"

Buck recoiled. "No, I reckon I ain't," he stammered.

"All right then," Wiley said, mounting the wagon, "why don't you boys go throw rocks in the creek or somethin' while we get on with our chore?" He clucked the horses into motion and drove around the bewildered men. Now I really understood why everyone liked and respected Wiley Jones.

Bob and Mary Lou Hollowell's home place was a shambles. In the daylight, the bullet holes in the house were evident. The broken glass in every window frame offered mute testimony to the abuse they'd witnessed. The men out front had torn down the fences to get the pile of lumber blocking the road. In the absence of any constraint, cows and pigs wandered aimlessly through freshly plowed corn and wheat fields. "They did a job of work on this place, didn't they?" Wiley observed.

I tried to express my outrage, but no words came. Milt simply stared in wonder.

Wiley halted in front of the shattered house. With a glance over his shoulder, he suggested, "I'll just rest easy here for a spell. You boys get the goods loaded." He turned in the seat to face the men behind us.

Milt and I scrambled down and into the house. "This place is a wreck," I managed to say.

"This's all happened since the night I was here," was Milt's whispered apology.

In the back hallway, we found two large trunks. "That Wiley's a bad one, ain't he?" I marveled.

"He ain't bad, Jimmy. That is, he ain't mean," Milt said. "When he was the law, he gained a reputation for being tough and fair. Buck and that bunch out there have seen him in action before. The Silent Brigade might not fear no judge or jury, but that don't take in Wiley Jones." An eerie emotion crept into my stomach as we carried a trunk past the bedroom. This house that had been a sanctuary to me now seemed haunted. Milt must have had similar feelings. "Spooky, ain't it?"

"Let's get this stuff and get the hell out of here," expressed my attitude.

Milt and I made three trips into the house to get the goods loaded. When we had it all in the wagon, Wiley drove back through the gate to where Buck Tandy and the other men were watching. Wiley doffed his hat to the men on guard as he nonchalantly drove around the road block.

* * * * * *

On the outskirts of Princeton, we had to halt for an east-bound train to cross the road. "That'd be the 2:47 comin' in from Paducah," Wiley announced, consulting his pocket watch. "Right on time, too."

When the train cleared the road, Wiley clucked the horses into motion and drove on into town. The train was stopped even with the depot when we arrived. Milt and Wiley began unloading the trunks while I arranged with the station agent to hold the goods until Bob Hollowell called for them. Wiley was lounging against the wagon watching the passengers come off the train when I returned. "Where'd Milt go?" I asked

"Said he had some errand to run." Wiley answered. "He said that you could come out to his place this evenin', if you want." He was looking at the train over my shoulder. Suddenly, Wiley's face lit up. "Johnny Miller," he shouted, "get yourself over here."

I turned to see a tall, handsome man wearing a black broadcloth suit of clothes approaching us. His face mirrored Wiley's big smile. "Wiley Jones, you old pole cat! What are you up to?" He and Wiley shook hands warmly.

"Not much, Johnny," Wiley said. "I ain't seen you since old Hector was a pup. What's a big city lawyer like you doin' around here?"

"Just slummin'," Miller laughed. "Actually, I've got a little business here in town."

"Let me introduce you. This here is Jimmy Singleton." Miller extended his hand. "John is an old friend of mine," Wiley explained. "He grew up here'bouts, but's been practicin' law over in Paducah for quite a while now. Come on over to my office, Johnny. I hope you've got time to visit a spell."

"I always have time for an old chum like you," Miller said.

"What do I owe you, Wiley?" I asked, assuming my business was done.

"Walk Johnny over to the office and we'll figure it up," Wiley said climbing into the wagon. He clucked to the horses and pulled away.

"You say you're name is Singleton?" Mr. Miller asked as we moved away from the depot. "I thought I knew all the families in the county, but I don't know any Singletons."

"I ain't from around here. I just kind of wandered up, you might say."

"Is that so? What do you do here in town?" Mr. Miller didn't actually seem interested; it was more as he was just making conversation.

"Oh, I don't do anything here in town. Some nice folks out in the country took me in." I really didn't want to talk about it.

"Yeah? Who might that be?"

"Bob and Mary Lou Hollowell," I answered, glad that we had arrived at the stable.

Mr. Miller stopped dead in his tracks, an astonished look on his face. "You live with the Hollowells?"

"Well, I did up until a few days ago. Why?"

"Mary Lou Hollowell was in my office yesterday. She said she was in a fix." Wiley was seated behind his desk as we entered the office. He slid an invoice across to me. "You boys gettin' acquainted?" he asked.

I pulled Bob's money from my pocket and paid the bill. "Strangest damn thing, Wiley," Mr. Miller said. "I never heard of Bob or Mary Lou Hollowell until yesterday, and today, I meet a friend of theirs."

"It's stranger than you might think," Wiley said. "I reckon nobody holds too much again' Bob, but you'd have to burn the woods and sift the ashes to find another friend of Mary Lou."

Miller sat in a straight chair, dropping his brief case to the floor. "It is strange. I was just telling Jimmy that I thought I knew most of the folks in this county. I know plenty of Hollowells, but I never heard of Bob before yesterday. Strange, indeed." He eyed each of us for a moment, then went on, "As a matter of ethics, I generally do not discuss one client's business with another, but, Wiley, you're an old friend as well and a kind of officer of the court. Jimmy here is what you might call a ward of the Hollowells', so ...." His voice trailed off.

"Yeah, so what?" Wiley leaned forward, placing his elbows on the desk.

"So, like I just told Jimmy here, she was in my office in Paducah yesterday."

"What'd she want?" Wiley was interested.

"Well," Miller hesitated. With a glance at me, he went on. "She wanted to retain our firm to represent her should the plant bed scraping incident ever come to trial. I generally wouldn't mention it, but ... well, the fact is that I just couldn't believe the fantastic tale she told."

I was happy to hear that. It meant that Mary Lou wasn't seriously injured and had recovered her spunk. "I don't know what she told you," I volunteered, "but, it couldn't be more fantastic than the truth."

Mr. Miller turned to stare at me. "Did you witness the affair?"

"No," I admitted. "I was out of town, but I've talked to some that did." The look that Wiley shot me made me wish I hadn't said that.

"I just find it difficult to believe that these ruffians would wantonly destroy property in the manner Mrs. Hollowell said."

I started to answer, but Wiley beat me to it. "Me and Jimmy here just come from the Hollowells' place. I seen it for myself," he said. "Johnny, there stands the house, riddled by bullets, windows and doors smashed, fences broken, stock wandering at will through the unguarded, growing crops. Bob and his family, usually industrious and careful, gone and not daring to come back even to see his old sick mother in her home close to his." There was a note of genuine sadness in his voice.

"I understand she's under indictment for a plant bed scraping," Mr. Miller said, shaking his head. "Why doesn't the county attorney get Judge Crumbaugh to issue a writ directed to the sheriff of McCracken County? He ought to know that he could then arrest her and return her here for trial. Hell, everybody knows she's in Paducah, and it's only forty-six miles away."

That was a good question.

"They got no real interest in prosecutin' her," Wiley commented. "The night riders just wanted to shut her up. The fact that she saw fit to get out of the county suits 'em fine. If they've managed to run her off, they're content."

"And," I added, "since the whole of this county is in the, uh, night riders, she's got no chance at gettin' a lawyer or a fair trial." I nearly said "Silent Brigade" rather than "night riders."

Mr. Miller's face reflected grave concern. "It's a sad commentary on the state of affairs that such an outrage should have been perpetrated in Kentucky and that the victims could find no lawyer who would dare to bring their suits for damages against those they pointed out as the actual assailants." I was beginning to like Mr. John Miller.

"If there are any lawyers around who aren't in with 'em, then they're afraid of 'em," I said.

"Well, it's a sad state of affairs," was Miller's final comment before we all fell silent.

My business finished, I made my exit from Wiley's office. I walked out on the sidewalk deciding what to do next when a shout brought me up short. I turned to see Mr. Miller, briefcase in hand, hurrying after me. "Hold up, Jimmy, I want to talk to you," he puffed. A mixture of excitement and trepidation filled me as I waited for him to catch his breath. "Walk along to the bank with me, son." We fell in step along the walk. "Do you know where Mr. Hollowell is?"

I hesitated to answer that. Miller seemed to be all right, but I felt a serious obligation to protect Bob and Mary Lou. Sensing my reluctance, he halted and touched my arm, turning me to face him. "I'm trying to help." His sincerity was evident.

"Yes," I sighed, "I know where he is. Do you want to see him?"

"All in good time, my boy." We resumed walking. "I just wanted to make sure you were a true friend. I told you that Mrs. Hollowell stopped in my office?"

"Yeah. You said that she wanted you to defend her for the plant bed scrapin'. Are you gonna do it?"

"There's not too much worry about on that charge. In the first place, it'll probably never come to trial. In the second place, I'm sure the governor will grant her a pardon. Just between us, do you know if she's guilty?"

My first impulse was to shout, "She's not!" I suppressed that, however, and said, "I actually don't know. I was out of town when it happened."

Miller frowned. "She impressed me, son. I told her that, as her attorney, I had to know the truth, and that, under the law, I could not be forced to violate her confidence. I advised her that even if she was to any extent involved, a full confession of all she knew about the alleged offense might be of the utmost importance to her and her family."

I could just imagine Mary Lou full of righteous indignation. "What'd she say?"

"To my astonishment, she fell on her knees, right there in the office, held up her right hand and said: 'I swear to you that I had nothing to do with the scraping of that plant bed, have no knowledge of who did it and am as innocent of that charge as an unborn child — so help me, God!' I was impressed and I believe her."

We'd arrived in front of the bank. "So," I said, "you don't think she has any legal problems?"

He paused with his hand on the door. Leaning out, he glanced both ways to make sure no one was within hearing. "Not on that score. But, what she really wanted me to do was bring suit against the parties that shot her and beat her husband."

She'd sure as hell have problems with that!

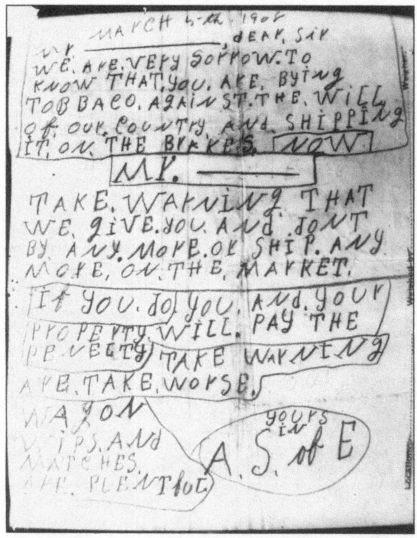

Although lacking in linguistic technique and penmanship, this message is quite clear. It was written to a non-member tobacco farmer in March 1908 at the twilight of the Black Patch Wars. Soon the "Night Riders" would have their victory. (Copy photo by Getter. Courtesy of the Kentucky Historical Society.)

Chapter 13

Sunday, April 21, 1907

B ob was sitting in a ladder-back chair at the table when I entered Archer's kitchen. I was glad to see that he was up and around, but I noticed that he was leaning forward with his elbows on the table so that his back did not touch the chair. "You wanted to see me?" I asked.

He smiled broadly. "Yep. You've done a good job of helpin' wind up the business around here. I don't know what I woulda done without you. Jim, you've done a man's work." I beamed with pride. It was the first time he'd called me "Jim."

I pulled the wad of money I'd collected for his property from my hip pocket and dropped it on the table. "I wish I could have done better. There's $140 there and that's mighty little for all the goods I sold."

"A man just has to take what comes in life," he sighed. Picking up the crumpled bills from the table, he went on, "You're right, this represents pennies on the dollar for what all our stuff was actually worth, but I guess considerin' the circumstances...." His voice trailed off. I shifted uncomfortably to the other foot, not knowing what to say. Bob studied each bill as he smoothed it on the oak table surface and placed it on the stack. When he'd inspected them all, he gestured at a chair. "Sit yourself down, there's some things we need to talk over."

I pulled a chair from the table and sat opposite Bob. His face looked pained — not with physical discomfort, but reflecting the agony within. "What's on your mind?" I prompted.

"Jim," he began, "you know that Mary Lou and I both like you, and in many ways, we consider you as our own son." I didn't care much for where this conversation was going. "And, like I said, I don't know what I would have done without you for the last two weeks." He paused, looking out the window, obviously reluctant to go on.

"Where's everybody?" I thought maybe I could change the subject.

"Gone to church," he sighed. "Don't worry, there's nobody around but me and you." After a pause, he shifted his eyes to mine. "I don't know how to tell you this, but the fact is that Mary Lou and I have decided to take the night riders' warning and get out of the country. We're moving to Oklahoma." He looked deeply into my eyes, awaiting my reaction.

"Oklahoma? Why do you want to go there?" I wasn't surprised at the location, just that Mary Lou would let them run her off.

"They's lots goin' on out there, son. The government's giving away free land, and a man can get a good start. Maybe build up a little ranch, maybe ...." Again his voice trailed off.

"What's to become of me?"

A small sob escaped his lips. "That's the hard part. The situation bein' what it is, I just can't afford to take you along. I don't know what to say, but the fact is, I've done all I can do."

Even though I had half expected this turn of events, I felt as if I'd been orphaned again. My eyes dropped to the floor. "I know you have," was all I could think to say.

Bob slowly rose and walked around the table to place a hand on my shoulder. "I'm going to Paducah to join my wife this afternoon. You're welcome — matter of fact — I'd like to have you come along. Not only would I enjoy the company, there'll be plenty of opportunities for a young man like you in Paducah." He squeezed my shoulder so hard it hurt, but I was determined not to wince.

With the Louisville experience behind me, I was not intimidated by the prospect of a big city, and besides, he might be right about the chances. Aside from Lorena, there weren't many opportunities around here. Feeling more at loose ends that I had in quite a while, I said, "I think I'd like to ride along."

"Fine," he enthused. He seemed genuinely pleased. "When they get back from church, I'll get Price ready and say my good-byes. Then we'll head for the depot."

"If it's all the same to you," I said, "I'll just go on back to town now and meet you at the station. I've got some good-byes to make, too."

He smiled for only the second time this morning. "That's right. I forgot about you and that pretty little gal. Well, the train leaves at 1:30."

* * * * * *

The widow Haynes' boarding house just did not seem as homey as Mary Lou's had. I'm not sure whether the boarders were not as friendly or the absence of Mary Lou's sociable attitude was the difference, but it was not the same. The widow Haynes hung around the parlor for a few minutes, providing her obligatory polite conversation before she made her exit and left Lorena and me alone. When Mrs. Haynes was gone, Lorena crossed the room and sat next to me on the sofa. She slipped her hand into mine. "I was beginning to think you didn't like me any more."

My pa always told me that when you didn't know how to say what you had to say, the simplest thing to do is to just say it. So, I just blurted out, "We've got a problem. A big problem"

"What's that?" Her smile faded.

"Well, you know that I've been helping Bob get his affairs together?"

She nodded.

"What he's been trying to do is get things straightened out so he can join Mary Lou in Paducah."

"I know. So?" A look of concern crossed her face as I hesitated.

"So," I sighed, "he and Price are leaving for Paducah today." I was ready to tell her that they were going on to Oklahoma from there, but she interrupted.

"I've assumed all along that they'd be leaving," she said, her smile returning. "There's no problem, you can just move in here with me." I don't know what my facial expression told her, but she quickly added, "I've already spoken with Mrs. Haynes about it."

"What'd she say?" I asked. I was having difficulty believing Lorena would suggest such a thing either to Mrs. Haynes or me.

"She wasn't real fond of the idea at first," she said. "It took a while, but once I convinced her that you and I were serious, she said she understood and that she'd try to smooth it over with the other boarders." Lorena snuggled against me, seeming perfectly content.

Some emotion within me, male ego I guess, rebelled at the idea of her having made up my mind. I wasn't sure that I liked the sound of "serious," either. "I'm going with Bob on the train," I said, suppressing my urge to inform her that I'd make my own decisions, thank you very much.

"That's fine," she purred, rubbing my chest. "I'll have ever'thing arranged by the time you get back."

With a deep sigh, I grasped her wrist and moved her hand away. She sat upright giving me a questioning gaze. "Lorena," I said, "I don't know that I'm coming back." There, I'd said it.

Her look of askance gave way to shock. "But...I thought...." she sputtered.

"Lorena, I just simply don't know. I'm poor as a church mouse. I've got no trade and no money and now nowhere to live. I don't know what's to become of me, but I can tell you right now that I ain't about to move in here and let you support me. I might not have anything else, but I do have some pride."

Her eyes filled with tears. "I'm offering you a place to live," she sobbed.

I felt like the biggest cad in history. Mixed emotions of fear, uncertainty, longing and emptiness churned within me. "I know you are," I choked. "And, I appreciate it. But, the fact is, I just don't know what to do."

She stood and turned to face me, tears streaming down her cheeks. "Well, just go on to Paducah, then. See if I care." With that, she turned on her heel and ran from the room. In the emptiness that filled the room, I think I felt more alone at that moment than I did even when my parents died.

* * * * * *

The train's engine was puffing steam beside the platform as I stepped up from the street. I spotted Bob standing at the station office door, holding Price's hand. He waved me over, looking as if raising his arm caused pain. "Get ever'thing taken care of?"

"Yeah," I mumbled. "How you doin', Price?" I still didn't like the kid, but I thought I could at least be civil.

"OK," he said brightly. "We sure are glad you're comin' along." Maybe Bob had coached him to say that or maybe he was maturing a little. Whatever the case, the boy apparently had done some growing up this spring. Bob said something that was lost in the clanging of the bell. "All aboard for points west," a conductor shouted above the din.

"That's us," Bob yelled into my ear. Clutching Price's hand, he started toward the passenger car. The crowd boarding the train seemed huge. I couldn't imagine why all these people were in Princeton or why they were leaving, but it reminded me of the station in Louisville. I stayed right behind Bob as bodies pushed me in various directions climbing into the car. The interior was standard — it may have even been the same one in which Lorena and I rode. Bob choose a seat facing forward, motioning me opposite, facing him.

In a few minutes, everyone had settled in place and the train rolled slowly rearward as the brakes were released. Suddenly, the car lunged forward as the engine caught. Price was thrown toward me, then recoiled hard into his seat back, just as had happened to me the first time I rode the train. I smiled as Price rubbed the back of his neck. At least he did not whine. A glum silence settled over us as the train picked up speed. Bob and I avoided eye contact, neither of us knowing what to say. I had no inkling of what might be on his mind, but my head was reeling with fear for my uncertain future. Staring at nothingness beyond Bob's shoulder, some kind of motion caught my attention. As my eyes focused, I saw that it was the Paducah lawyer, John Miller, waving at me. A trifling smile and a hand motion summoned me to him. Price was mesmerized by the scenery out the window as I stood. Bob looked up at me, his eyes questioning. "I think I'll get some air," I announced.

I made my way down the swaying aisle to where Mr. Miller sat alone in the seat. "Jimmy," he said, "sit a spell with me." He slid against the window to his right and patted the seat beside him with his left hand.

"You got your Princeton business wrapped up?" I asked, sliding in beside him.

"Well, I accomplished the purpose of my trip," he replied. After a pause, he asked, "Is that Mr. Hollowell you're with?"

"Yes. Would you like me to introduce you?"

Mr. Miller recoiled, almost banging his head on the window. "No, no, not at this time," he said. "He looks as if he has enough on his mind at present."

Glancing at Bob's hunched shoulders, I agreed. "I suppose we all do."

Mr. Miller turned his gaze out the window for a moment. Then, turning back to me, he said, "I told you that Mrs. Hollowell wants to retain my firm to represent her?"

"Yes. Are you going to do it?" He didn't give me a very satisfactory answer when I'd asked him that before.

He shook his head sadly. "I can't. I have two partners in the firm. One of them is running for state office and the other owns property in Caldwell County. Hence, each, for his own reasons, is unwilling for our firm to accept the case."

A wave of rage rose up in my chest. "Then why are you so interested in what happens to them?"

An enigmatic grin appeared on his face. "What I should have said is that I cannot provide legal counsel *at this time*." He looked directly into my face, his eyes asking if I understood.

"Do you mean to say that you might take the case later?"

His grin widened. "Let's just say that things do change. Do you know what the Hollowells' plans are?"

I hesitated to answer that, but decided that he was actually trying to help. "Yes. They plan to move to Oklahoma." I suppose that uncertainty must have been etched on my face.

His grin had faded and he faced me in earnest. "You'll pardon my being so bold, but I'm not sure that I understood your situation. I take it that you're living with the Hollowells?"

"Well, I was." I paused, unsure of how to go on. "I'm not going west with them," was the best I could think of to say.

"What are your plans?" I was impressed by his show of concern.

"I don't know," I sighed. "Bob said that they couldn't afford to take me along. He thinks I might be able to find something in Paducah."

Miller turned to the window, his chin resting in his hand. A silence seemed to descend over the car as he viewed the passing countryside. At length, he turned back to me. "Tell you what. I might be able to help you out. To begin, I'll send you over to a friend of mine at the stable. His name's Adam Smoot, and he's been looking for someone to help out around there. It might not be real pleasant work, but it'll pay enough to put food in your mouth. I suspect that Adam'll let you live upstairs in the loft, too. What do you say?"

It was the best offer I'd had so far, but I didn't want to make any commitment before I even got a look at the place. "I never fancied workin' in a stable," I said.

"Well, you think it over." His smile had returned. "Anybody in town can tell you where my office is. Come by and let me know."

I rose to leave. "I do thank you for the offer," I said. "Truth to tell, I'd like to find something better if I can, but it's nice to have an option to fall back on, even if it's not a job I'd relish."

"Keep in mind what I said — things do change," was his parting comment.

* * * * * *

Mary Lou was waiting on the platform as we descended from the car. The small bandage on her neck did not detract from her beauty, and the beaming smile on her face told of no suffering on her part. Price rushed into her arms and her smile widened as she greeted us.

She hugged her son fondly and stretched out her hand to Bob. He entered the three-way embrace. In a moment, her gaze fell on me. "How are you doing, Jimmy?"

"I'm OK," was the best I could muster.

"Jim's been a world of help to us, honey," Bob said. "I don't think we would've made it out of Caldwell County without his support."

She disengaged herself from Bob and Price and extended her hand to me. I thought she meant to shake hands, but when I took her hand, she pulled me into an embrace. "Thank you so much," she whispered. My spine tightened until she released me.

"What's the plan now?" Bob asked.

"I've made all the arrangements," she announced. "We're leaving for Oklahoma on tomorrow morning's train." Price jumped in the air and clapped his hands with glee.

Bob was more somber. "Are you sure that's what you want?"

A porter approached with the little baggage we had. I picked up Bob's grip and my knapsack as we walked out of the depot. Mary Lou was deep in thought the entire time. After we'd walked a few minutes, she finally answered Bob's question. "I suppose it's best that we put some distance between us and all this trouble. However, I have no intention of letting those ruffians get away with this outrage." Her face turned red as anger rose within her.

We'd reached the entrance of the Palmer House Hotel. Mary Lou turned to me. Tears replaced her anger of the previous moment. "I'm so sorry that you can't go with us," she sobbed. It was the first time I've ever seen her cry.

"It's all right," I said, fighting back my own tears. "You folks have been mighty good to me, and I suppose it's time for me to move along." I hoped that my voice conveyed more optimism than I felt.

Mary Lou looked deeply into my eyes, tears streaming down her cheeks. She looked as if she wanted to say something, but merely gasped "Good-bye," and disappeared into the building, dragging Price along. Bob's chin dropped to his chest. "Jim, I don't know what to say. I mean it son, we wouldn't have made it without your help."

A deep sigh escaped my lips. For somebody who had so little experience with good-bye scenes, I'd had enough for one day. "It's been nice knowing you," I said. "I'll never forget you."

Bob stuck his hand in his pocket and handed me a paper-wrapped package. "Good luck to you, son," he said as he turned on his heel and entered the door.

Alone on the sidewalk, a sense of abandonment swept over me. In the course of one day, I'd deserted —or been deserted by — every person I knew. I walked aimlessly along the street. Oblivious to the bustle of the city, I don't know how long I wandered along. At length, a boy hawking newspapers drew my attention. Inspecting my pockets, I found that I had ten cents more than the price of a paper. I made the purchase anyway, thinking that the classified ads might offer me something. A few yards down the street, I found a bench and sat to examine the paper. A half hour of searching brought me no hope of any kind of a job. By the time I finished with the paper, the sun was sinking behind the buildings, and I was hungry. It was a desolate feeling.

Rising from the bench, I remembered the package Bob had given me. My hands shook as I opened the wrapping. Inside, I found a small New Testament and two five dollar bills. At least I could get something to eat.

* * * * * *

After I'd eaten a forty-cent meal in a restaurant, the world seemed somewhat brighter. Although the newspaper had yielded nothing, I still had the stable offer Mr. Miller had given me. I still didn't relish the idea of a stable job, but it seemed preferable to a night on the street. A passing couple informed me that Smoot's stable was two blocks away.

Blindfolded, you can tell when you're in the stable area. If I'd walked one more block, I wouldn't have had to ask. Adam Smoot turned out to be a barrel-chested man with huge hairy arms, a round face, and a kindly smile.

"My name's Jimmy, uh, Jim Singleton," I announced. "Mr. John Miller said that you might have a job for me."

Adam looked me over head to toe. "Well," he drawled, "I have been needin' some help around here. Pay's three dollars a week and a spot in the loft. It's damn hard work. Are you sure you're up to it?"

"Yep," I lied. I wasn't at all sure.

"All right then, we'll give you a try. Anybody that John Miller recommends can't be all bad. I'll get you a blanket and you can make yourself to home up there." His eyes clicked up to the loft.

The loft was none too homey, but it was warm. And dry. The skies had opened up and a steady downpour was drumming the tin roof. Taking stock of my situation, I decided that things could be a lot worse. After all, I was warm and dry, and had a full stomach. With all of that and the money Bob had given me, I thought I should be reasonably content, but as I drifted off to sleep, I found myself wondering if I'd ever see Bob and Mary Lou again. Or Milt. Or Lorena.

Chapter 14

Tuesday, August 13, 1907

The weeks turned into months as the dog days of summer slipped off the calendar. Adam Smoot proved to be pleasant enough, I had a decent spot to sleep, and the work, although smelly, was not too hard. I didn't enjoy being around a stable all the time, but it beat fooling around with dark fired tobacco all to hell. I spent my days mucking stalls, throwing down hay, and mending harness. Nighttime was the worst. I hadn't made any friends here in town, so there wasn't much to do. As far as I could find out without directly asking, there was no local chapter of the Silent Brigade. I'm not sure if I was happy about that — I was glad that they weren't doing any local harm, but I did miss the camaraderie of the meetings.

This morning showed the promise of being just one more oppressively humid day. I'd already managed a pretty good sweat just sweeping out the tack room when I heard Adam call my name. I dropped the broom and headed for the office, hoping that he had an errand for me to run. Adam met me in the runway before I reached the office. "They's a couple of fellas up there to see you," he announced.

"Who? There's nobody I know around here."

"I don't know who they are," he said. "Just don't kill all day jawin' with 'em. We've got work to do, you know."

"Okay," I said as I walked on to the office. Inside stood Milt Oliver and a tall thin man who looked vaguely familiar. A sly grin spread over Milt's face when I entered. "Jimmy, how the hell are you, son?"

My face mirrored his smile. "I'm doin' all right. Damned if I ain't happy to see your ugly hide." He wrung my hand.

"This here is Sanford Hall," Milt said indicating his companion. "I don't know if you two have ever formally met." Milt leaned out into the barn to see if anybody was around. "Where's your boss?"

"I don't know. Out back smokin', I'd guess."

"Sanford's a member of another lodge. I thought maybe you might have seen him at some of the meetin's."

Sanford took a step toward me and extended his hand. I looked into his face and knew that I had seen those eyes peering out of a mask before. "How you doin'?" I asked as we shook hands. He smiled faintly but said nothing.

"Can we talk a spell?" Milt asked after an awkward silence.

"Well, I reckon we can," I said. "Have a seat." I indicated the sway-backed cane bottom chairs in front of Adam's desk.

Milt shifted uncomfortably to his other foot. "I was hopin' for a little privacy," he said, his eyes darting around the room. Sanford simply eyed the dusty floor at his feet.

"How long you gonna be in town?"

"I don't know," Milt answered, "we really ain't got no plans."

"Well, if you can wait 'til this evenin', we'll go out to supper. They's a quiet little place up the street here where they know me. We can talk there."

Milt eyed Sanford who just shrugged his shoulders. "All right, we'll hang around."

"Great," I said. "Come on back by here about 5, and I'll be ready to go. It'll be good to have a chance to catch up."

"We'll see you at 5," Milt said as the two of them exited the office.

For the first time since I began working there, the afternoon hours flew by. Despite the heat and flies, I worked steadily to be sure I'd have all my chores done before Milt returned. I had no idea what he wanted to talk about, but I really didn't care — I was ready for some socializing.

About 4:30, Adam appeared in the door of the stall where I was working. "Got an errand for you to run this evenin', son."

Damn! The one day of my life I have plans, he has to decide there's something else for me to do. "What is it?" I asked.

"Some goods come into that need deliverin'."

"Can I do it in the mornin'?"

He looked puzzled. "I thought you'd enjoy a little wagon ride."

"Ordinarily, I would. But, I'd planned to have supper this evenin' with some friends."

Adam Smoot was a good man and a good boss. As long as I did a passable job, he pretty much let me do as I pleased. "Well, I figured that you'd be 'specially anxious to take this ride."

"Why?" The broad smile on his face told me that he was up to something.

"It's for some folks over in Caldwell. I imagined that you wouldn't mind takin' a little ride over that way."

Adam and I hadn't gotten to know each other real well, but we had had a few personal discussions. We'd talked about the night riders and all, but I'd never told him about my Silent Brigade affiliations. As far as I knew, he knew nothing about that. I knew that Mr. Miller had told him about my living in Caldwell County and my relationship with the Hollowells. At this moment, I wished I'd never mentioned Lorena to him. I could see that I was in for a round of teasing. "Can the delivery wait 'til tomorrow?" I repeated.

"Hell, son, it ain't ever' day that you get a chance to let the breeze cool you off on the way to get all heated up again. Don't you want to go?"

"'Course I want to go." I hadn't seen Lorena in several months and I didn't leave her on very good terms at that. If I hadn't made the commitment to Milt, I'd have been off like a shot. "Won't tomorrow be soon enough?"

Apparently Adam thought he'd tortured me enough. "Oh, I reckon so. They don't know that the goods come in today anyhow. Go ahead and knock off for today so you can get cleaned up. You can run that stuff over to Caldwell in the mornin'."

"Thanks, Adam," I shouted, shoving the pitchfork into the rack. "I'll be up and ready to go bright and early."

"I 'spect you will," he chuckled, walking away.

I'd finished washing up and was waiting out front when Milt and Sanford Hall came around the corner. "Evenin', Jimmy."

"Howdy, Milt. Sanford. You boys ready for some supper?"

"Lead the way," Milt said. Hall had still not said a word in my presence.

I started down the sidewalk toward the restaurant. Milt and Sanford fell in step across the walk. "So," I said, "what's the big mystery? What the hell are you up to?"

Milt turned to look behind us. Seeing no one following, he replied, "Jimmy, what do you know about the Hollowells?"

"What do you mean? I know a lot about the Hollowells."

"I mean have you heard from them?"

"No. Hell, Milt, you know the Silent Brigade run them out of the country. All I can tell you is that they went to Oklahoma."

We had reached the restaurant. Conversation stopped as we found a table and ordered. When the waiter left, Milt leaned across the table toward me. "They's a lot of talk goin' around Princeton," he whispered.

"Talk about what?"

Sanford Hall leaned into the center of the table, his face near ours. "They say that Mary Lou Hollowell is bringing some kind of suit against the Silent Brigade members that raided her." Although he spoke softly, his voice was gruff and his dark eyes were glowing.

"Why are you askin' me? I ain't seen nothin' of 'em for several months now. And, besides, don't ever'body know that a suit would be useless since ever'body involved belongs to the Silent Brigade?"

Milt leaned back in his chair. He started to speak, but paused as the waiter delivered our food. When the man was gone, he leaned forward again. "Don't be coy with us Jimmy. We know that you know that Miller man."

I did not like the tone of his voice. "What the hell's goin' on here? Did you two come to threaten me?"

Sanford spoke first. "No, nothin' like that. We're just concerned for our own health, that's all." His voice was softer now.

"No, Jimmy," Milt said. "It's just that we thought you might know somethin' that's for sure. The rumors are flyin' thick and fast."

"Why?" I said. "I told you, they've gone to Oklahoma. Ain't that what the Silent Brigade wanted to accomplish?"

"That Miller is up to somethin'," Hall said. "He's been makin' a lot of trips to Princeton and he's been seen talkin' to people that makes the lodge leaders nervous. We thought you might know what he's doin'."

"I don't know nothin'. The last I talked to him about it, he said he had no interest in the case." I decided not to mention that grin I remembered Miller had on his face at the time.

Both men leaned back in their chairs and seemed to relax. "Well, we just thought you might know," Milt sighed, turning his attention to the meal before him.

Taking my cue from that, I sawed off a hunk of roast beef. "Honest, I don't know nothin'. I did talk to Mr. Miller a couple of weeks ago, but it was just 'how are you?' and stuff like that."

We finished our meal in chit-chat conversation about the events around Princeton. They filled me in on all the local gossip. I started to ask about Lorena, but I figured they wouldn't know anything, so I held my questions. Over a final cup of coffee, I asked, "What are you two so worried about, anyway?"

Milt and Sanford exchanged a knowing glance. "Well," Milt said, "let's just say that all hell may be about to break loose."

Now it was my turn to question. "All right, quit holdin' out. Tell me what's goin' on."

Milt heaved a sigh. "Ever since that raid on the Hollowells', I ain't felt good about this lodge business. Seems to me it just got out of hand. Now they're raidin' and beatin' folks just 'cause they don't like 'em. It ain't the fun it was to begin with."

Sanford leaned in and rested his elbows on the table. "I'm fed up with 'em myself. Milt told me about the talk you and him had about doin' somethin' about all this mess," he said. His demeanor was deadly serious. "I want to do somethin', too."

"I've got the same question I had for Milt — what can a few of us nobodies do?"

Sanford shifted uncomfortably in his chair. Glancing around, he said, "Truth be told, I ain't got the courage to take 'em on. What I was hopin' for is to help Mrs. Hollowell do somethin'." His deep sigh told me that he was glad to get that off his chest.

"Well, I don't know that she has any plans to do anything. But, you're right, if there's anybody that's got guts enough to face up to 'em, it'd be Mary Lou."

We stood from the table and left the restaurant. On the sidewalk, Milt turned to me. "Jimmy, don't breathe this to a livin' soul, but we've already set some things in motion."

"Like what?"

Milt shot a questioning look at Sanford who simply looked away. "I ain't at liberty to say at the moment." He paused, then went on, "For now, let's just leave it at this: if you get a chance to talk to Mr. Miller, try to find out what, if anything, the Hollowells are up to. If they are gonna try to take on the Silent Brigade, Sanford and me are willin' to do what we can to help."

We made our good-byes and I headed back to the stable loft. Lying alone in the straw, my mind wandered back to the oath that we'd all sworn at initiation to the Silent Brigade about violent death and an unmarked grave. In view of the possible consequences, Sanford Hall's frank admission that he didn't have the requisite courage was impressive . As powerful and as far reaching as the Silent Brigade was, I had to confess to myself that I wasn't sure whether I had enough courage to make any move against them either.

Chapter 15

Wednesday, August 14, 1907

B right sunlight pouring through the front of the stable told me I'd overslept. Getting hurriedly dressed, I wondered why Adam had let me sleep so late. I scrambled down the ladder expecting him to start yelling for me, but found only the sounds of the horses snorting. Thinking that perhaps he'd overslept too, I ran to his shack back of the stable. All was quiet here also. After I pounded on the door, Adam's weak voice called, "Get in here!"

He was awake but still in bed . "What's wrong?" I asked.

Adam propped himself up slightly. "I'm sick," he whispered.

"You want me to go for the doctor?"

"Yes. Get the hoss doc."

"The horse doctor?" I said incredulously. "Don't you want the people doctor?"

He sank back on the pillow. "No sir. The people doc, he comes in and asks you what's wrong, and you tell him. Then he'll prod and poke and ask if it hurts and you say yes or no. After a while, he'll decide what's wrong with you. Now the hoss doc, he ain't used to asking his patients no questions. The hoss doc, he has to know what he's doing. No sir, you get me the hoss doc." He managed a smile.

"I'm serious, you want me to get the doctor?"

"No. I'll be all right. Finish up your chores first. The goods for you to take to Caldwell are in the wagon out back. When you're ready, hitch up the grays and take that stuff over to the feed store in Princeton.

You needn't be in any hurry 'bout gettin' back — you can visit a spell with your friends over there, if you want."

"Are you sure you ain't gonna need me to be here?"

He seemed to perk up a little. "I'll get dressed here in a bit. I reckon I can sit in the office as good as I can lay here."

"Well, if you're sure, I wouldn't mind seein' some of my friends." I had Lorena in mind.

* * * * * *

The long ride to Princeton gave me plenty of time to organize my thoughts. Lorena and I hadn't left each other on the best of terms, and I wasn't sure what kind of reception to expect. Hell, she might not even still be there for all I knew. As the wagon creaked and bounced over the ruts in the road, I found myself wondering — for the first time — how I really felt about her. Did I love her? Did I really care about how she felt about seeing me again? The miles rolled by as I questioned myself about my motives for seeing her. Somewhere in the midst of my contemplation, the thought occurred that I didn't even have to let her know I was in town. Before I came to any conclusions, I was stopping in front of the feed store. Milt Oliver was leaning against the door frame.

"Jimmy! What the hell are you doin' here?" He was all smiles.

"Just makin' a delivery. What the hell are you doin' in town?"

"The owner of this place is a friend of mine," he answered. "He had to go somewhere today and asked me to mind the store."

"Well I'm glad you're here," I said. "This stuff's for the store."

"Good," he exclaimed. "That'd be the goods old man Brock ordered last week. Purdy told me to expect it." He walked to the back of the wagon to help me unload the crates.

I climbed over the board into the wagon bed. "What'd you think of Paducah?"

Milt stopped and peered quizzically at me. "Well," he grinned, "I allow it's a right smart place they got over there, but it ain't never gonna amount to nothin' 'cause it's just too far away."

"Milt," I said as I pushed the last crate along the wagon bed to him, "can you tell me any more about what we discussed yesterday?"

Although we were alone in the street, a look of panic covered his face. "Shut up!" he mouthed, snatching the crate from the wagon. He turned and carried the crate inside. I followed him in. After checking to ensure that no one would overhear, Milt said, "Damn, son, don't you know that loose talk is liable to get us killed?"

"I'm sorry. I guess I've gotten used to bein' in Paducah."

Milt heaved a sigh of exasperation. "Well, this here is Princeton. If you plan to stay alive, you'd best watch your mouth."

"Yeah, I will. There ain't nobody around now, so tell me what's goin' on."

A look of alarm crossed Milt's face. "All I can tell you, Jimmy, is that Sanford's made a move, and I encouraged him. Word'll be out about it soon enough, but I hope that nobody finds out who's behind it. If it does, Sanford, and probably me, are as good as dead." His voice clearly reflected the terror within him.

"Well, Milt, I'm willin' to do whatever I can to help."

* * * * * *

All thoughts of Milt's problems evaporated from my mind while I drove the wagon to the widow Haynes' boarding house. I wasn't sure how long I'd be staying, so I just parked on the street out front. A trickle of cold sweat ran down my back as I twisted the doorbell.

Mrs. Haynes regarded me with all the affection she'd display for a dead rodent. "Can I help you?" She gave no intention of opening the screen door.

"I'm here to see Lorena."

"I'll see if she's in." She turned abruptly and left me standing on the porch. I'm sure that she damn well knew whether Lorena was there. I guessed that she was providing Lorena with the opportunity not to talk to me. After what seemed like hours, Lorena appeared in the hallway.

"Jimmy! How good to see you." Her voice gave no clue of her feelings. She opened the screen door. "Please come in."

I followed her into the parlor on the left of the hall. She sat in an easy chair, so I took the sofa. "I happened to be in the neighborhood, so I thought I'd stop by," I said.

"That's nice." She smiled faintly. "How've you been?"

"Oh, I'm doin' all right. I'm workin' at the stable in Paducah, you know."

Her back was ramrod straight in the chair. "That's nice," she repeated.

If this was going to be the run of the conversation, why didn't she just have Mrs. Haynes tell me she wasn't here? I decided we might as well get it over with. "I've missed you," I opened.

Her posture softened somewhat. "Oh? I would have thought you'd have plenty to keep your mind occupied in the big city."

"I haven't seen much of the city except on errands. Fact is, I haven't seen much of anything but horse droppings."

That seemed to break her resolve. She laughed aloud. "I've missed you, too. I didn't realize how much I'd come to depend on you until you ran off."

"I didn't run off," I cried, taken aback by the comment. "You know I had no choice."

She stiffened again. "I seem to recall offering you a choice."

"Please, Lorena, let's not get into that again. I only came because I miss you and to see how you're gettin' on."

"I'm doing fine." She paused, then said, "I was engaged for a while."

"What?" My image of her sitting around pining away was shattered.

"Engaged. You know, to be married."

"You said 'was.' I take it you're not still."

"No, I broke it off."

I was in shock. Fearing that the question was too personal, I asked "Why?"

She hesitated a moment before answering. As she spoke, the hardness in her dissolved and she became the girl I had known before. "I just didn't love him." Her words were barely audible.

Mixed emotions filled me. "You gave up on me pretty quickly, didn't you?" My wounded pride demanded attention first.

A firm resolve covered her being. "Well, you did abandon me."

"Abandon? Damn it, you know I had to go." This conversation had a familiar tone. "Quit avoiding the point. The whole thing happened pretty fast, didn't it?"

"I'm not avoiding anything. Use whatever terms you like. I was left at loose ends, and I had to do something."

Coming to the point, I asked, "Well, you picked a hell of a thing to do. Who were you engaged to, anyway?"

"That's not important." She was avoiding eye contact.

"If it isn't, just what the hell do you consider important?" I expected it'd take a while for her to compose an answer.

As if she'd anticipated the question, she spoke right away. "What's important is that we've come to where we are right now. You're here and I'm here. I told you, I didn't love him. I love you, and that's all that matters."

At that moment, some of the questions that had been turning in my mind were answered. And while some new concerns occurred, I knew that I did love her, and I knew why, too. " I appreciate your courage in facing up to the fact that you couldn't marry someone you didn't love." I hoped that my voice reflected the admiration I felt for her.

"It wasn't an easy thing to do," she said. "It's never fun to hurt someone you care about."

Callow as I was, I caught the intent of that remark. "Yes, I know. I didn't intend to hurt you either, but a man has to do what he has to do."

She laughed again. "That's exactly what I said to my fiancé." Her smiled faded. "He didn't see much humor in it. It was very difficult, Jimmy, but ...." Her voice trailed off.

"But what?" I was fishing.

"But it's you I love." A tear rolled down her cheek.

I'm not sure if that was what I was casting for, but it's what I caught. I moved over to her chair and put my arms around her. She responded by reaching her arms around my neck and turning her face to me. I brushed the tears from her cheeks and kissed her as tenderly as I could manage. "I love you, too."

We held the embrace for a long while without speaking. At length, I said, "So what do we do now?"

She let me go and composed herself in the chair, straightening her skirts and smoothing her hair. "Well," she said slowly, "I have been giving that matter some thought."

"And?"

She looked directly into my eyes. "I have an idea I hope you'll like. How do you feel about coming back to Princeton?"

I feared that she was going to open the topic of my moving into the boarding house again. "My job's in Paducah," I replied, trying to keep emotion out of my tone.

"It just so happens," she said, "that I bought Helton's hardware store last week. I need somebody to run the place." She awaited my response with a bemused smile.

"Did you have anyone in particular in mind?"

She swatted the air toward my face. "Don't you be coy with me. I want you to come back here and take over management of the store."

Again, I was taken aback by this unexpected turn of events. "What kind of arrangement did you have in mind?" I asked.

"We'll be partners. It's a real money maker, Jimmy. We'll split the profits. We'll both have a nice income, and as a bonus, there's an apartment over the store. That'll give you a place to live. We can go have a look at it right now." She seemed pleased with herself as she stood.

My head was swimming. "Well, it's gettin' late," I said, stepping back. "I'd better get Mr. Smoot's wagon back to Paducah."

"Does that mean you don't want it?" She was crestfallen.

"No, no. I don't mean that at all," I exclaimed, moving toward her. "It's just that this is a bolt out of the blue. I'll have to think about it and even if it is all perfect, I still have to get the wagon back."

With a coquettish flip of her hair, she said, "Don't think too long. I do need, and I will find, somebody to run the store."

"Tell you what," I said, my arms encircling her waist. "I'll be back this weekend and we'll have a look at the place." I drew her to me. I said nothing more, but my mind was resolved as a deluge of lace, perfume, warmth, and soft femininity pressed against me.

* * * * *

The streets were empty when I drove into Paducah. I wasn't sure what time it was, but the lack of activity in town said it was late. A light was beaming from Adam Smoot's office, though, so I knew he was waiting for me. I pulled into the runway and while I was unhitching the horses, Adam came out of the office. "I was beginning to think the hogs ate you," he called.

"You did say I needn't hurry," I replied. "It was good to see some old friends."

"And how is she?"

"She's fine." I emphasized the word "fine," believing he'd catch my meaning.

"That's good," he said. "Good for a man of your age to sow some wild oats, you know." He opened the stall door.

"Yeah, and hope like hell they don't grow," I laughed, guiding the horses inside. "How you feelin'?"

"Just a bit too much fun last night," he said turning toward me. The smile faded from his face. "You're gettin' pretty popular around here."

"Huh?"

"They's some folks waitin' to see you. They come by here lookin' for you this afternoon. I told 'em you was out of town, but I'd send you up when you got back."

"Up where? Who is it?" I couldn't imagine who'd be looking for me.

"A stoop-shouldered man, a good-lookin' woman, and a kid. I

didn't know 'em. They said they was stayin' at the Palmer House." I turned and headed for the door. "It might be too late to go visitin'," he shouted at my back as I ran out.

Chapter 16

Thursday, August 15, 1907

The Palmer House's desk clerk confirmed that it was the Hollowells. He said that they were there all right, but the hour was a little late to be calling. I spent a restless night in the loft and had my morning chores finished before Adam appeared in the office. "I'm goin' up to the hotel," I announced.

"Son, you've got work to do around here. Them stalls need muckin', you know."

"I'll get to it when I get back," I said walking out the front. So what if he was mad — I didn't figure to be working there much longer anyway.

The town was bustling. Wagons and carriages clogged the street and the sidewalks were lined with people. I made my way through the throng and into the lobby of the Palmer House. Approaching the desk, I asked the clerk, "Are the Hollowells in?"

"Yep," he replied. "They checked their mail about 10 minutes ago, then went in to breakfast."

"Thanks," I shouted over my shoulder, dashing into the dining room. The room was not crowded. I spotted Bob, Mary Lou and Price right away. I was halfway across the floor when they saw me. Bob jumped to his feet, smiled widely, and waved enthusiastically. Mary Lou looked up at him, a puzzled look on her face. She turned her head to follow Bob's gaze until her eyes fell on me. She smiled and waved, but did not get up. Bob took a step toward me and extended his hand. "Jim, how are you, son? It's good to see you again."

"I'm doin' fine," I said as he pumped my hand. I glanced at Price, then Mary Lou. "How are y'all?"

Price grinned, but said nothing, Mary Lou's smile widened as she said, "All better now that we're back in Kentucky."

Bob shot her a frown and resumed his seat. Indicating the empty chair at the table, he said, "Sit, son. Want some breakfast?"

"No thanks," I replied. "I already ate." After a moment, I asked, "So what are you doin' back here?"

Bob started to answer, but a glare from Mary Lou closed his mouth. She looked great — I'd forgotten how beautiful she was. A high collar hid whatever scar her wound had left, and I soon saw that she'd recovered spiritually, as well. "There's several factors," she said. "The most important is that this is our home, and I won't be run off."

I glanced at Bob. I knew that pursuing this conversation would irritate him, but I had to ask, "Aren't you afraid of the night riders?" I should have known better. Anger rose in her as quickly as mercury in a thermometer on a spring morning.

"Those nocturnal ruffians better watch out for me," she exploded. "I know just who they were! If they think they can get the best of me with a shot gun, they've got another think coming." She was sputtering with rage.

"Now you've done it," Bob commented. "It took me all morning to calm her, now you've got her boiling again."

"Maybe bein' back here ain't good for her health in more ways than one," I joked.

Bob smiled. "Well, as a matter of fact, it's my health that was of concern."

"How's that?"

He heaved a deep sigh. "I've not been the same since ... well, since we left here. Mary Lou finally badgered my doctor into suggesting that returning to Kentucky might just be the required remedy."

That made no sense. "I don't understand. Why would coming back into the danger here be a good remedy?"

"My family's here, son, and it's home. Besides, being ... leaving under the circumstances that we did .... Well, it preys on a man's mind." His voice betrayed the anguish the whole situation had caused.

"And I don't aim to let 'em get away with it!" Mary Lou was still incensed.

Her voice had become so loud that everyone in the restaurant was staring at us, so I thought I'd change the subject. "So, how'd you like Oklahoma?"

"I didn't like it," Price offered.

"We all hated it," Mary Lou spat. "It's flat and dry and dusty. What scrubby little trees they've got are so far apart that the woodpeckers have to tote a lunch."

"They's a lot of land out there, Jimmy. It's poor, though, relative to the fertile soil of Kentucky. Like I said, this is home." Bob's face reflected the sadness within him.

"What's been going on around here since we've been gone?" Mary Lou asked in a lighter tone.

"Oh, not much that I know of," I replied. "I actually don't worry about politics and such very much."

"Have you seen Lorena?" She was finishing her meal.

I could not suppress a grin. "Well, yes. As a matter of fact, I saw her yesterday."

"That lascivious leer on your face tells me you've got more to say," she observed.

As she spoke , Bob pulled his watch from his pocket and snapped the case open. Before I could answer Mary Lou, Bob announced that it was time for his appointment. We all stood, and Mary Lou, Price and I wandered out to the lobby while Bob paid the bill. "All right, young man," she said, "let's hear it."

The grin spread over my face again. "Well," I stammered, "bein' over here, I hadn't had much chance to get to Princeton."

Price was either bored or realized that he was hampering the conversation. He wandered over to a sofa and entertained himself by tracing the pattern in the fabric with his finger. "So?" Mary Lou insisted.

"Mr. Smoot had me run an errand over there yesterday," I said. "I stopped by to call on Lorena while I was in town."

"At last." She feigned impatience. "We come to the point."

"We did have a heart-to-heart talk," I went on. "It seems as how she'd missed me as much as I'd missed her. We kinda decided we'd better do something about that."

"And what did we decide?" She seemed genuinely interested now.

I really didn't want to answer that. Bob saved me by picking that moment to appear from the dining room. Replacing his wallet in his coat pocket as he approached us, he said, "We'd better get on over to Mr. Miller's office."

Mary Lou looked irritated. "I suppose you're right," she said.

Then turning to me, "Walk along with us. You're not off the hook yet."

"I'd better get back to work," I said as we exited the hotel. Outside, I turned left while Bob and Price walked in the opposite direction.

"Another few minutes isn't going to matter," she said gripping my arm. "Walk down this way with us." I should have remembered that once Mary Lou Hollowell got her mind set on something, you might as well resign to agree with whatever it was. With a sigh, I let her guide me along behind the family. "Go on," she demanded. "What did you and Miss Lorena Leeson come up with?"

I slowed the pace a bit. If I was going to have to tell her, at least I didn't have to announce it to everybody in town. "She's bought the hardware store," I said. "She wants me to run it for her."

"And the two of you plan to live in the upstairs apartment, I suppose." I could not detect any disapproval in her voice.

"We didn't discuss that. I told her that I'd be back this weekend." Looking around, I realized that we were in the middle of the business district. I had not been to this part of town before. A few yards ahead of us, Bob and Price had halted under a sign announcing the law firm of Miller and Miller. "What's this?" I asked. "I thought Mr. Miller had several partners."

"John Jr. earned his law degree a while back," Bob said. "Mr. Miller dissolved his previous firm and took his son into a new practice. We're late," he said to Mary Lou.

"We'll take this up again later," she told me as they entered the office.

Turning to walk back to the stable, I found myself wondering if the formation of the new firm was what Mr. Miller meant when he and I talked on the train. As I recalled that conversation in my mind, I remembered that he'd implied that his partners had been holding him back from representing the Hollowells. Now that that encumbrance was removed, he'd be free to accept whatever clients he saw fit to work with. Maybe Milt and Sanford Hall knew what they were talking about, after all.

Adam Smoot was in his office with several of the regular loafers. I entered via the stable door hoping to avoid the wrath I knew he'd built up while I was gone. He saw me walking through the runway and called, "'Bout time you got back here! Work's piling up." That was his standard example of stable humor. The remainder of the day passed pleasantly enough and by the time I finished my chores, he'd forgotten about being angry.

"Who was them folks you spent the morning with?" he asked when I entered the office.

"They're the ones who took me in when I first came to this part of the world."

"That was the woman who tried to tell tales on the night riders?" His voice was mixed with admiration and wonder.

"That's her," I replied.

"I thought so. I'd heard she was a looker. I also heard that the night riders run them plum' out of the state. Are they just back for a visit?"

"I'm not sure what their plans are." I wasn't about to tell him anything.

Adam rolled his chair back and placed his muddy boots on the desk. Rearing back, he said, "Speakin' of plans, I get the feelin' you've got somethin' to tell me."

"What makes you think that?" I wasn't sure I was ready to discuss my plans with him..

"Them bein' here, for one thing," he said. "And you ain't seemed too interested in your work since you come back from your visit with your little sweet thing, for another."

I guess he had me. "Well," I said slowly, "I might be movin' back to Princeton."

"I thought that might be," he said dropping his feet to the floor. "How long do you plan to be around?"

"I don't know. I'm gonna visit with the Hollowells some more this evenin'. Then I'm goin' to Princeton after work Saturday."

His response was not as I expected. Rather than anger, his tone was of indifference. "I hope ever'thing works out for you. Let me know," he said as he rose to leave the office.

Adam had been good to me. A quick internal debate told me that I was only fooling myself by thinking that there was still a question in my mind about moving to Princeton. Realizing that, there was no need to try to string him along. "I don't expect that I'll be back Sunday."

He stopped at the door and stared at me for a moment. "No, I don't expect that you will," was his parting comment.

I locked up the stable office and headed for the Palmer House. Bob was seated on a sofa in the lobby, reading a newspaper. "Did you get things arranged with Mr. Miller?" I asked to announce my arrival.

He lowered an edge of the paper and peered at me. "Yeah, I guess ... I don't know, Jimmy. I just don't know about this whole business."

"What's goin' on Bob? I know what you said this mornin' about Kentucky bein' home and all, but don't you know that Mary Lou's under indictment back in Caldwell for scrapin' them plant beds?"

"Of course, I know it. And she knows it too, but you know how hard-headed she can be. Lettin' them run her out of our home just don't sit right with her. You know as well as I do that once she gets something in her mind, you might as well let her have her way." A sigh of resignation finished his comments.

There was nobody near us, so I felt free to talk. "Bob," I began, "I don't know anything definite, but somethin's goin' on back in Caldwell, and it don't look good. I think there's great danger for you here."

He laid the newspaper aside. "What are you talkin' about?" There was concern on his face now.

"Like I said, I don't know anything for sure, but I do know that John Miller has been makin' some of the Caldwell night riders mighty nervous."

"I don't see how that concerns us," he said. "Surely Mr. Miller has other clients. Anyway, we've had no contact with him until today."

"However that might be, they seem to think that he's up to something on your behalf, and you showin' up here just confirms it."

Before he could answer, Mary Lou and Price arrived. "Hello, Jimmy," she said. "Did you have a good day?" She seemed in fine spirits.

"Oh, it was all right," I said. "How about you?"

She smiled broadly. "Everything's just fine. We're going for a little ride to look around town. Care to come along?"

I didn't relish the idea. "What are you looking for?" I asked.

"Somewhere to live," she answered, ushering Bob and Price toward the door.

* * * * *

Packing my meager belongings didn't take very long. Throwing my knapsack over my shoulder, I descended the ladder from the stable loft for the last time. No great sense of melancholy accompanied me as I walked into Adam's office to say good-bye. He was alone, working on the books. "Well, I guess this is it," I said.

"Did you get ever'thing finished up?" he asked looking up from the ledger.

"Yep." I could see that this wasn't going to be a sentimental farewell scene.

"Here's your pay," he said sliding an envelope across the desk. "We'll miss you around here."

I checked the contents of the envelope and stuffed it in my pocket. "I'll miss you, too." It seemed like a good thing to say.

Without rising or looking up, he extended his hand to me. "Good luck to you, son."

"Thanks." I waited another moment, but he was still focused on the figures in front of him. "Well, I'll see you," I said.

"Yeah. See ya."

I inhaled my last whiff of stable air and walked onto the sidewalk. I'd expected some sense of loss at leaving my job, but a feeling of relief came over me as I walked toward the Palmer House. Unsure as I was about the future, I think I'd discovered that there is no security in this world anyway, so one might as well move forward. A few hundred feet down the walk, I met the Hollowells going in the opposite direction carrying their grips. "Where are you started?" I asked.

Mary Lou smiled widely. "We've taken a house down the street," she replied. "And Bob's found him a job." Eyeing my knapsack, she said, "Looks like you're moving, too."

"Yeah. I'm goin' back to Princeton."

Her smile faded. "Jimmy, you watch yourself over there. Those lawless ruffians are riding for a fall."

I wasn't sure what she meant by that, but I was impressed that she'd show concern for me. "Oh, I'll be all right," I said. "You'd best be careful around here, too."

"Those cowards don't have the guts to come after me." I could see the ire rising in her. "Let's get on," she said to Bob. "Jimmy, you take care of Lorena and come see us when you can." She hugged me awkwardly and turned away.

Bob hesitated a moment as Mary Lou and Price walked away. "Jim, I'd appreciate it if you'd keep the fact that we're here under your hat," he whispered.

"Don't worry, Bob. You know that I'm not gonna do anything to hurt you. If I can help in any way, just let me know."

He dropped his grip and shook my hand. "Thanks, son. It's good to know that we have at least one friend." Mary Lou had stopped a few yards away and was waiting impatiently.

"I think maybe you've got more friends than you realize." As Bob peered quizzically at me, I wished I hadn't said that. He looked as if he was going to ask what I meant when Mary Lou yelled at him.

With a sigh, he picked up his grip. "Don't be a stranger," he said.

"I won't. I'm sure Lorena will want to visit you," I said as he walked away.

I took a minute to watch them move on down the walk. Whatever else one had to say about Mrs. Mary Lou Hollowell, the lady had courage. If I'd been through what she had, I think I'd have found some way to be happy in Oklahoma. Walking toward the depot, I resolved to find some way for me to be happy in Kentucky.

The eastbound train arrived at the station just as I turned away from the ticket window. I stood aside as a rush of arriving passengers exited the cars. Once I was aboard, the engine's bell announced my departure from Paducah. As the train picked up speed, it occurred to me that this was the first time in my life that I was going to something rather than running away. It felt good.

Chapter 17

Monday, August 19, 1907

My first night as proprietor of the L & J hardware store had passed peacefully. Waking up in a room of my own was a strange experience, and I lay in bed for a while just soaking in the ambiance. Lorena had not broached the subject of her moving in with me, and at this moment, I was glad I was alone despite the yearning I felt. I arose and dressed. Rummaging around the place, I discovered that she'd even gone so far as to stock the larder for me. With a good breakfast under my belt, I ventured downstairs to face my inaugural day in a store. Just as I reached the foot of the stairs, I heard someone knocking on the front door. I raised the shade and found myself looking into Lorena's eyes. "I thought I had my first customer." I smiled as I unlocked the door.

"Good morning, Mr. Business Man. Does the first customer of the day get any special treatment?" she asked, throwing her arms around my neck.

"Well, seein' as how you're so early," I said, pulling her to me, "I suppose we might come to some agreement." I pressed my lips to hers.

She held the kiss for a long moment. Then, pulling away, she said, "You'd best make sure the boss doesn't find out about it." Although her tone was playful, I wasn't sure how to take that comment. She walked to the side of the store and behind the counter. "Do you know how to run a cash register?"

"You know I don't know anything. I told you that somebody would have to show me what to do. Do we have any employees?"

"I let the previous staff go. Come on over here and I'll show you how to ring up sales." She seemed irritated.

"You fired them? Why?" As soon as the words were out of my mouth, I wished I hadn't asked. I knew she wasn't upset by my ignorance of cash registers, so it had to be the question that she didn't like.

"You and I can manage," she replied.

Why didn't she want to answer that? I didn't know who the previous owner was. Perhaps that had something to do with it. At any rate, we had enough to discuss at the moment and she was the boss. In case she was just trying to assert her authority, I decided not to pursue the issue. She showed me how to work the cash register and then we spent the next couple of hours discussing the layout of merchandise, pricing, charge accounts, business insurance, ordering supplies, and a hundred other topics I'd never considered before. My head was swimming by the time she'd covered all the items she had in mind. "Lorena, I'm not sure I can handle this."

Exasperation must have shown in my voice. She dropped the business-like attitude she'd had for the last hour and put her arm around my waist. "You'll do fine. I'll be right in the back if you have any questions."

"What? You're going to work here?" The possibility had not dawned on me.

"Why, yes, of course." She looked surprised that I'd ask. "Somebody has to keep the books, you know."

"I understood that I'd be runnin' the place."

"You will. I promise to stay out of the way. I'll just do the accounting and help whenever you need me. A woman has to do something with herself, after all." The tone in her voice reminded me of Mary Lou. What had happened to that silly girl who watched the stars from the porch with me so long ago? With a quick peck on my cheek, she went into the office at the rear of the store.

Inspecting my new domain was a treat. Brand-spanking new merchandise of all varieties filled every shelf and bin. Nails, fencing material, leather goods, horse shoes, guns and shells, harness, and even fabric occupied their niches along the walls. Each of the areas exuded its own peculiar aroma and the mix was intoxicating. I was going to like this — if I could keep all the details straight. My reverie was interrupted by the tinkling of the little brass bell over the door. I rushed to the front to see J. T. Jackson entering the store.

He stopped dead in his tracks when his eyes fell on me. "Jimmy Singleton! What in the pure-dee hell are you doin' here?"

"Didn't you see the new sign out front? This store has changed ownership."

"And you're the new owner?" he said, wonder in his voice.

"Not exactly, but I'm workin' here. What can I do for you?"

"Seein' you is such a shock, I pert nigh forgot what I came in for. I need two pounds of ten-penny nails."

I weighed out the nails from the marked bin and dumped them into a paper poke. I was behind the cash register before I realized that I had no idea what to charge. "Uh, J. T., I'm new at this. Do you, uh, happen to know what these things cost?"

He laughed aloud, much to my embarrassment. "You got some things to learn about business, son. They's four cents a pound, but I'd advise you not to take the customer's word for nothin'."

I thought about asking Lorena to verify the price. But it crossed my mind only momentarily. J. T. was probably right about not taking a customer's word, but I'd trust him this one time. I rang up the eight cent sale and gave him two pennies change for his dime. I was proud of the way I handled the cash register. "Thanks, J. T.," I said, beaming.

"You're welcome," he mumbled, picking up the poke. "Say, are you back here for good?"

Knowing what was coming, I answered evasively. "I'm not sure. I'm just workin' here, sorta on trial."

J. T. removed his hat and scratched the top of his head. "Well, we've missed you at the meetin's," he said. "They's a lot of activity goin' on and we need all the riders we can get. I hope you'll be comin' back to us."

That was just as I feared. While I had somewhat longed for the fraternity of the Silent Brigade, I had no desire to get mixed up in the violence that they were now perpetrating. "Like I said, I just don't know."

He started to the door. "I'll let you know when the next meetin's gonna be." Relief covered me when he was out the door.

Only a few customers came in through the rest of the morning. I managed to get through it without having to go ask Lorena anything, and I was happy to see that she kept her promise to stay out of the way. I was surprised when I heard her call from upstairs. "Lock the door and come on up," she yelled, "it's dinner time."

I threw the bolt on the door and flipped the sign to "closed." Half-way up the stairs, the aroma of fried chicken wafted into my nose. "How'd you get up here?" I asked.

Lorena busied herself in the kitchen. "Oh, I came up while you were waiting on a customer. How's it going?" She seemed perfectly at home.

"I'm doin' all right. Mighty nice of you to fix this spread." The chicken and mashed potatoes she sat in front of me made my mouth water.

"A workin' man needs a good meal. Eat." She loaded another plate and joined me at the table.

As I was hungry, I made no protest. I guess she was hungry also because we ate with little conversation. When I'd finished, I said, "Lorena, I didn't know you were such a good cook. Are you holdin' out anythin' else on me?"

She wiped her mouth daintily with a napkin and looked directly into my eyes. "You never can tell." she said. "There might be some other things up my sleeve."

Thinking I'd make a joke, I said, "Oh, yeah? What's for dessert?"

She smiled and stood. Taking my hand and pulling me toward the bedroom, she said, "It's not on the table."

* * * * *

After that dinner break, it was hard to concentrate on work. Lorena had insisted on an inventory of the merchandise when she bought the place, and I thought it prudent to check it against the actual goods on hand. I was knee deep in bridles when I heard the door bell. "I'm back here," I yelled from my corner.

Milt Oliver walked over to me. "I heered it, but I didn't believe it," he commented.

"What's that?" We were both grinning from ear to ear.

"J. T. come by the feed store and said you was workin' here. I told him that it couldn't be so, that you was in Paducah as of last Friday. He said I could just come see for myself, so here I am."

"You're workin' at the feed store?"

"Yeah," he replied. "They seem to need me to hold the fort down now and again."

"Well, as you can see, I am workin' here."

"So it do appear. Why didn't you tell me?"

"I wasn't sure myself when I saw you last week. This deal just sorta fell in my lap. You were a part of my decision, though. I've missed palin' around with you more than you'd think a body could miss somethin' as ugly as you are."

"I'm glad you're back. What is this deal that fell in your lap?"

After a quick glance to ensure Lorena wasn't in earshot, I answered, "You know my friend, Lorena?"

"That little gal you went to Louisville with?"

"Yeah. Well, she bought this place. She's got some money her parents left her. She and the bankers decided it was a good investment, I guess. Anyway, she bought it and then she asked me to run it for her."

"Too sweet to turn down, huh?"

A blush crept up my neck. "It beats the hell out of muckin' stalls," I said.

"I'd say it does," he mused looking around the store. "You got any coffee in this place?"

"Grab yourself a chair and I'll rustle some up." Milt moved toward the stove in the middle of the floor while I ran upstairs. When I returned, he was sitting with his feet propped on the side of the stove. I handed him a mug.

"Thanks," he said. He was quiet for a few moments, content to stare into the empty cavity of the stove. At length, he spoke softly, "Jim, are you sure you told me all you know about the Hollowells?"

"I told you all there was to tell when we talked about it." I hoped he would not interpret my meaning.

To my dismay, he did get it. "I take it somethin' changed since then?" He shifted his feet to the floor and his gaze to me.

"Milt," I began, looking into his eyes. "You're a good friend and I owe you some things. But I've got other friends, too, and other obligations."

He stared intently. "The Hollowells?"

"Please don't press me. I can't tell you anything."

"I guess you don't have to," he said with a sigh. "J. T. said that the word was out that they were living in Paducah. I just wanted to know if you knew if it's true."

A deep sigh escaped my lips. "Just between you and me?" I asked.

"I sure as hell ain't got any interest in helpin' do 'em harm, if that's what you mean." I could see that he meant what he said.

"It's true. They arrived last week, just after you and that Hall man came to see me. I swore not to tell anybody, Milt. I'm trustin' you."

"There's no need to worry about me." He paused, then continued, "What the hell is the matter with them? Don't they know that the Silent Brigade ain't gonna let them stay around here?"

"I don't know. Bob and Mary Lou both said that they just weren't happy in Oklahoma, that Kentucky was home. There was somethin' about Bob's health, but I think that was just a handy excuse. It was clear to me that Mary Lou never did plan to stay away."

"As far as I know, there's nothin' scheduled yet, but you can bet there'll be a meetin' about this." Concern was evident in his manner. "Do you think she's got sense enough to keep her mouth shut?"

"She'll do whatever she's a mind to," I said. "Keep her mouth shut about what?"

"You heard about Ned Pettit and Steve Choate, didn't you?"

"The last I heard, they were in jail. Were they tried?"

"I guess you could call it that," he sighed. "Both of 'em pleaded guilty and swore that Mrs. Hollowell paid 'em $10 each to scrape them plant beds. They're servin' a year in state prison now."

"I don't believe that she'd hire somebody," I said. "Not that I'd put scrapin' them beds past her, but she ain't cowardly enough to pay somebody to do her dirty work."

Milt scooted his chair around to face me. "What do you mean by that?"

"I mean that if she was of a mind to scrape a plant bed, she'd probably do it herself, and in broad daylight, too. That woman ain't afraid of the very devil himself. It'd be my guess that it was just a sham that the Silent Brigade set up to discredit her."

"What makes you say a thing like that?" Milt seemed interested.

"Like I said, she'd do it herself if she was a mind to." Then I had a thought. "You know, Milt, I never did think Steve Choate had any business in the Silent Brigade."

Milt snorted. "I don't know that any of us did."

"I guess you're right about that," I agreed.

"I've heered it said that Mary Lou's got more guts than brains." He shook his head in awe. "I wouldn't doubt but what you're right, but do you think Steve and that Pettit man would go to prison for a mere $10?"

"They would if they was scared enough."

"I reckon they would," Milt said. "I guess it's better to be alive in prison than sleepin' at the bottom of a lake someplace. Mary Lou does have guts, don't she?"

"I had to admit that she's got more courage than I do," I said. "If it'd been me, I'd have just stayed in Oklahoma. You got any idea what J .T. and them might try to do?"

"Nothin' other than they might try to enforce the arrest warrant that's out for her." He was studying the floor at his feet now.

"You don't really think they'd do that, do you? That trumped up charge won't stand up in court." I was incredulous.

"You've forgot 'we fear no judge or jury.' With all the law in their pocket, they can do 'most whatever they want to. There'll be a meetin' soon. Do you plan to go?"

A shiver went up my spine. "J. T. invited me back into the fold when he was in this mornin'. I can't see how I can get involved, but I don't see how not to, either."

"I've got the same problem," Milt said sadly. "The last few times, I've managed to beg off on one excuse or another, but I don't know how long I can get away with that. I'd hate for 'em to get the notion that I was tryin' to back out."

"I see what you mean," I agreed, "But it'd be worse if they got the idea that a man was tryin' to spy on 'em."

"Oh, Lord," Milt cried. "If they got a thought like that, a man'd wake up dead the next mornin', no question."

"What are we gonna do?"

Lorena chose that moment to appear from the office. "Hello, Milt, isn't it?" Her voice was full of charm.

Milt jerked the hat from his head so violently, I thought maybe he'd pull some hair along. "Yes, miss," he said loudly, leaping to his feet. "How good of you to remember," he stammered.

"Any friend of Jimmy's is a friend of mine and of the L & J hardware, too. How do you like our store?"

Milt was as ill at ease as a long-tailed cat in a room full of rocking chairs. I giggled at his bashfulness as he made a show of looking around. "It's fine. Looks like you've got a lot of new stuff in here."

Lorena smiled indulgently. "It's pretty much the same stock as before, but I do have some ideas for new merchandise. Well, I must get back. Stop in again, Milt."

"I will, I'll do that." he stuttered as she walked away, her skirts swishing. I knew she was doing that just to torment Milt and I could not suppress a laugh.

The levity did not last. It took a few moments before Milt's embarrassment faded. Checking to ensure that she was out of earshot, he turned to me again. "Does she know anything?"

"I told her the Hollowells were back," I admitted.

"You ain't doin' too good for somebody that swore to keep a secret, are you?" He was teasing me in retribution for laughing at him.

"No need to worry about her," I said. "I'll take care of that."

"Quit changin' the subject."   There was no humor in his voice. Then he repeated my question, "What are we gonna do about the meetin's?"

"Damned if I know," was all I could say.

Chapter 18

Friday, December 6, 1907

A t last our long awaited weekend had arrived. Since the day I'd come back to Princeton, Lorena had been talking about going to Paducah to visit the Hollowells. We hadn't gone not so much because I didn't want to go as it just wasn't ever convenient. At first, I thought we ought to give the Hollowells and the situation some time to settle down. Then I became so involved in the day-to-day operations of the store that I never felt that we could get away. Now, with a couple of months experience under my belt, I was really looking forward to getting away and to seeing Bob and Mary Lou, too.

The morning had been typical of days in the store. After dinner, my plan was to loaf around until time for the afternoon train to Paducah. Seated by the stove, I had almost dozed off when I heard the bell. Before I was fully alert, J. T. Jackson was seated beside me. After checking to make sure no one was around, without preliminaries, he said, "Be at the Nabb school at dark tonight."

It was the demand I'd been dreading for months. "Can't make it tonight, J. T.," I said as calmly as possible. I thought I had a good excuse.

He glared at me. "I don't want to hear 'can't.' We need you tonight."

"I'm sorry," I lied. "We're goin' out of town this evenin' — already bought the train tickets and everything. I just can't do it tonight."

J. T. assumed a slightly less menacing posture. "We're gonna have some fun. You wouldn't want to miss it."

It crossed my mind to tell him that I didn't think we had the same idea of what was fun, but that thought was short-lived. "What's happenin'?" I asked, knowing he wouldn't say.

"The boys are goin' for a little ride. Should be a hot time." He was grinning from ear to ear.

His attitude suggested some hidden significance to that remark, but I wasn't about to ask. "It does sound like fun, but Lorena and I have been plannin' this trip for weeks. She's upstairs packin' right now. And havin' bought the tickets already ...."

"Well, I guess we can get along without you this one time," he said, rising. "How's things goin' in the store?"

A silent sigh of relief went through me. I felt sure he could have gotten ugly. "It's doin' fine," I replied.

"I got to get on," he announced, turning for the door. He grinned again and said, "You go on back to what you was doin'. Matter of fact, that ain't a bad position for you to stay in."

"Huh?"

"I'd advise you to keep your head down," he laughed as he went out the door.

Mystification over what he was talking about kept me in my chair for a few minutes. He did not seem to be threatening me, so I didn't have to worry about that. Not yet, anyway. From what I heard, I was sure the Silent Brigade suspected no danger from Bob and Mary Lou, so Paducah should be safe. I went to the stairs and yelled, "Lorena!"

"What is it?"

"Are you through packin'?"

"Yes. Why?"

"Come down and keep an eye on things for a while. I've got to go down the street." I started for the door.

I heard her voice and I knew she'd be asking where I was going. I hurried outside before she got down stairs. A few days before, Milt had told me that he was working at the feed store for a few days. I wanted to find out what he knew about what was going on. Bright sunshine bathed the street creating a beautiful late fall day. I was glad winter hadn't set in yet, but I did wish I'd taken time to get my coat. I walked briskly to the feed store. Milt was sitting in the office, his feet up on the desk. "Workin' hard?" I asked.

"Hardly workin'," he laughed. "I'll learn 'em to go off and leave me in charge."

"In that case, I'm surprised I caught you awake." My smile faded. "Say, Milt ...."

"Yeah, I know," he interrupted. "J. T. was in here to see me, too."

"What'd you tell him?"

He looked out the window, avoiding eye contact. "I told him I'd be there at dark." After a pause, he added, "But I ain't gonna do it."

"You had nerve enough to lie to him?"

He laughed humorlessly. "That took less guts than to tell him straight out that I wasn't gonna show up. What'd you tell him?"

"I told him the truth — I'm goin' to Paducah this evenin'."

"That's right. Y'all are gonna visit the...." Seeing my eyes flash, he said, "Yeah. Visitin'. J. T. bought that?"

"Yeah. Surprised me some, but he seemed satisfied. How do you figure to get away with not showin' up?"

"I've done it before," he sighed. "When they get all fired up, they don't pay much attention to who's there and who ain't."

I sat on a stack of feed sacks beside the stove and warmed my hands. "You got any idea what they're up to?" I asked, coming to the point of my comming here.

His eyes flashed with fear. "I'm afraid I do, but I really don't care to talk about it out loud."

"There ain't nobody here but us chickens." I tried to make it sound light.

"Yeah, I know. But the walls do have ears. They's been rumors for over a year now. If it's what I think, it don't make no difference to us, anyway. We'll talk about it tomorrow." I could see that he was uncomfortable and I understood how he felt so I didn't press him.

"I won't be back until Sunday," I reminded.

"Well, we'll know what's goin' on for sure by then, won't we?"

* * * * *

There couldn't have been a more agreeable day for a train ride if we'd ordered it. The late afternoon sun imparted a pastel hue on the pastures and fallow tobacco fields. Although the November winds had stripped the trees, there was as yet no hint of winter in the air. Everyone in the car seemed in good spirits and the ride passed pleasantly.

When we arrived at the Paducah depot, Lorena asked her first question of the trip. "Are we going to stay with the Hollowells?"

"No," I replied. "I don't know where they live or even if they have a spare bedroom. And since they don't expect us, I thought we'd just check into the hotel." I failed to mention that I didn't care to hear what Mary Lou would have to say about us sleeping together.

She seemed content with that answer. "How far is the hotel? Can we walk?"

"It's close enough to walk," I laughed, "But seein' as how you brought enough baggage to stay a month, I think we'll take a cab." As I looked for a driver, it occurred to me that I had moved up in the world. For a boy that had nothing less than six months ago, I was taking cab fares and hotel bills in stride.

The Palmer House hadn't changed and I felt right at home. After I registered — as Mr. and Mrs. Singleton — and the porter took the grips away, I asked the clerk if he happened to know the Hollowells. "No," he said scratching his chin. "I thought I knew everybody in town, but I don't know of nobody by that name." He continued to scratch while he thought. "Now they is a family name of Holman down the road here, but I don't 'spect them's the ones you want. Used to be a Sam Hillerman lived down by the river, but I think he died. Where these folks you're looking for from?"

To cut short what would be, no doubt, a long conversation, I simply said, "Never mind," and walked away.

Lorena was unpacking her dresses when I got to the room. "Oh, Jimmy," she gushed, "this is so exciting. We needed to get away from the store, don't you think?"

"Yeah," I agreed. "It'll do us good, and it'll be good to see Bob and Mary Lou, too."

"Oh, yes. It will. It's been almost a year since I've seen Mrs. Hollowell. Did you find out where they live?"

I flopped down on the bed. The springs were soft and I bounced two feet in the air. "No." I said. "The clerk was willin' to recite the history of the county, but I didn't stick around for it. I don't know how we'll find 'em."

She hung the last garment in the closet and turned toward me, arms akimbo. "Why don't you look in the telephone directory, silly?"

That idea hadn't occurred to me. We'd discussed getting a telephone in the store, but hadn't done it yet, and I was not accustomed to such new-fangled devices. "Good idea," I said.

I motioned for her to join me on the bed. With a mischievous grin, she crossed the room and lay beside me. I threw an arm across her chest and was about to get serious but she playfully slapped my wrist.

"Plenty of time for that," she said. "Go look in the telephone book now. We'll see if they want to meet us for supper."

Reluctantly, I let her go and went back down to the lobby. Almost as reluctantly, I approached the desk. The clerk was sorting some papers. "Can I help you?" he inquired with a frown.

"Where's the telephone book?"

"Right here behind the desk." He went right on sorting the papers.

"Well, can I see it?" I tried to keep the irritation out of my voice.

"Oh. Of course." He was grinning like a 'possum under a red wagon. "You didn't say you wanted to see it." He handed me the thin volume. There was no listing for Hollowell.

"Lots of folks ain't got telephones, you know." His grin continued. "Find what you was lookin' for?"

"Yes, I did. I got Hillerman's number," I said, turning away. I won that one!

Lorena had put on her best dress and was ready to go out.. "Did you get the address?" she asked.

"No. They're not listed. They probably ain't got one of those things installed. But, I did get an idea."

"What's that?"

"Their lawyer, John Miller, was listed. He'll know where they are."

"Good thought," she said. "Did you call him?"

Not particularly wanting to admit I was uncomfortable with telephones, I replied. "If we go right now, maybe we can catch him before he goes home for the evening."

* * * * *

"Is John Miller in?" I asked the young man at the reception desk.

"Do you want Senior or Junior?"

"Uh, Senior, I guess."

"Yes, he's here. May I tell him who's calling?" He was very polite and professional.

"Jim Singleton," I said as he disappeared behind a door with a bumpy translucent glass pane. In a few seconds, he opened the door and motioned us inside the office.

"Mr. Miller," I said, entering the room, "do you remember me?"

"Of course. Adam Smoot tells me you did a good job over at his place." He smiled broadly while extending his hand.

"Well, thank you for the recommendation. I needed a job at the time. I'd like you to meet my, uh, friend, Lorena."

"Welcome to the firm of Miller and Miller. Please have a seat." He gestured across his desk toward the chairs. When we were seated, he asked, "What can I do for you folks?"

"We're looking for the Hollowells."

He jumped up and quickly crossed to the door which was ajar. Closing it, he returned to his seat. "The Hollowells?" John Miller seemed puzzled, which confused me. I knew that he was aware of my relationship with Bob and Mary Lou.

"Yeah," I said. "Bob and Mary Lou. Do you know where they live?"

His eyes dropped to the surface of his desk. "What do you want with them?"

"They're good friends of both of us," I said waving my hand between Lorena and myself. "We've just come to visit, but don't know where they live. I thought you could help."

Miller leaned into his desk and put his elbows on the top. "There's people other than you looking for the Hollowells," he whispered.

"Yes, we know," Lorena said. "Let me assure you, Mr. Miller, that we mean them no harm." She flashed her most charming smile.

"I didn't mean to imply that I thought you did," he said. "I only mean that we do not wish their whereabouts to become common knowledge."

"Do you mean that you think we might be followed?" I asked.

He leaned back in his chair and hesitated before he spoke. "I mean that I'm not at liberty to tell you where they are."

"But we've come all the way over here on the train," Lorena protested. "We can't go running all over town ...." He halted her with an upraised palm.

Leaning toward us, he said, "I can tell you this. They're not in Paducah."

* * * * *

The next morning we decided that we'd stay for the weekend anyway. Paducah was a big city — relative to Princeton — and with some money in my pocket, I thought we could have some fun. The lobby was buzzing with activity when we came down for breakfast. Men and boys were running hither and yon through knots of people engaged in animated conversation. I grabbed a passing bellboy by the arm. "What's goin' on?" I asked.

"Ain't you heard?" he replied.

"If I'd heard, I wouldn't be askin'. What?"

He jerked his arm from my grasp. "The night riders raided Hopkinsville early this mornin'," he said as he dashed away.

"Well! That explains it," I said aloud to myself.

"Explains what?" Lorena asked.

"Oh, uh," I stammered. "There's been rumors about that ever since the Princeton raid a year ago."

"That's right," she agreed. "I've heard it discussed at the boarding house table."

To get some details, I bought a newspaper as we entered the dining room. The lead story explained that about 1 AM, approximately 250 masked riders —evidently gathered from all over the Black Patch — had converged on the city of Hopkinsville. The details of the raid were similar to the Princeton affair in that the city police, the telephone office and the fire department had all been efficiently neutralized while the main body of riders burned the Tandy & Fairleigh and Latham warehouses, both full of Trust tobacco. Damages were estimated at $50,000. The most interesting part of the article was the reporter's speculations that as Hopkinsville had its own local militia company and given that the city officials were strongly opposed to the night rider movement, such a raid could only have been accomplished with the aid of "citizen sympathizers."

Lorena was keenly interested and had me read much of the article to her over breakfast. When we'd finished eating, she asked, "Do you think we'd better get back home?"

"I hate to spoil the weekend," I said, glad that she made the suggestion already in my mind.

"Me too, but there's no telling what this might precipitate. I think we'd better go protect our property." Although not panicked, she was concerned.

"I agree. Let's pay our bill and get to the depot."

* * * * *

After dropping Lorena at Mrs. Haynes', I headed for the feed store, assuming that Milt would be staying there. A gruff, "What is it?" answered my knock.

"It's me, Milt. Open up." The door opened a crack and he eyed me through the slit.

Opening the door fully, he managed a wry smile and said, "How the hell am I supposed to know who 'me' is?"

"It always works."

He smiled humorlessly as he checked the street and closed the door. "Well, you've heard?"

"Yep. Is that what you thought was gonna happen?"

He crossed the room and sat on a stack of sacks while I took the only chair. "Yeah. They've been plannin' to raid Hopkinsville for some time."

"I can see why you didn't want to talk about it. I've heard rumors about it, but I never knew if it was just talk or what."

"I can tell you it weren't just talk. I know for a fact that they tried to do it the middle of last month."

"Are you serious?"

He lay back on the sacks. "I didn't know what they was up to at first. If I had, I wouldn't have gone. By the time I figured it out, we was halfway to Hopkinsville and I couldn't get out."

"What happened?"

He sighed deeply and closed his eyes. "Like I say, we was halfway there when a big wind come up. Seems as how about that same time, they got word that the Hopkinsville militia company had been alerted and was waiting for us. Of course, in view of that, they didn't want to risk the wind causin' the whole town to burn, so we turned back."

"That was civic minded of 'em," I giggled. "Bein' afraid of the armed militia couldn't have had nothin' to do with the decision, I suppose."

Milt opened his eyes and stared at me. "They ain't cowards, Jim. You'd be mistaken to think so. It's just that they don't need to risk a regular battle to accomplish their goals."

Shifting back to last night, I asked, "You didn't go, did you?"

He sat upright. "Hell no!" he roared. Then more quietly, "Like I told you, I just didn't show up. I'm sure that nobody missed me in all the excitement. Have you heard all about it?"

"No," I said. "I read what was in the Paducah paper about burnin' the two warehouses, but it didn't tell a whole lot. What else do you know?"

"I talked to Sanford Hall this mornin'," he said. "He said that there was a lot of events that didn't make the papers."

"Like what?" Now I'd hear the good stuff.

"Like they beat up a man by the name of Lindsay Mitchell."

"What for?"

"He's a buyer for the Trust, but I think they whipped him just for fun. It's tricks like that that convinced me to distance myself from 'em."

"What else?" I wanted to hear it all.

"Lots of things," he said with a sigh. "At least one person was shot by accident, but an employee of the L & N Railroad was shot on purpose. He was tryin' to move some railroad cars to keep 'em from burnin'. One of the riders ordered him to stop and when he didn't, the rider shot him."

"Is he dead?"

"I don't know. I suppose nobody hung around to find out. They did do one good deed, though. Evidently the fires were about to get out of hand, so they turned the fire department out and let 'em save some buildings."

"That was big of 'em. So it didn't come off as smooth as our raid last year?"

"You ain't heard the worst of it yet. A couple of the night riders got shot up. One of 'em's dead, and another one might not make it." There was neither excitement nor sadness in his voice.

"How'd that happen?" After the kind of organization I'd seen, I couldn't imagine Doc Amoss' planning being less than perfect.

"Apparently some of the local citizens or maybe the militia chased a bunch of the riders as they left town. The way Sanford told it, it was a regular pitched battle out on the road someplace. Anyway, I hear one's dead, and some others wounded, including Doc Amoss."

"The 'General' himself? Oh, Lord," I exclaimed. "That'll make 'em madder than a centipede on a hot rock."

A chill fell over the room. Milt got up and threw a lump of coal into the glowing embers in the fireplace. "Damn right it will. I'm more scared now than I was before." Turning to face me, he continued, "That ain't all that's gonna aggravate 'em. The Governor ordered the Hopkinsville militia to active duty to guard the place."

"The hell you say? Governor Beckham ain't showed any interest in the affair the whole four years he's been in office and now he's takin' a hand with only a few days left in his term?"

"I guess he figures to let the new governor, Willson, deal with it," Milt sighed. "I know for a fact that the Silent Brigade ain't happy to see a damned Republican come in office, and with the militia out .... Well, I'm scared."

When I got back to the store, I picked a double barreled shotgun from the rack and took it with a box of shells upstairs. Before I went to bed, I loaded both barrels and propped the gun against the wall within easy reach of where I lay.

Chapter 19

Saturday, March 5, 1908

T he days and weeks following the Hopkinsville raid brought an es calation in what was now being called the "Black Patch War." A week after the raid, we got word that Governor Willson replaced the Hopkinsville militia company with a company from Louisville. The loafers around the stove seemed to think that he did that because he thought that non-local soldier guards would be more effective than the boys from Hopkinsville. Just before Christmas, word came in that one of the soldiers had accidentally shot a resident. Most of the local folks being Democrats and Willson being a Republican, the stove wasn't the only thing hot after that. Early in January, the night riders carried out an unexpected raid on Russellville, burned two more tobacco ware-houses and got away with only minor injuries to the citizens. In re-sponse, Governor Willson ordered the militia — which had been con-fined to Hopkinsville — to Marion, then Eddyville and Kuttawa. From what we read in the papers, the entire Black Patch was rife with ten-sion. Every train that stopped in Princeton seemed to be loaded with soldiers, and just their passing through caused a lot of friction here. It was easy to see that the people in the towns where they were posted didn't care for their presence. Rumors from those towns had it that the soldiers spent most of their time flirting with the local girls and for sure the boys didn't care for that. From the talk I picked up, I felt sure that I wasn't the only one sleeping with a weapon within reach.

On this windy, cold Saturday afternoon, Lorena had taken the week's receipts to the bank after dinner. I was sitting sleepily at the stove filling out an order when the door flew open, admitting a blast of frigid air and Milt Oilver. He slammed the door and walked to the stove, taking a chair opposite me. Even before he spoke, his ashen face told me something was wrong. "Well, the fat's really in the fire now." I was surprised at the lack of emotion.

"What is it?" I asked, laying my work aside.

In response, he rolled his weight to one side and produced a folded paper from his hip pocket. Wordlessly, he handed it over to me. As I opened the first fold, the heading, "The United States of America" appeared. "What is this?" Excitement rose in me.

"It's just what it says. It's a summons to appear in court." His entire body was shaking.

Glancing down the page, the first item I noticed was that the summons was in response to a petition filed by Robert H. Hollowell. By God, Bob had gotten up the nerve to file! "I can't believe he'd do this," I said.

"Why not? Hell, you know what happened." There was a tone of resignation in his voice.

"Yeah, but I mean I'd never of thought it of Bob. Mary Lou, maybe, but not Bob."

"Humph!" he snorted. "She's filed one just like it."

"There's two suits?" After I said that, I realized that as they'd both suffered injuries, it only made sense for them to file separately. Apparently Milt thought so, too. He simply nodded.

"There's a bunch of names here." I remarked, eyeing the document.

"Twenty-nine of 'em," Milt said. "It's ever'body who was in on the Hollowell affair, including two of 'em who've died in the meantime."

"And Lula Hollowell, too!" I could envision the pleasure Mary Lou took in having her sister-in-law included.

"Well, John's wife was there," he said. "As a matter of fact, I suspect she was one of the ring leaders."

"Do you know what the petition says?" I was wide awake now.

"Our lawyer, Mr. Ruby Laffoon, read it to us," he replied slowly. "Bob accused us of shooting up the place, whipping him and running them out of the state. He's seeking $50,000 damages."

I let out a whistle. "That's a hell of a lot of money."

"Yep. Mary Lou's petition asked for $50,000, too."

"Well, hell, Milt. There's been other suits and nothin' come of 'em. I don't see that you have much to worry about." I was experiencing mixed emotions — I thought Bob and Mary Lou were due some justice, but Milt was my friend, too. I knew that Milt was in on the raid, but I also knew that he took no active part.

Milt shook his head. "That's what ever'body thought. They thought we was safe. But, that was all county and state court. You'll notice that this is from the United States Government— it's federal court, Jimmy. Federal!"

I examined the summons more closely. It directed the Marshal of the Western District of Kentucky to warn these men that failure to answer and appear in court in Paducah on April 20 amounted to confession or contempt. I understood why he was scared. "How'd they manage to get into federal court?" I asked.

Milt stared at the red hot sides of the stove. "The Hollowells moved across the river to Indiana. Residents of one state filing again' residents of another automatically goes to federal court."

Mary Lou Hollowell had struck an incredible blow against the night riders! While they thought they were— and it was true — beyond the reach of the law in the Black Patch, she was the only one who'd thought of federal court. The move to Indiana explained why we couldn't locate them in Paducah, and why Miller didn't want to talk about it. "Do you understand exactly what this means?"

"The Silent Brigade's employed some lawyers," he answered. "When we met with them, they explained some. What it boils down to is they ain't got the federal judge in their pocket, and the jury will be called from the whole district, not just local counties."

"Wow! Looks like the Silent Brigade underestimated Mary Lou, don't it?" My own respect for her had gone up a notch, too.

Milt shifted his gaze from the stove for the first time. Looking directly into my eyes, he said, "The rooster ain't crowed yet."

"What do you mean?"

"I ain't at liberty to discuss it, but the Silent Brigade ain't exactly helpless, you know." There was determination in his voice now.

"I understand," I said. "But, take some advice from a friend. If I was in your shoes, I'd try to put some distance between me and whatever they plan."

"You mean run?" A shocked look crossed his face. "Hell, I can't do that! It's United States court — why, they'd track me down!"

"No," I apologized, "that ain't what I meant. I was just suggestin' that I'd try to stay out of whatever response they're cookin' up."

He managed a weak smile. "Thanks, but your name ain't on that list." He pointed at the document in my hands. "This is serious business, and I guess a man will do whatever he can to try to get out of it."

"I guess he would," I agreed.

Milt was silent for a few minutes. At length, he sighed and said, "I think you ought to watch out for yourself, too."

"Nobody thinks I'm involved, do they?" I asked, amazed.

"No," he replied, studying the stove again. "But, all them boys named there with me — John Hollowell, B. Malone, Bill Larkins, and all of 'em — they ain't overlookin' the fact that you was part of Mary Lou's family, so to speak. They're madder'n a bunch of wet hens over this. There ain't no tellin' what they're liable to do."

* * * * *

Milt had been gone less than five minutes when Lorena returned, puffing from the brisk walk. "The town's all abuzz out there," she announced, removing her coat. "What's going on?"

The cold air had imparted a pink flush to her cheeks and she looked lovely. Since we'd begun working together in the store, we'd had the opportunity to get to know each other better. Before, I'd simply thought of her as a person that I liked, but as time passed, she and I grew more in love, and I was just beginning to fully appreciate her qualities. She was beautiful, sexy, charming, witty, and intelligent. All in all, she was quite a package. I felt lucky to have her, and a little guilty that I'd never told her any of these things. Realizing that I hadn't answered her question, I said, "Bob and Mary Lou Hollowell have filed a suit on the night riders who shot up their place and ran them off."

She joined me at the stove. Warming her hands, she asked, "Why in the world would they do that? Everyone knows they've got all the law in their ranks, so there's no chance of beating them. I didn't think Mrs. Hollowell was stupid enough to endanger herself and her family again."

"The reason we couldn't find them was that they moved to Indiana," I told her. "Since they're across the river, it'll go to federal court, and that's beyond the control of even the night riders."

She looked at me in wonder for a moment, then burst into laughter. "What's so funny about that?" I asked.

"Mrs. Hollowell has outsmarted 'em, that's what," she roared.

"They thought they had everything and everybody under their control. Good for her!" She clapped her hands with glee.

"I feel the same way, but let's don't be countin' our chickens before they hatch," I warned. "The night riders ain't just gonna roll over and play dead on this thing."

"What can they do? The federal court isn't intimidated by them like the local courts are. Mrs. Hollowell's beat 'em, that's all there is to it." She was delighted.

"Well, Mary Lou's still under indictment here in Caldwell County for scrapin' that plant bed," I reminded. "The federal court meets in Paducah, which means that she'll have to set foot on Kentucky soil. I'll bet they'll try to arrest her when she does."

My thoughts did not dampen her enthusiasm. "Let 'em try. No trumped up local charge is going to supersede a federal case. This is just delicious — she's outsmarted the whole bunch of ruffians. I knew she could do it, and I knew she would, too!."

I wished I felt as comfortable about it all as she. "Lorena," I said, intending to tell her about Milt's warning.

"Yes?" Honey dripped from her voice as she turned toward me and smiled.

"I love you," I said. No point in spoiling her mood or unduly alarming her.

"It's mutual," she said, throwing her arms around my neck. Despite all the trouble going around, life was not all bad.

* * * * *

Monday dawned bright and sunny with a promise of spring in the cool air. The station agent sent a boy to tell me that a large order for the store had arrived at the Illinois Central depot. Because most of the goods were ordered by one customer, I decided to hire a wagon and return to the store with the balance of the merchandise after I'd made the delivery out in the county.

"How are you this morning?" Lorena asked as she reported for work.

"All better now that I get to see you," I said with a smile, reaching for her.

"Behave yourself!" She slapped playfully at my hands. "Anything going on this morning?"

"The stuff Deaton ordered has come in. I'm gonna deliver it if you can hold the fort down here."

"I think I can handle it. How long will you be gone?"

"Shouldn't take more'n half a day. If I get goin', I 'spect I'll be back by the middle of the afternoon."

"No problem," she said. "I'll stay right here until you get back." She kissed me on the cheek and walked into her office at the back. My heart swelled as I watched her walk away. I was a lucky man.

"Good Mornin'," Wiley Jones greeted me from his perch behind his desk.

"Mornin', Wiley. You got a wagon ready for me?"

"Sure do, son." He rose and walked with me into the runway of the stable. The odor of the place brought back memories. I was just as glad to only have to endure it for as long as it took to drive out. The horses were hitched to the wagon, snorting in the morning air. Wiley patted the neck of his mare as I climbed onto the wagon. "You be careful out there, Jim," he said. "There's lots of meanness goin' on."

"Yeah, I know," I replied, flipping the reins. "I'll keep my eyes peeled."

I'd driven about three miles when the left rear wheel began to squeak. I stopped and looked at it but couldn't see anything wrong. The hub felt pretty warm, but the wheel didn't seem loose on the axle. I had to get the goods delivered, so I decided to press on and give Wiley some grief about his wagon when I got back to town.

"Got a problem there, don't you Jim?" Josh Deaton called as I pulled in front of his barn.

"What'd give you that idea?" I said, feigning ignorance.

"The way that wheel's screamin', a man'd think a deaf mute woulda noticed it." He was laughing. "I heered you comin' ten minutes ago."

I jumped from the wagon to the ground. "It's been makin' a little noise, but I knew you needed this stuff, so I decided to try to make it on out here and back to town," I said walking to the rear of the bed.

Josh joined me at the rear wheel. A wisp of smoke was coming from the hub and it smelled burnt. "Looks bad," he said. "We'll let it cool off while we unload this stuff, then we'll have a look."

After an hour, we had the fencing and supplies unloaded and stored in the barn. Josh walked to the rear of the wagon and tugged on the wheel. "It don't look good, Jim. We'll have to pull the wheel, then we'll see for sure what the problem is."

Wiley Jones' ears must have been burning as I cussed him under my breath while we propped up the wagon's axle on firewood so the wheel could be removed. The day had warmed and we were both sweating profusely by the time the chore was accomplished. Just as we sat to rest, Josh's wife yelled out the back door that dinner was ready. "Let's eat a bite," Josh said, pulling off his gloves.

Knowing that Josh would be offended if the offer was refused, I followed him to the pump at the rear of the house. Splashing cold well water on my face felt good. We washed up and went inside. The table was set with two plates, a platter of pork chops, fried potatoes, milk gravy, two vegetables, biscuits and butter. "Have a seat, son and dig in," Josh said tucking a napkin into the neck opening of his bib overalls.

I followed suit and ate a hearty meal. I wanted to thank his wife, but she had disappeared when we came inside and was still nowhere in sight as we went back out. After inspecting the wheel hub, Josh announced, "It's the bearing, all right. It's got to be replaced. Is this your wagon?"

"No," I replied. "It belongs to Wiley Jones and he can have it. I'm gonna give him what-for when I get the damned thing back to him."

"Don't blame you none," he laughed. "Well sir, all I see we can do is pack this hub with grease and put the wheel back on." He scratched the back of his head as he spoke, pushing his hat forward.

"You think it'll make it back to town like that?" I was concerned.

"Maybe. You'll have to take it slow. I suggest you stop and let it cool off ever' few minutes. It's burned some in there already. If it gets hot again, the wheel's liable to just fall off on you." Josh accepted the situation stoically.

"Damn!" It came out louder than intended.

"Just calm down, son. By the time you get to my age, you'll have learned not to waste energy on things that can't be helped." His voice was soothing.

I thought I had a right to be upset. I was thinking up some choice words for Mr. Wiley Jones, but rather than risk having to hear more of Josh's philosophy, I simply said, "I've got things to do this evenin'."

"Well, I hope you can do 'em in the dark," he said, moving toward the shed to get the grease.

Dusk was settling in by the time we'd replaced the wheel and removed the firewood props. When I at last got started, I was tempted to whip the horses into a run, but I knew that I'd better heed Josh's warning to take it slow. After each ten minute interval, I stopped and sat until the hub was completely cool. Even when I was moving, the ground seemed to crawl by inch by inch. Stars were twinkling in a deep blue sky when I finally reached town. Not only had I wasted the day, I knew Lorena would be upset by my being so late.

The stable was completely deserted. I yelled, but there was no answer. It was strange for Wiley not to be around. He knew I had his wagon out and was overdue. I went to the office and pounded on the door, thinking he might have fallen asleep in there. No answer. I thought about just leaving the horses hitched to the wagon, but none of this was their fault. My anger boiled higher as I put the horses away and pitched them some hay. Having to do stable work again did not improve my frame of mind, either. Wiley Jones was in for the cussing of his life when I found him.

Empty streets were all I saw on the walk back to the store. I calmed somewhat with the expectation that Lorena would have a good supper ready for me. She'd said that she'd stay there until I returned, and I knew she would. I rounded the corner and stopped, stunned. Where the store should have been, there was only a pile of black, smoldering ashes. I ran to the front, not knowing why. There was nothing there — the store had burned to the ground. Twisted strips of tin roofing offered mute testimony to the intense heat that had ravaged the building. When I inhaled deeply in a gasp, the acrid odor stung my lungs and sent me into a fit of coughing which, in turn, brought tears to my eyes. Once the tears started to flow, a flood poured forth from the depths of my being. Sobbing, I realized that this wouldn't have happened if I'd been back as I planned. Damn Wiley Jones and his junk wagon to hell! I thought of going to take it out on Wiley, but deep down, I knew it wasn't his fault. As I stood there coughing and crying, the feeling soaked in on me that my entire world had been destroyed. By fire. Again. Although it seemed impossible, I sank even lower as I thought of all the events of the last 18 months that had helped build the world that had just vanished in smoke. How did this happen? My mind raced. Had the Silent Brigade made good on the threat to take out their vengeance on me? Was it an accident? I stood there, bewildered until at last I remembered what was really important. When I did, my heart froze within me— where was Lorena?

Reversing my direction, I dashed to Mrs. Haynes' boarding house. I jumped up on the porch and rang the bell. When the door did not open instantly, I began pounding on the frame, tears of frustration streaming down my cheeks. I beat on the door with all my might, yelling. After what seemed hours, the widow Haynes appeared in the hall.

"Land's sakes, mister, keep your shirt on," she said opening the door. "Decent folks would ...." Seeing my face, she stopped in mid-sentence. Her eyes widened and her hand flew to her mouth. "Oh," she cried, "it's you."

"Where's Lorena?" I demanded.

"Why, she's, uh ...."

"Well," I insisted "Where is she, damn it?"

Mrs. Haynes chin dropped to her chest. "I'm sorry," she sobbed. "Miss Leeson's dead."

My heart stopped. "What?"

She was weeping. "Burned up in the fire. May the devil himself take them that caused it. She was a fine young lady ...."

She may have said something else, I don't know. My whole being was numb as I turned away. Without conscious thought, I walked back to the street and sat down on the sidewalk. Dead? My mind went into denial. She couldn't possibly be dead — she was so alive only a few hours ago. As paralyzed as my mind was, rationality kicked in. The store had burned completely to the ground and she had said that she'd stay there until I got back. There was no doubt that she was in the store when the fire started. Maybe she got out. Mrs. Haynes wouldn't lie to me, would she? No. Why would she tell me that Lorena was dead if she wasn't? Dead! I don't know how long I sat there before I noticed that a cold rain had started. I was soaked to the skin and shivering.

Perhaps the need for heat put me in motion. I wandered aimlessly along the street, placing one foot in front of another without conscious thought. The pungent taste in my nostrils first made me aware that I was back at the site of the store. The "ping" that accompanied each rain drop's impact on the tin roofing drummed in my head as loud as thunder. My mind snapped. I screamed at the top of my lungs and ran.

Exhaustion finally stopped me. I was covered in water, rain or sweat. I slumped into the doorway of whatever building it was. Gasping for breath, reality set in again. She's dead. Where was she? I wanted to see her. I wanted to tell her all the things I hadn't said. At least, I had to tell her good-bye. Where would the body be? I decided the funeral emporium was the best bet. Taking stock, I found my bearings and headed in that direction.

The building was totally dark. I guess it must be the middle of the night by now, but I didn't care. I pounded the door until the glass rattled. A light went on inside and a figure in a night shirt appeared in the door. "My God, you'll wake the dead," he said as the door swung open.

If that was an example of morticians' humor, I was in no mood to appreciate it. "Is Lorena Leeson here?" I demanded.

"You mean the young lady that burned in the hardware store?" When I didn't answer, he continued, "Yes. The remains are here."

"I want to see her," I said, stepping inside. Judging from the look of terror on his face, I suppose that my appearance frightened him.

"Now, see here. After a fire like that ...." he began, stepping back.

I cut him off. "I've got to see her." The loudness of my voice made the crystal gas light fixture overhead jingle.

With a sigh of resignation, he led the way into a dark room. He turned up the light until a dim glow illuminated a pine box along the opposite wall. "There it is if you've got to look. Lock the door on your way out," he said as he turned away.

My blood turned to ice water as I walked across the room. The lid of the coffin was just lying in place, not nailed. Marshaling my resolve, I ignored the icy hand gripping my heart, slid the lid aside and peered inside. Sometimes my determination gets the better of good judgment. I wish I hadn't looked.

Chapter 20

Tuesday, March 8, 1908

Whoever invented the English language made a mistake with the word "funeral." I can tell you for a fact that there ain't no fun in it. For a fun thing, watching that pine box descend into the ground rates right up there with having the blacksmith pull a tooth. The widow Haynes, a couple of her permanent boarders and I were all that showed up to bid Lorena Leeson a final farewell. Rain poured in buckets, of course, and it was a gloomy day. The preacher made it clear that while he didn't personally know the young lady, he felt sure that God would forgive her for whatever her sins might have been. Mrs. Haynes made polite enough to say "hello," and that was about the extent of the conversation, although she did offer me a ride back in her carriage. As I was having difficulty dealing with my grief, I declined, preferring to walk.

Trudging along through the cold rain and mud, many sad emotions raged within me. I'd lost not only my love, but my job and home as well. The home part had been relatively easy to cure — I'd rented a room above the bank. One of my thoughts was that a rented room wasn't much of a home, but it was about as close as I'd been for a while. The main source of my dispair, however, was the question in my mind about whether I'd really loved Lorena. I'd tried to convince myself that the idea that I didn't love her had only popped into my head as a defense mechanism. But try as I might, I wasn't totally convinced. A deep melancholy had settled in on me by the time I got to town.

"Jim!" A voice called from the alley as I walked between two buildings.

I stopped and peered into the rain and fog. "Who is it?"

"It's me," Milt Oliver said, stepping out from beneath the steps on the side of the building just enough for me to see his face. "Come back here," he yelled.

"Hell, Milt," I shouted above the din of the rain, "it's rainin' out here." I walked a few steps toward where I'd seen him.

"I can see that, you damn fool," he said gripping my arm and pulling me under the stairs. "I want to talk to you."

"Let's go inside." I was already soaked and the cold was sinking to my bones.

"Can't risk bein' seen with you," he replied.

"Well, I ain't stayin' out here. Wait a few minutes and then come on up to my place." I turned away before he could protest and ran to my room.

I'd just dried my hair and changed clothes when a soft knock sounded at the door. "Come on in, Milt," I called.

"Keep your voice down," he said, stepping inside and quickly closing the door.

"What are you so jumpy about?" I asked, tossing him the towel.

He caught it and began rubbing his head while water dripped from his clothes onto the floor. "You're a marked man."

I think I would have rather been alone, but that was an interesting comment. "Sit by the fire and explain that," I said.

He pulled a chair up to the fireplace and hesitated a long moment before answering. "You were seen talkin' to that Miller man yesterday." His voice was soft.

I was a little shocked. "Hell, I just happened to meet him on the street. Why does that interest anybody?"

Milt scooted his chair closer to the fire. "The boys know what Miller's doin'," he said.

"I'd think they sure as hell would," I exploded. "His having those summons served on them made it pretty plain, didn't it?"

"Yeah, but that ain't it. What'd he say to you?"

I wasn't sure I wanted to answer that. Milt was a friend, and I trusted him, but given all the devilment that had been going on, I thought it was probably best not to trust anyone. Miller had said that since he was sure that the defendants would try to impeach Mary Lou's character, he was trying to round up some who'd testify on her behalf. I decided to play Milt along a bit. "What do you mean, 'that ain't it?'"

Milt looked from the fire into my eyes. "They aim to make damn sure that nobody —and I mean nobody — don't contradict the picture they're gonna paint of Mrs. Mary Lou Hollowell. Some of 'em figure that you might try to do that."

He was being honest with me. They did know what Mr. Miller was doing in Princeton. "We talked about that," I replied honestly. "He said that while he'd love to have me testify, given what my relationship with the Hollowells was, it'd be about the same as them testifyin' to their own character. So, his plans don't include me."

"I'm glad to hear that," he said, staring into the fire again. "I don't know that it'll get you off the hook with the Silent Brigade, but I'm glad to hear it." He seemed weary.

I decided to let him in on all I knew. "Mr. Miller did tell me one thing that's interestin'."

"What's that?" His gaze snapped to me.

"I guess you know that most lawyers think that neither husband nor wife can testify for the other?"

"That's what Mr. Lafoon said." I had his full attention now.

"Well, Mr. Miller seems to think otherwise. I reckon he aims to have 'em speak for each other."

Milt's eyes went back to the fire. "He'll need 'em," he said softly.

"How's that?" He now had my attention.

"Ever' one of us defendants will have an alibi and two or three witnesses to back it up." He spoke matter-of-factly.

We fell silent while I considered the odds of sixty or seventy witnesses for the defense against three for the Hollowells. "Has this thing got the boys worried?" I didn't know if he'd want to tell me, but I was curious.

He continued to stare into the fire. "I wouldn't say 'worried.' There's been a bunch of meetin's on it, but it's more like Doc Amoss is just irritated by the suits. His attitude is like he's, oh, I don't know, subdued."

"That's interestin'. What does he talk about at the meetin's?"

Milt presented a strange sight. His clothes were beginning to dry, wreathing his slumped figure in steam. He looked up at me, alarm in his eyes. Then his look softened. "It is interestin'." he said. "They've laid a levy of 50 cents a head on all the members to help pay the lawyers' fees."

That statement provoked a laugh from me. "What's funny about that?" Milt asked.

"It's just strange," I replied, "that this whole nasty business got started because the farmers couldn't make any money. Now they're chargin' 'em to help pay for the trouble that their own efforts caused."

Milt did not see any humor in the situation. "I've got a job, so it don't matter much to me, but I know it's damned hard for many of the boys to come up with any cash at all."

"Yeah, I guess it is. You say they ain't worried?" I asked to get off the money aspect.

"Nah. They ain't too worried about this particular suit. I'll tell you, though, you were right — they're sure as hell surprised."

"About a suit in federal court?"

"That's right," he nodded. "They thought that whatever crimes they'd committed were all against the state or county. Federal court never occurred to anybody."

"Except Mary Lou Hollowell," I laughed.

"I've got to hand it to her," he agreed. "Our lawyer explained that the only way to get into federal court was for it to be residents of one state again' another for more than $10,000. She did ever'thing just right." He paused, shaking his head. "She outsmarted 'em, good and proper."

"I learned long ago that she's as smart as she is pretty. I'd say nobody doubts it now." Conversation lagged while we each digested our thoughts. Remembering what Milt had said earlier, I asked, "What did you mean that Doc Amoss ain't worried about this *particular* suit?"

"Well," he began, "he figures they ain't much chance of the Hollowells winnin'. What he is worried about is that this suit opens the gates for other folks to follow the same path."

"I can see that," I agreed. "But, it seems to me that this one is cut and dry. Between you and me and the gate post, the ones charged are guilty as hell, ain't they?"

Milt shot me a hard glare, but it only lasted a moment. "Yeah, I reckon so," he admitted. "But, accordin' to the lawyers, that don't matter."

"What do you mean, 'that don't matter?' It matters if you're guilty, don't it?"

He studied the floor for a moment before answering. "According to the lawyers, it's who's on the jury, not the facts, that counts. They said we needn't be worried."

"If my name was on one of them summonses, I'd be worried," I said.

He allowed himself a sly smile. "Them summonses served by the Unites States Marshall scared the hell out of ever'body right off, but they figure we still have an ace in the hole in the plant bed scraping indictment against Mary Lou. According to the talk I've heard, they plan to have her arrested and hauled back to Caldwell County the minute she sets foot on Kentucky soil. Even if that fails, they're sure that they'll never have to appear in court. The Silent Brigade's confidence is supreme. I've heard them say openly that if somehow we do have to appear, the federal court will never hand down a judgment against us, and even if it does, we won't have to pay it.

"I don't understand," I said. "I thought you'd be facing jail."

"Our lawyers don't think they can bring any criminal action against us in federal court," he explained. "After all, we ain't committed no offense against the United States. So, this is just a civil proceeding. The worst they can do is order us to pay some money, and, like I said, they don't think the court will do that."

It took me a few minutes to think all that over. "I can't see how they've got that figured," I said. "I know that the Silent Brigade ain't got control over Walter Evans, the federal judge scheduled to hear the case. The jury selection will include the whole western half of the state, I don't reckon they'd be able to control that, either. Where the hell does this supreme confidence come from?"

Almost completely dry, Milt moved his chair a few feet back from the fire. "The lawyers have got a few tricks up their sleeves. Like I told you, we've been advised to make sure that ever'body's got an alibi for the night of the Hollowell raid. You'll understand if I don't tell you ever' last little detail, won't you?" A sly grin accompanied that comment.

"I guess so," I said. I was interested, but decided not to press him. "Let's talk about something more pleasant," I suggested.

His face broke into a wide grin. "All right." he said. "I hear tell that you're gonna be one of the richest men in the county. How do you plan to spend all that money?"

"Damn! Word spreads quick in town, don't it? I only talked to the lawyer this mornin'."

"What's the deal?" He was leaned back and relaxed now.

"I didn't know it, but Lorena had written a will that left all of her worldly possessions to me. So, not only did I inherit an annual income of $4,500 from her trust fund, but sole ownership of the hardware store, too. The store was destroyed, of course, but she'd also purchased an insurance policy on the building as well as the contents. I don't know what the settlement'll be, but I guess I'll get a nice check from them."

"That makes the whole situation a little easier to deal with, I reckon?"

"You know the old sayin' —money won't buy happiness. I guess I'll be able to do as I damn well please, but the money won't help me deal with the grief."

He let that sink in for a moment, then as if to change the subject, he asked, "You gonna stay here?"

A deep sigh escaped my lips. "I don't know, Milt. I'm gonna go to Paducah to attend the trial, if there is one. Then, maybe I'll rebuild the store, maybe... I just don't know. How 'bout you?"

He looked nearly as sad as I felt. "Despite what the lawyers say, myself, I'm scared as hell," he said. Then, managing a wry smile, he continued, "Havin to answer these charges ain't the barrel of monkeys I've been led to believe. Seems to me that it could work out that the United States government will be payin' my rent for a long time."

Chapter 21

Tuesday, April 21, 1908

S trips of white canvas covering tobacco beds bordered nearly every
field I could see from the train window — as sure a sign of spring
in the Black Patch as the proverbial robin. There'd been talk around
Caldwell County that the Silent Brigade was going to send an army of
500 men to Paducah as a show of force. There were plenty of men on
the train I'd seen around, but nothing like the predicted number. Despite the discomfort their presence caused, I felt relief. As soon as the
train left Princeton, I felt as if a great weight had been lifted from my
shoulders. I realized that I'd have to go back to deal with the bank and
insurance company, but I now knew that getting away from that place
would be a good thing for me.

Not much had developed on the legal scene in the last few weeks.
Price Hollowell had filed a suit similar to the ones his parents had
instituted. Price was seeking $25,000, bringing the total of the three
actions to $125,000 — a hell of a lot of money!. From the talk I'd
heard, the night riders still weren't worried. That attitude surprised me
in that they clearly were going to have to appear in court, but they
seemed to think that there was no danger of a judgment against them.
Mr. Miller had decided to have Bob's case come first. His reasons
were a mystery to me — all of the talk and animosity revolved around
Mary Lou. Maybe that was his reason. The Princeton newspaper had
published a statement of support for the defendants, telling what fine,
upstanding citizens they all were and how they were clearly innocent

of the crime. The statement was signed by everybody who was any-body in Caldwell County — the county judge, presidents of both local banks, the mayor, and even two Baptist preachers. In view of the fact that I knew damned well that half of those who signed that document were members of the Silent Brigade, I thought it was more of a farce than people who merely knew those charged were guilty. In fairness, I guess that if I thought I had to stay in Princeton, I'd have signed it too, if they'd asked. Maybe that was another reason I was glad to be out of there.

The trip to Paducah seemed to take forever. I suppose the train was making its regular speed, but we seemed to be crawling. With the trial of the night riders against Bob Hollowell scheduled to begin this morning, tension hung in the air. None of the defendants were aboard, but some of the looks I was getting from the men who knew who I was were quite unsettling. I'd noticed, though, that one didn't hear the phrase "we fear no judge or jury" being repeated very often these days.

At long last the engine whistled for Paducah. Eager to leave the company of the Silent Brigade members on board, I jumped up to be first out the door. As soon as the train slowed sufficiently, I leapt to the platform.

The depot was bedlam. I think most of the people of Kentucky and several surrounding states were milling around the arrival area. To my surprise, the State Guard was also in attendance, quietly standing around to see that order was maintained. Apparently Governor Willson was making good on his promise to put a stop to the lawlessness. I made my way through the pressing throng and headed for Mr. Miller's of-fice. He and two other men were just coming out the door as I ap-proached. They looked neither left nor right, but marched determinedly away. "Mr. Miller," I yelled.

He stopped and turned to look at me. Apprehension turned to re-lief on his face when he recognized me. "Jimmy Singleton, what are you doing in town?"

"Same thing as ever'body else," I laughed, shaking his hand.

"Well, we're on our way to the federal courthouse right now," he said. "Walk along with us." After a few steps, he indicated the younger man by his side. "Have you met my son, John Jr.?"

"No, I haven't," I replied, shaking hands with the handsome young man.

"And this is George Du Relle," Miller said, indicating the distin-guished-looking other man.

"That's a familiar name," I said.

"As well it should be," John Jr. said with a smile. "Mr. Du Relle used to be the chief justice of Kentucky. He's the United States district attorney now, and I'm happy to say, our co-counsel on this case."

"Wow! I'm impressed."

"George has been of invaluable help to us. What's the word from Caldwell County?" Mr. Miller asked.

"I don't know much," I answered. Thinking that it wouldn't be anything he didn't already know, I volunteered, "The night riders all plan to present an alibi."

All three men laughed. "I'm sure they do," Mr. Du Relle said.

We'd reached the court house. "Do you think the Hollowells have a chance?" I asked as we started up the stone steps. The building was surrounded with people in various modes of dress — farmers, blacksmiths, businessmen, and some women. The militia was on watch here, too.

"It's our job to see that they do." He halted at the top of the first flight of steps. Following his lead, we all turned to face the street. In a few minutes, a closed carriage pulled up at the walk below us, the drawn curtains concealing the occupants from view. The door opened and a huge man appeared from within, followed by another. They posted themselves on each side of the door, their eyes darting quickly from one person to another. In another moment, Price Hollowell hopped from the carriage to the ground. Then Bob stepped out and turned to hold Mary Lou's hand as she stepped down. The profusion of noise that had been in the air a moment ago was gone as all heads turned toward the Hollowells. Mr. Miller smiled and waved them up to where we waited.

"My God," I exclaimed, "ain't you afraid they're going to arrest her for the plant bed scrapin'?" I knew that was the plan.

"We've already won that battle," John Jr. laughed. "When they arrived yesterday morning, we called the sheriff and told him that she was waiting in our office if he wanted to talk to her. He was a mite surprised."

"What happened?" I was surprised, too. To notify the sheriff seemed dangerous to me.

"Oh, he showed up right away with a grin on his face and a warrant in his hand. We had all the paperwork prepared and had arranged for a resident of Princeton to be there too. The sheriff served the warrant, and the Princeton man signed the bond." Delight was evident on his face.

"So what does that mean?'

Mr. Du Relle answered. "It means that they can't take her to jail in Princeton as bond has been posted. It also means that these defendants are going to have to answer this charge before she'll have to appear in Caldwell County court — the next session's in June. That gives us plenty of time to try these cases two, or even three times, if necessary."

The Hollowells were at the top of the steps. "What it really means," Mr. Miller added with a smile, "is that all the hopes the defendants had pinned on that trumped-up warrant are gone." I think that the Silent Brigade had figured that if the attempt to haul Mary Lou to Princeton failed, at least she'd have to appear in this case under arrest and guarded. That wasn't going to happen —they might be in more trouble than they thought. I was impressed; John Miller and George Du Relle knew what they were doing

Mary Lou's face lit up when she saw me. She rushed up and hugged me, whispering how glad she was to see me. Dressed in the finest she could purchase, she looked spectacular and didn't seem to have a care in the world. Bob, on the other hand, appeared scared and was deep in thought as we shook hands. Price didn't even look up. "Sorry, to hear about your troubles," Bob said, releasing my hand.

I simply dropped my eyes to the ground — I didn't want to talk about it.

"I was just sick when I heard about Lorena being killed," Mary Lou said. "She was such a lovely young lady and I had high hopes for her future."

A dagger went into my heart at the mention of Lorena's name. I was impressed that Mary Lou would leave her own problem to try to comfort me. "My troubles seem pretty small compared to yours," I commented.

Mary Lou turned her brightest smile on me. "Well, I think we'll all be just fine," she bubbled.

"We'd better get inside," Mr. Du Relle said, moving toward the court house.

"Yes," Mary Lou agreed, falling in step. "After all the trouble we've put them to, we wouldn't want to keep all these fine, upstanding citizens waiting for their just desserts." We all moved through the lines of soldiers posted along the walkway.

You wouldn't have thought so many people could be packed into one court room. People of all descriptions filled the benches, stood in the aisles and blocked the doorways. "Hanging from the rafters," my pa would have said. This trial was without doubt the event of the decade in this neck of the woods. The defendants, all twenty-seven of them, were seated at the front of the room. Predominately farm boys, they presented an uncharacteristic picture dressed in their Sunday-go-to-meeting clothes, faces scrubbed and hair brushed. My bonds of friendship for Milt Oliver were a little strained seeing him sitting up there with the rest of the defendants. Lula Hollowell, the lone female on that side of the aisle, stood out like a sore thumb. In stark contrast to Mary Lou, she was attired in a plain dress and was totally unattractive. Her attitude was totally divergent, also. While Mary Lou sat serenely with a faint smile on her face, Lula's flush cheeks showed her to be as mad as a centipede on a hot rock. When Bob's eyes occasionally met his brother John's, both men looked away quickly. Mr. Miller found me a seat directly behind their table. The third brother, Archer, smiled weakly and waved when I saw him seated a few rows behind me. The strain of this brother-against-brother situation was plainly etched on his face.

The first order of business was to impanel the jury. As each prospect was called, the lawyers for each side would put various queries to him, questioning where he might stand on the night rider troubles. Many were dismissed, and some selected. One such man was W. A. Gresham of Kuttawa. "What do you know about this violence being perpetrated by the night riders?" Miller challenged.

Gresham shifted uncomfortably in his chair. "Nothin' much," he replied.

"You live in Kuttawa?"

"Yes sir." The man was so ill at ease that I actually felt sorry for him.

"Right in the hot bed of the most troubled area of the Black Patch?"

"Uh. I don't know. I guess so." Gresham seemed confused.

"So, your residence is in one of the most troubled areas of the state, you're in daily contact with the people of the region and you know nothing of the lawless activities?" Miller's voice was insistent.

"I just ... well ... I don't know nothin'." Gresham stammered.

Miller retreated to the table. "This man's one of 'em," he said to Mary Lou. "I'm going to dismiss him."

"No," she insisted. "Bob and I have known him for a long time. He's a family friend, and Lord knows we need friends here."

"You saw how nervous he is. I'm sure that the night riders have gotten to him. I say we pass."

"I agree," Mr. Du Relle added.

"Absolutely not!" Mary Lou almost shouted. "I'm the best judge of character here, and it's my life on the line. We need Mr. Gresham."

Turning to the court, Mr. Miller announced, "This man is acceptable," resignation in his voice.

Throughout the remainder of the jury selection process, Mary Lou argued with her attorneys on nearly every point. The vehemence of her disputes made all within hearing wonder why she had bothered to retain counsel. At length, twelve men acceptable to both the defense attorneys and Mary Lou were chosen. Bob sat demurely by as if he was a mere bystander in the process.

With the jury in place, testimony for the plaintiff began. Bob Hollowell was the first on the stand. Prompted to tell his story, he said: "The first I heard of the approach of the mob was the shooting up of the tenant's house on my place. Then the mob moved nearer and I heard someone order them to close in around my house. My wife and I were ordered to come out. We stayed in the house until we heard someone say, 'Bring the coal oil.' When we went out, I saw George Brown and my brother, John, and another man on the porch. All three of them ordered us to go out into the yard. Brown shook his fist in my wife's face and told her that she had been before one grand jury but would never have a chance to go before another. He said, 'The Association came here to win and, by God, it will win.'

"Brown said, 'You have worked against the Association, but you must join it. We will give you one week to join. If you tell who is here tonight, we will kill you.'

"John Gray held a pistol on me while Milt and Wallace Oliver took hold of my arms and dragged me to the wood yard and made me take off my clothing. They kicked me and cursed me and called me a 'plant bed scraper.' They voted to give me 'fifty.'

"Marion Brown and Malachi Pickering whipped me while John Gray held a pistol on me the whole time." Bob's voice cracked with emotion while tears streamed down his cheeks.

"After they all left, we crawled back to the house. My wife and my child and I were sitting on the floor when brother John, the Olivers and Jim Hyde returned and ordered us to leave the country." His flow of tears increased and he concluded, "I begged John to leave us alone." If there were any impartial observers in the court room, they had to be moved by Bob's plight. His appearance was of such helplessness that Miller's reasons for having his case first became clear to me.

Mr. Miller begged the court's indulgence while he paused to give Bob an opportunity to compose himself. When Bob was ready, Miller asked, "Can you identify the assailants?"

Bob seemed to gather a modicum of resolve. Indicating the defendants, he said, "There they are right there."

"All of them?"

"Yes sir, all of those men there." He pointed. "And Lula Hollowell, too."

"No more questions," Miller announced.

The defendants' attorney, Ward Headly, rose from the table and approached the stand. "How do you know these defendants were your assailants?" His voice was booming.

Bob looked surprised. "Why, I saw them," he said.

"Were the men who assaulted you masked?"

"No."

"They wore no disguise of any kind?"

"No."

"Did you not tell Archer Hollowell, George Petty, Lee Robertson, and others that the assailants wore masks and that you did not recognize any of them?"

"Your Honor, we object!" Mr. Du Relle shouted. I remembered that at Archer's house right after it happened, Bob had told me that they were masked.

"Overruled." Judge Evans' voice was stern. "The witness will answer the question," he said to Bob.

"I was still in Caldwell County," Bob mumbled. "I refused to name them for fear I'd be killed."

"Well, then, if they were masked, you wouldn't know who they were, would you?" Headly was smiling.

"They weren't masked," Bob said weakly.

"Then please tell this court why you previously said that they were." His voice was forceful.

Bob heaved a great sigh. "I told you, I was afraid they'd kill me if I made an attempt to identify them," he said softly.

John Miller called Price to the witness stand. Price related the same story his father had told, but the boy's perspective was even more pitiful. He said, "I heard them shootin up Steve's place. We stayed in the house until they called for coal oil and matches. We went out on the porch, Momma leading the way. George Brown, Uncle Johnny and Aunt Lula were on the porch. Some men took Papa away. A man named Jim shot at Momma. Sid Smith kicked her off the porch. I begged them not to shoot her any more. Uncle Johnny grabbed me by the hair and told me that if I screamed anymore, he would cut my throat." I could almost picture the horror that the night had held for him as he attempted to describe his emotions. "Uncle Johnny," sitting directly in front of Price listened with a disinterested expression. Like Bob, Price dissolved into tears by the time he was finished. Using the same technique as before, Miller stalled the court to give Price a chance to gather his wits. "Just two more questions," Miller said, kindness in his voice, "can you identify the persons who did this to your parents?"

"Yes," Price sobbed. "That's them right there." He indicated the defendants.

"You're doing fine, son," Miller said. "Now, did they wear masks or any kind of a disguise?"

"No. They said they wanted us to know who they were."

"Did you ever say that you did not recognize the men?"

"No, I never said that."

"Your witness," Miller said, glaring at the attorneys across the way. Mr. Laffoon whispered something to his partner, Ward Headly. Headly answered him, the passion of their discussion written on his face. After a few moments, Judge Evans boomed, "Mr. Laffoon?" Laffoon whispered one more line to Headly, who nodded. "No questions for this witness," Laffoon announced.

I felt as much relief as Price did. Given our past relationship, I was none too fond of the boy, but my respect for the defense lawyers went up a notch when they decided to let him alone. As Price stepped down, the Hollowells' lawyers were whispering fervently. As close as I was, I couldn't hear what they were discussing. The Judge waited a moment, then said, "Mr. Miller, call your next witness."

Miller stood. "Your Honor, we'd like to recess for dinner."

Evans looked at the defense table. "Mr. Laffoon?"

"We have no objection, Your Honor."

Judge Evans consulted the clock at the back of the room. "This court is in recess until 12:30," he announced with a bang of the gavel.

* * * * *

When we filed back in after eating, Mr. Miller, his son, and Mr. Du Relle were still in the same positions at the table. Apparently they had remained in the court room discussing what they were going to do next. A rap of Judge Evans' gavel broke up their conference and called the court to order.

Mr. Miller stood and called the name of a Mrs. Mitchell of Paducah. An excited ripple went through the crowd as she made her way to the witness chair. When she was seated, Mr. Miller asked, "Do you know the plaintiffs in this case?"

"Yes sir," she replied. "I've known the Hollowells for more than ten years."

"Would you describe their character for the jury, please?"

"They're the finest people in Caldwell County," she said. "Bob Hollowell is a man of the highest order, kind and gentle. He's never offended a house fly. Mrs. Mary Lou Hollowell is one of the leading citizens of Princeton and highly regarded by all who truly know her."

"Do you believe they are telling the truth in this court?"

She moved back in the chair so that her spine was perfectly vertical. "There's not a single question in my mind that they are."

"So you think these defendants are guilty?"

"If the Hollowells say they are the ones, they are the ones." She glared at the defense table.

I heard someone behind me say, "That took a hell of a lot of guts for her to show up here," as Ward Headly rose to cross-examine.

"How long did you say you've known Mrs. Hollowell?"

"Ten years."

"How much of that time has she lived in Princeton?" His tone was challenging.

"The whole time." The witness squirmed in the chair.

"I don't think you understand me," Mr. Headly said. "What I'm asking is does she live in town all the time."

"Well, no," she answered hesitantly. "She just lives in town through the fall and winter."

Headly smiled. "Do you mean to say that she lives in town part of the time and somewhere else part of the time?"

"That's right. She stays out on the farm with her husband in the spring and summer, and in town the rest of the year."

"Well, that's interesting," Headly said rubbing his palms together. "If I understand you correctly, she lives in town without her husband for half the year?"

"She runs a boarding house. And her son goes to the school in town."

"What kind of a woman would you say it takes to forsake her husband for more than half the year?"

"We object!" Mr. Du Relle shouted.

"Overruled," Judge Evans said. "You brought up the character of the plaintiff."

"No more questions for this witness," Mr. Headly said as he retreated. Mr. Du Relle whispered something angrly to Miller.

This same scenario was repeated three more times with two other Princeton ladies and the man who had signed Mary Lou's bond offering testimony in support of the Hollowells' character. Everyone in the court room was impressed with the fortitude they displayed both in even appearing and the way they stood up to the lawyers' questioning. Evidently Mary Lou Hollowell wasn't the only courageous woman in the Black Patch. I know that I wouldn't have wanted to have to return to Princeton if I'd testified against the "upstanding citizens" on trial here. After the fourth witness had been excused, Miller and Headly entered into another whispered discussion at the table. It continued until Judge Evans instructed them to call the next witness. I was surprised that they'd managed to round up the four that had already appeared. The next move was even more surprising.

Rising slowly to his feet , Mr. Miller announced, "We call Mrs. Mary Lou Hollowell to the stand."

Sounds of amazement went through the spectators. "Your Honor, we object to this," Mr. Laffoon yelled above the din.

Judge Evans banged the gavel furiously. "Order in the court!" His booming voice quieted the throng.

On his feet, Mr. Laffoon said, "The gentleman knows that under the Kentucky Code of Practice, Section 606, governing the competency of witnesses, one spouse cannot testify on behalf of the other."

The Judge nodded. "Mr. Miller?"

Mr. Miller stepped forward, his finger stuck in a law book. "We have a precedent here, Your Honor. May we approach?"

Judge Evans waved them to the bench. After a few moments of heated conversation, the lawyers stepped back. "Objection overruled," the Judge announced. "I'm going to allow Mrs. Hollowell to be heard."

Yet another ripple went through the throng as Mary Lou stood. She walked to the witness chair in all her majesty, her beautiful head held high and fire in her eyes. She glared at the defendants as she placed her hand on the Bible and took the oath. Sitting, she turned slightly in the chair and smiled at the men in the jury box. Under Miller's questioning, she told the same tale as Bob and Price had already related, identifying every defendant. Unlike her family, her attitude was defiant.

"Did the assailants wear any kind of mask or disguise?" Miller asked.

"Not of any kind," she declared.

"Are you sure on that point?"

"Of course I'm sure! I was there, wasn't I?" The force of her reply seemed to drive Mr. Miller back a step.

Miller asked a few more questions and then sat down. I thought he looked like he was happy to get away from her. Her look of defiance stiffened as Mr. Headly stood.

"Is it a fact that you live with your husband only half the time?" I was surprised at how soft his voice was.

"I intend for our son to have the finest education he can get," she replied.

"An admirable goal," he said. "But I was asking about your living arrangements."

Her eyes flashed. "And I'm explaining why Price and I live in town part of the time," she spat.

"Very well. It is a fact, then, that you abandon your legal husband while school is in session?"

"I don't abandon anyone. I simply ...."

"Tell us about this house you manage in Princeton." His question cut her off.

"We are objecting to this line of questioning," Mr. Du Relle said.

Judge Evans leaned forward, putting his elbows on the rostrum. "Overruled. Once again, counselor, you opened the gate."

Miller and Du Relle exchanged frustrated glances.

Headly smiled broadly at Mary Lou. "You were about to tell us about this house you run in Princeton." It was the second time he'd used the term "house."

"I managed a boarding house for ladies and gentlemen before I was deprived of home and livelihood by those ruffians," she spewed.

"Are there rumors to the effect that more than room and board could be had at this 'boarding' house?"

"How would I know what rumors people tell?" she exploded.

"Is it not the fact that the attack against you was just simply an attempt by the decent citizens of the county to rid themselves of a woman of your character."

I thought Mary Lou was going to blow a gasket. With controlled rage, she said, "There they sit right there, why don't you ask your clients that question?"

"Rest assured that I intend to do just that," Mr. Headly said, returning to his seat.

"You may step down," Judge Evans said to Mary Lou. I felt pride in her — her head was just as high coming back as it had been going. She'd taken their best shot and came through it unscathed.

After a pause, Judge Evans looked at the lawyers. "Mr. Miller?"

"The plaintiff rests," he announced.

"In that case, court's adjourned until tomorrow morning." The room exploded with conversation as soon as the gavel hit the block. As I walked out of the court house, I was exhausted from the emotional drain. I could only imagine how Mary Lou and Bob and Milt must have felt.

Chapter 22

Wednesday, April 22, 1908

S pectators once again packed every available inch of space in the courtroom as the second day of the trial began. The first day's action was, of course, the topic of every overnight conversation. The consensus of the observers was that things did not look good for the Hollowells. In response to someone's comment at supper that Mr. Miller had rested too soon, I allowed that I could not think of anything else he could have done. The fact that he'd found four witnesses willing to risk all they had — literally, property and life itself — by testifying on their behalf amazed me. You had to figure that the Silent Brigade would exact retribution on them when this thing was over. Most people also seemed to feel that Miller had made a mistake by allowing Mary Lou on the stand, because as the Judge had said, it opened the gate for attacks on her character. I guess those that didn't know her as well as I couldn't understand that no force on heaven or earth would have kept her out of the witness chair.

John Hollowell was the first defendant to testify. Apparently Mr. Headly felt he had a lot of ground to cover today — he didn't waste any time.

"Do you know the plaintiff in this case, Robert Hollowell?"

"He's my brother."

"Is he a resident of the state of Indiana?"

John sighed. "I don't know whether he is or not. The last I heard, he was in Oklahoma."

"Your brother was formerly a resident of Caldwell County, Kentucky?"

"Yes."

"Do you know why he removed to Oklahoma?"

"So his wife would avoid prosecution for scrapin' the plant beds is what I understood."

"Do you have any ill will toward him?"

"Of course not. He's my brother."

"Where were you on the night of May 1 last?" Mr. Headly turned to face Mary Lou.

"I was at home." John's voice betrayed no emotion.

"Was anyone there with you?"

"My wife, Lula was there."

I could see the line of defense was just as Milt had told me to expect. John was attempting to establish an alibi for two of the defendants.

"Did you, by any act, cause any suffering on the part of the plaintiff?"

"No sir, I did not."

"Did you, by any act, cause the plaintiff to abandon his home or forsake his crops?"

"No sir, I did not."

"Did you, alone or with anyone else, shoot into the plaintiff's home or damage his property in any way?"

"No sir, I did not."

"Do you have sufficient knowledge to form a belief as to whether or not the plaintiff, either by loss of property or crops, was damaged in any specific sum of money?"

"No sir, I do not."

"Was the plaintiff forced to sell, or did he sell, any of his property in obedience to threats made by you or anyone else?"

"I know that he sold his property and moved away. I do not know why."

From my position behind Bob and Mary Lou, I could see that John avoided eye contact with either of them. I understood that, as every word he was uttering was a lie. You could almost see steam coming out of Mary Lou's ears. Bob sat stoically while Mr. Miller doodled on a pad.

"Do you know if the plaintiff sold his property at less than the actual worth?"

"I don't know what he got for it. He never said."

"Are you guilty, by any act, of placing the plaintiff in fear of losing his life or any fear at all?"

"No sir. None whatsoever."

"Do you know of any reason why anyone would want to harm your brother?"

"No sir. None whatsoever."

"Thank you, Mr. Hollowell. Your witness," he said nodding to Mr. Miller.

Given that I knew the defendants were all guilty anyway, and that John Hollowell was probably one of the ring leaders, it was perfectly obvious to me that this whole episode was carefully rehearsed. I wondered what the jury thought.

John Miller dropped his pencil and leapt to his feet. Charging toward the witness stand, he asked, "How far do you live from the plaintiff's home?"

"Oh, three hundred yards, maybe." John squirmed in the chair.

"And you say you were home on the night of May 1, 1907?"

"Yes, that 's right."

"Did you hear any shooting?"

John glanced uncertainly at Ruby Laffoon. "Yeah, I guess I did," he answered softly.

"Did you have any idea about what the disturbance was?"

"None at all." That answer was firm.

"Did you go out to see?"

With another glance at the lawyers, he said, "No, I didn't."

"Why not?" Miller demanded.

John twisted uncomfortably in the chair. "Well. uh, I just, that is, we — Lula and I — thought it was probably just some, uh, 'possum hunters."

"Did you suspect that it might be an attack on your brother?"

"Well, I don't know." After a pause, he said, "I suppose it might have crossed my mind."

"Well, then, even the next morning, did you go to see what had happened?"

"No."

"Why not?" Miller's voice became more insistent with each question. He had John twisting on a spit and was not going to let him off.

"Well, uh, I was busy that morning."

"Doing what?"

"It was in the spring of the year. I had to plow my 'baccer patch." Again, John appeared to be ready for that one.

"Did you lead a party of men to your brother's home one night in the fall of 1906?"

"Yeah, I guess I did." His chin dropped to his chest.

"For what purpose?" Miller stepped up to stand right at John's elbow blocking the witness' view of his attorneys.

"To try to talk him into joining the Association." John's answer was barely audible.

"Was any violence done that night?"

"No sir." John's head snapped up to look into Mr. Miller's eyes.

"Did Bob Hollowell join the Association?"

John's head dropped again. "I understand that he did the day after he was attacked." There was no emotion in his voice.

"But you know of no reason why anyone would want to injure the plaintiff?"

"My brother, Bob, is one of the most mild-mannered men in the county. I can't imagine why anyone would want to do him harm."

Mr. Miller stared into John's eyes for a full minute without saying anything. Apparently convinced that he'd made his point, he glanced at the jury, announced, "I'm through with this witness," and sat down.

Mr. Laffoon stood up. "The defense calls Lula Hollowell."

Lula walked slowly to the stand. She was wearing the same plain dress she'd appeared in yesterday. Her hair was clean, but unkempt. Overall, she presented a disheveled appearance. After she took the oath, she fixed Mary Lou with a contemptuous stare. Under Mr. Laffoon's guidance, Lula repeated the story her husband had told, the questions and responses just the same in every detail.

"Do you know the plaintiff's wife, Mary Lou Hollowell?"

"I'm sorry to say that I do," she spat.

"Do you know her well enough to speak to her character?"

Mr. Du Relle jumped up. "We object!"

Judge Evans rocked forward in his chair. "We covered this ground yesterday, counselor. Objection overruled." He nodded to Mr. Laffoon.

"Yes, I most certainly do," Lula said.

"And what would you say is her character?" Ruby Laffoon allowed himself a slight smile.

"She's a slut!" Lula screamed.

"Your Honor!" Miller and Du Relle shouted in unison.

The Judge banged his gavel. "Mr. Laffoon, I suggest that you advise this witness to control her emotions and her language."

"Yes sir," Laffoon said. Then to Lula, "Do you know of any reason why anyone would want to destroy the plaintiff's property?"

"I'd allow that the decent citizens of the county wanted to run the bit..., uh, her off." She glanced quickly at the Judge as she changed her wording.

"You'd say she was a disgrace to the community?"

"And the family, too." She placed great emphasis on those words.

"That's all. Your witness." Mr. Laffoon sat as Mr. Du Relle rose.

"Mrs. Hollowell, aside from the fact that you and the plaintiff are related by marriage, what is the relationship between you?" His voice was kind.

A look of confusion appeared on Lula's face. "I don't understand you," she said.

"I mean what do you think of Robert Hollowell?"

"Bob's a fine man. The only thing I've got against him is that wom...."

Du Relle cut her off. "We'll come to that. In your opinion, would anyone want to injure Robert Hollowell?"

"No. I don't know why anyone would."

"Then you think that the attack on the plaintiff was simply an attack against Mrs. Hollowell?"

"No question." She was adamant.

"Do you, of your own knowledge, know who might have perpetrated the attack?"

Again she looked confused. "You mean shot her?"

"That's close enough." Du Relle smiled.

"Why! It could of been anybody. Nobody likes her but the whoremon..."

"Your Honor!" Du Relle interrupted.

Judge Evans leaned toward the witness chair. "Mrs. Hollowell," he said, "you've been warned to watch your language. Another such outbreak and I'll hold you in contempt." Lula's face turned red as she swallowed hard.

"Given how you feel about your sister-in-law, would you have done this yourself?"

Lula had never impressed me with being too smart, but it appeared that she knew she'd better be careful with her answer to that. She glanced at Mr. Headly while she hesitated.

"Well?" Mr. Du Relle insisted.

Shifting her gaze to the questioner, she said, "I'm not a violent person."

"I think I've heard enough from this witness." Mr. Du Relle walked away.

Lula did not move, but continued to look toward the lawyer. After a few seconds, the Judge leaned toward her. "The witness is excused," he said.

Lula blinked, then apparently came out of the daze. Blushing, she got out of the witness chair and returned to her seat with the defendants.

The spectators were then treated to a parade of the defendants and their alibi witnesses to the stand. Mr. Headly and Mr. Laffoon alternated asking the same series of questions and Mr. Miller and Mr. Du Relle also took turns at cross-examination. Jim Hyde had Doctor Setzler at his house between midnight and 2 AM attending to a case of croup. John Turner had acute indigestion and had Doctor Morril with him from midnight until 3 AM. Buck Tandy's parents heard him going to bed shortly after the clock struck 12 o'clock. Sid Smith's wife and children saw him at home that night. Malachi Pickering was up all night with a sick horse. Through the morning, Wallace Oliver, Joe Murphy, and others droned away with their alibis. After the mid-day break, the trend continued with Urey Lacey, B. Malone, Richard Pool, Otis Smith, Firm Oliver, Bill Larkins, and the rest taking a turn in the witness chair.

Late in the afternoon, Mr. Headly called Milt Oliver's name. Milt stood and walked to the witness stand to be sworn. As he turned to face the gallery, I thought I caught a little wink at me. After he took the oath, Mr. Headly launched into the familiar routine of questions.

"Do you know the plaintiff, Robert Hollowell?" Headly asked.

"Yes sir. Not too well, but I know him."

"What would you say about the character of Mr. Hollowell?"

Milt was ready for this line. "I know him to be a fine man," he replied.

"Do you know of any reason at all why anyone would want to harm Mr. Hollowell?"

"No. None at all. As far as I know, ever'body likes Bob."

"Do you know his wife, Mary Lou?"

"Not as well as I'd like to." He grinned from ear to ear.

"Your witness." He turned Milt over to Mr. Miller.

Miller rose to cross-examine and followed his usual line for a while.

In response to the questions about his whereabouts on May 1, Milt responded that he was helping Teedy Murphy, another defendant, tend to a sick cow.

"What was the matter with the cow?" Miller asked.

"She had, uh, well, I don't know. She was sick, that's all I can tell you." Milt squirmed like most of the others had done.

"You're a tobacco farmer, is that right?"

"That's right, I am."

"Do you own any cows?"

"No."

"Have you ever owned any cows?"

Milt shifted uncomfortably in the chair. "No, can't say that I have."

"What do you know about doctoring cows?"

"Nothin'."

"Well then, why were you helping Mr. Murphy?"

"'Cause he asked me to." Milt seemed pleased with himself for that answer.

"What did you and Mr. Murphy do for the cow?"

"Uh. We, uh, well, we boiled some water on the stove." The laugh that the comment provoked from the gallery said that everyone present knew what was going on.

"This was at Mr. Murphy's home?"

"Yeah. Well, out in the barn." Milt grinned.

"What time did you get there that evening?"

"It was 9:30."

"What time did you leave?"

"Just after 2 AM." He answered the last two questions without a moment's hesitation.

Mr. Miller walked toward the table, then suddenly turned on his heel. "What did you have for supper last Tuesday night?" A hint of a smile glinted at the corner of Miller's mouth.

Milt's face went blank. He hadn't been coached for that question. "Good Lord, I don't know."

"Did you see Teedy Murphy on January 12, 1908?"

"Possibly. I don't know."

"What color shirt did you wear on October 18 ,1907?"

"I don't remember." The confidence Milt had brought to the stand was gone now.

"Would you mind explaining to this court, Mr. Oliver, how it is that you can't remember any details of your life from six months ago or three months ago or even last week but yet can recall your exact whereabouts and companions for a particular evening nearly a year ago?" Miller's voice went up a few decibels on the last phrase.

"Well, uh, I guess ...."

Miller let Milt sit there in silence for a few moments. "Well, never mind, Mr. Oliver. I think the jury knows the answer to that question. You are dismissed."

More of the same filled the rest of the day. By the time the defense rested, more than 65 witnesses had testified and each one had a perfect alibi for the time of the attack. Most of them had also indicated that they believed that whoever had done the dirty deed was out to injure Mary Lou, not Bob.

The jury retired to deliberate. I had not even been able to get out of the room when the foreman walked back into the court. "Your Honor," he addressed the judge, "must our verdict be unanimous?"

"That is correct," Judge Evans replied.

The foreman frowned. He nodded and returned to the jury room.

I wandered outside to await the jury's return. It was a lovely evening; the air was soft and gentle as occurs only in Kentucky and only in the spring. I sat on a bench and inhaled the fragrance wafting from a nearby stand of crab apple trees. Worn out from the strain of the last two days and sitting in the dusk, I closed my eyes and tried to relax. In a little while, I became aware of someone sitting beside me. My eyes popped open wide, fear of the Silent Brigade uppermost in my mind. The handsome young man smiled. "Hope I didn't startle you," he said.

"That's all right," I sighed, rubbing my eyes. "I'm a little jumpy, I guess."

"I suppose we all are." He extended his hand. "I'm Sam Bailey. This is nasty business, isn't it?"

"Jim Singleton," I responded shaking hands. "It's a mess, all right." I noticed that he had a pad of notes under his arm. "Keepin' track of the trial?"

"I'm a newspaper reporter," he said. "Got to have notes to write the story. What's your interest in this case?

"I'm a friend of the Hollowells."

"Is that so? I didn't think they had many friends in town." He pulled a pencil from his vest pocket. "In that case, do you have any observations you'd like to state for the record?"

I decided I'd better see where this Sam Bailey stood. "Have you been there?"

He looked puzzled. "At the trial? Of course, I told you, I'm a reporter."

"Sorry," I said. "I guess I didn't realize that newspaper reporters were normal people."

He laughed. "Normal enough to eat supper. Want to go get a bite?"

* * * * *

Sam told me that his opinion was that the defendants were as guilty as sin, although he wasn't sure he'd report it that way. He said that what he'd write depended on the verdict the jury brought in. It was fully dark now, stars twinkling in the deep blue sky as we walked back toward the court house. I was thinking that I did not understand the newspaper business. Why would what he wrote depend on the outcome of the case? A shout from the court house doorway drew our attention, but we were too far away to hear what he said. We quickened the pace. "Jury's comin' in!" the man repeated as we reached the bottom of the steps.

I rushed up the steps and into the building. The jury was moving back into the box in single file when I regained my seat. Tension was thick in the room as the Judge called the court to order. When everyone was settled, Judge Evans faced the jury. "Mr. Foreman, have you reached a verdict?" His voice was stern.

The foreman stood. "Well, no sir, we ain't," he said.

The Judge looked shocked. "What do you mean?" he boomed, his voice filling every corner of the room.

"We're hung." The man's voice was barely above a whisper.

"Hopelessly deadlocked?" Judge Evans did not look happy.

"Yes. Hopelessly." With that, the foreman sat down and mopped his brow with a bandanna.

Judge Evans released a deep sigh. The defense lawyers were grinning and shaking hands all around. Miller and Du Relle stared at the Judge. "In that case," he began slowly, "I have no choice but to declare a mistrial."

A whoop went up from the defendants. Judge Evans glared at them as he smacked the walnut block with his gavel. "Quiet!" he roared. "I do, however, have some leeway in other matters. For one thing, I'd like to comment for the record that I find it remarkable that twenty-seven defendants, all of whom say they had no idea that they'd ever be sued, and forty-some witnesses can remember each and every detail of what they were doing at 2 AM on a morning nearly a year ago. I never knew, nor imagined, that such a memory existed. If all their testimony is true, their memories so far surpass mine that I am ashamed of it. I'd also like you gentlemen to know that I am personally appalled at your apparent lack of concern for a man who is, by your own admission, a fine citizen and a credit to the county. Although Robert Hollowell is a neighbor of many of you and a relative of some, not one of you offered to lend any aid of any kind to him at any time."

The smiles on the defendants' faces faded. "That said," the Judge continued, swiveling to face the jury, "I usually thank the jury for doing their duty as citizens, but in this case, I cannot do that. If you gentlemen believe the testimony of the defendants and their alibi witnesses, that should settle it — the defendants are not guilty. On the other hand, if you believe their testimony was fabricated, that likewise settles the case — they are guilty. If alibi testimony can be fabricated, it is easier still to fabricate character testimony. But you gentlemen decided neither way. All I can say to you is that you're dismissed." Then turning back to face the defendants, he said, "I hereby declare this case a mistrial and schedule it to be heard again on the eleventh day of May, 1908."

Chapter 23

Wednesday, May 6, 1908

M r. Singleton," the clerk called as I walked through the hotel lobby. "I have a letter here for you." It struck me as interesting how I'd become accustomed to being called "Mister" in two short weeks.

The return address told me that it was the long awaited settlement from the insurance company. I moved away from the clerk's prying eyes and tore the envelope open. Inside was a check for $18,573.06 — the payoff on the hardware store claim and the land sale. My arm trembled as my brain tried to deal with such a sum. Glancing around to see if anyone was watching, I decided I'd better get this money to the bank.

I rushed down the sidewalk, the check burning a hole in my pocket. A sense of relief washed over me after I'd endorsed the check and deposited the money. As I turned to leave the bank, John Miller called to me. I had not talked to him since the trial.

"How you doin'?" I asked.

"Fine," he replied. "You've decided to stay in Paducah, I take it?"

"Until the next trial anyway. After that, I'm not sure what I'll do."

"Well, I'd like to see you stick around," he said with a smile. "I hear you're a wealthy man now and I can always use another rich client."

I realized that he was just joking. "I hope I don't have need of your services, but I'll keep it in mind. Besides, I'd think you'd be pretty busy right along now."

"Yes." He smiled broadly. "Robert Hollowell's case is due next week, you know."

"Yeah, I know. Are you ready?"

He glanced quickly around the lobby. "Let's walk down to my office," he suggested. On the sidewalk, he apparently did not feel free to discuss the case. We chatted about the weather and such until we were behind the closed door of his office. "Judge Evans did us a big favor, you know."

"How's that," I asked, taking a chair across the desk from him.

"By scheduling the hearing for only three weeks from the previous one. He could have put it on the docket for November if he'd wanted to." He leaned back in his chair. "As it is, the Judge ensured that they'd not have time to haul Mrs. Hollowell back to Caldwell County."

"Good God," I exclaimed. "If he'd scheduled it for November, neither she nor Bob would still be alive by the time it came up."

"You're right. And Judge Evans knew that too."

"Where are Bob and Mary Lou?" I asked. Their welfare was constantly in my thoughts.

The smile faded from his face as he leaned toward me. "I know why you're asking, but all I can tell you is that they're safe."

"That's all I was asking," I said. After an uncomfortable pause, I asked, "Are you going to do anything different this time?"

"One thing I've learned in my career, is that if you want different results, you'd better try something different." His smile returned.

"Care to discuss it?"

He moved his chair back and put his feet up on the desk. "I'll damn sure not allow Mary Lou Hollowell on the witness stand again."

I laughed. "You'll play hell keeping her off."

"I'll keep her off if I have to hog-tie her," he laughed. "If she doesn't get on the stand, they won't have an opening to attack her character. That was one of the mistakes I made the first time. I simply will not allow it to happen again." He seemed perfectly at ease.

"One of the mistakes? What else did you do wrong?"

"I allowed her to override my judgment," he said seriously. "Mary Lou Hollowell has a lot of attributes, but being a good judge of character isn't one of them."

I put my elbows on his desk. "What are you talkin' about?"

"That damned Gresham — the one she insisted on including — is the one who hung the jury." He spoke emphatically.

"How do you know that?"

"Some of the jurors told me so, for one thing. One man told me that ten of them were ready to award Mr. Hollowell $40,000 within ten minutes, but that Gresham would not agree. He said that they kept reducing the amount hoping that Gresham would give in, but he wouldn't do it. They finally worked the suggested amount all the way down to $5,000, but it was still no good."

"I guess he was serious," I commented. Then, remembering what Mr. Miller had said, I added, "You said, 'for one thing.' What else did you find out?"

Miller let his feet drop to the floor and stared at me. "Can you keep your mouth shut?"

"If I couldn't, I wouldn't be alive today." I looked directly into his eyes.

Apparently he was impressed with the sincerity of my statement. Wordlessly, he pulled open a desk drawer and handed me a sheet of paper with words typed on it. The letterhead was "Commonwealth of Kentucky, Governor's Office." The letter, dated May 5 and addressed to Mr. Miller, read:

My Dear Sir:

I send you herewith a copy of a communication received by me. It is corroborated in a great many details by information from my secret service. I believe the man is writing the whole truth as far as he knows it. He is not interested in the case and I am not, and I merely send you this for your information. It need not be acknowledged, and it should be carefully guarded to avoid danger to the life of the man who sends it, who does not give me his name, but gives me much useful information. The letter is printed with pencil to avoid detection.

The letter was signed by Augustus E. Willson

"Wow! What does the letter say?"

"It's a long letter," Miller said, pulling several crumpled sheets from his desk drawer. "And it tells a lot. For one thing, it says that Denny Smith, the Commonwealth Attorney over in the Caldwell district is a night rider and assists them in the courts in every way he can." He looked up from the letter to me. "I've suspected that for sometime now." Then returning to the letter, he read, "'Dr. David Amoss led the raid on Hopkinsville and was wounded (by his own men) behind the right ear.' I thought that to be true, also. Now here's something that'll interest you. According to this, Steve Choate, Mary Lou Hollowell's tenant, who was accused of scraping the plants beds while in her employ, was recruited into the Silent Brigade for that single purpose." He looked up at me.

"You mean just to be accused of scrapin' the plant bed so he could say she paid him to do it?" That was incredible.

"Yes. According to this letter, the boys are taking up collections at the meetings to raise money to support Choate's family while he's in prison."

"I didn't know that." I'd said that before I thought about it.

Mr. Miller glared at me. "I take it you did know some of this." He paused and stared at me for a few seconds. Looking directly into my eyes, he asked, "You've been there, haven't you?"

I was flabbergasted. Miller knew more about the whole situation than even I had given him credit for. Trying to return his unblinking gaze, I decided to be honest. "On my bended knee," I said.

"I thought so." He handed me a sheet of the letter. "And finally, there's this. Read the part I've underlined there."

The childishly scrawled pencil writing said, "W. A. Gresham of Kuttawa one of the jurors who tried this case, took the night rider oath ten days before the trial, and promised to hang the jury until hell froze over, regardless of testimony." I handed the sheet back to Mr. Miller.

"So, how much of this can you verify?" he asked.

"I'm not gonna testify," I declared.

"We've already been through that. I don't need you, I just want to know if you know what's true here." He was sincere.

"All right," I sighed. I told him about how they'd caught me under the Nabb school and forced me to join. "Mr. Smith is one of 'em. I've seen him at the meetin's. Doc Amoss is the main night rider, for a fact. He's the man that directs ever'thing. I'd already got away from 'em before the Hopkinsville raid, so I don't know anything about that or him bein' wounded. I learned that this Gresham existed at the same time you did. I never heard of him before." It felt good to admit to all that. Confession is good for the soul.

"Do you have any idea who might have written this letter?"

A *little* confession is good for the soul. I suspected that Milt Oliver probably wrote the letter, and I knew that the Silent Brigade would kill him instantly if they found out. I looked deep into my conscience and lied. "None at all," I said.

"Well, I don't either," he sighed. "It really doesn't matter, though. Enough of what he said is known to be true to do the trick. Armed with this information, I'm ready to go to trial."

"Aside from what I've told you, how do you know all the stuff in that letter is true?" I didn't see how it could be verified.

"There's a couple of reasons. For one thing, it fits exactly with many of the things the Hollowells have told me in confidence. Facts which were not made public on the witness stand nor elsewhere are also told in this letter by one of whom they know nothing. I've not mentioned this letter to the Hollowells. Secondly, the writer says that he writes at the risk of his life but will furnish additional information if the Governor will give him a pardon. Finally, he says, 'I must be protected financially and bodily if the situation should demand it.' I'm convinced that the man's serious."

"I see that it's good to know these things," I said, "but how will it help Bob?"

Miller again leaned back, a satisfied smile on his face. "They're running scared right now, Jim. The first trial convinced them that they are not beyond the reach of the federal court. I'll make damn sure that they do not have any of their members on the jury this time. You heard what Judge Evans said — he left little doubt about how he felt. He even went so far as to say that he'd not allow any man who was a member of any kind of association on the jury this time. With an honest jury, I've got 'em!"

* * * * *

I lay in bed that night thinking over all Mr. Miller and I had talked about. The fact that Gresham had been recruited to hang the jury was not really too surprising. After all, the Silent Brigade had sufficient power to ensure that he'd be called as a prospective juror. All along, I'd been impressed with the intelligent planning and excellent execution of John Miller, but here was evidence of the same level of mentality on the part of some night rider — probably Doc Amoss. Because there was no way he could ensure Gresham's selection to the jury, Amoss must have counted on Mary Lou's obstinacy for that — how ironic that is. The really interesting part of the letter was the stuff about Steve Choate. I knew that being intelligent wasn't a requirement for Silent Brigade membership, but Steve really never did have a clue of what was going on. I suppose they probably explained to him that he'd have to take a little vacation at the state prison and I'm sure they didn't give him too much choice in the matter. I found it incredible that the Silent Brigade would dream up such an elaborate plan just to bring an indictment against Mary Lou. Maybe Lula was behind the whole thing — hell hath no fury and all that.

As I tossed and turned, thoughts of that letter would not let me relax. Governor Willson had said that the party who wrote the letter had no interest in the Hollowell case. If that were true, it wasn't Milt. But how would Willson know? The letter was signed only with a cryptic "S.R." Whoever wrote it certainly was a member of the Silent Brigade.. The secrets and names revealed in the letter left no doubt about that The fact that he wrote the letter demonstrated plenty of courage, too, although not enough to allow him to sign his name. The last thought I remember going through my mind before I went to sleep was, "Who could have written that letter?"

Chapter 24

Monday, May 11, 1908

O nce again, spectators were hanging from the rafters of the court
room. Everybody occupied the same positions as before: Bob,
Mary Lou, Price and their lawyers on one side of the aisle, twenty-
seven defendants and their lawyers gathered on the other. As I made
my way to the seat Mr. Miller had saved for me, I saw many of the men
I'd known from Princeton in attendance, along with plenty of others
who'd "been there." Turning to squeeze between the rows of chairs, a
vaguely familiar man nodded to me. I smiled, not recognizing him
initially. Then I remembered that he was the man Milt had brought to
Smoot's stable; his name was Sanford Hall. Apparently Mr. Miller had
had a serious talk with Mary Lou. She looked fine, but was not dressed
as flashily as the last time, and seemed to be making an attempt to
present a less defiant appearance.

This case began just as before — interviewing prospective jurors.
Any one of them who was from the Black Patch area was dismissed
out-of-hand by Mr. Miller — without consulting Mary Lou. I suppose
Judge Evans had taken a hand in the process as most of the men hailed
from other regions within the western district of Kentucky. When all
was done, six men from the city of Louisville proper and six more
from the same area — more than two hundred miles away — occupied
the jury box. Miller had his lowest jury!

Judge Evans saw fit to lay down some ground rules for the attorneys. He warned the defendants' lawyers that he would tolerate no

such outbursts as Lula Hollowell had exhibited in the previous trial. Then, he informed the plaintiff's attorneys that they would be required to prove that each defendant was an actual participant in the attack. I made a note to ask Mr. Miller why the Judge did that.

As before, Bob Hollowell was first on the stand. It seemed to me that they might as well have had the court recorder read the previous testimony — this was identical in every respect. I could see in the jurors' eyes that Bob's demeanor convinced them that he was a victim.

Mr. Du Relle next called Price to testify. About halfway through his story, a great commotion occurred behind me, drawing everyone's attention. Turning, I saw Sanford Hall making his way toward the front of the court room. Weaving between the spectators, he approached Mr. Miller and whispered something. All eyes in the room were glued on the pair as they conferred. In a moment, Judge Evans said, "Mr. Miller, would you mind telling the court what's going on?" Silence descended on the crowd.

"One moment please, Your Honor," Miller said, returning his attention to Hall. After a few more whispered words, Miller stood to face the judge. "I'm sorry for the interruption, Your Honor. This man here," he said, indicating Hall, "is to be a witness for the plaintiff. I am informed that a detective is in the corridor attempting to execute a Lyon County arrest warrant against Mr. Hall."

"A detective?" Evans roared. "What's the charge against this man?" The defense attorneys, Mr. Headly and Mr. Laffoon, were all smiles.

"I don't know," Miller answered. "I've only just been informed of this development."

"And this man is your witness? Get the detective in here," the Judge demanded. "We'll just get to the bottom of this."

All heads turned toward the doors at the back of the room. A United States marshal opened the doors and escorted in a small, bald man. The man made his way down the aisle and stopped just behind the rail, directly in front of the judge.

"Now then," Evans boomed. "What's your name sir?"

"Will Baker," the man answered nervously.

"All right, Mr. Baker," the Judge said. "What's this all about?"

"I have a warrant executed in Lyon County for the arrest of Sanford Hall."

"What's the charge?" the Judge again demanded.

Baker unfolded the paper clutched in his hand. "Sellin' bootleg whiskey," he read.

"What?" Evans voice filled the room. "Let me see that."

A clerk stepped forward, took the warrant from Baker and handed it up. After reading, Judge Evans fixed Baker with his sternest glare. "This warrant charges Mr. Sanford Hall with selling illegal spirits in Princeton in April, 1906."

Beads of sweat popped out on Baker's bare pate. "Yes sir," he stammered.

"Would you tell me why, more than two years after the fact, you see fit to try to execute the warrant at this particular time.?" The force of his voice was awesome.

"Uh, I just ... I don't know." Mr. Baker obviously wished he was somewhere else. "Your Honor," he stammered, "I wish to state that I've been taken advantage of here. I was only told to serve the warrant and that Mr. Hall could be found around the federal court house. I was not informed that he was a witness in this case."

Judge Evans rose partially from his chair. As he leaned over the rostrum, Baker apparently thought the Judge was coming after him. He retreated a step. "How dare you," Evans roared, "interrupt these proceedings with this petty issue." He waved the paper in the air before his face. "**Get out** of my court room and don't you **dare** show your face here again for **any reason**! Do you **understand** me?" Anger showed in his flushed face. The smiles were gone from the faces of the defense attorneys.

Mr. Baker did not hang around to reply to the Judge's question. The man was short, and the sight of his little legs pumping at a rapid clip was comical although no one dared laugh. Judge Evans resumed his seat and heaved a deep sigh. Glaring at the defense attorneys, he said, "Now, where were we?"

Mr. Du Relle stood and took a moment to settle himself. I thought he was trying to suppress a giggle. He resumed his examination of Price Hollowell. His testimony was also the same as before in every detail. Price's description of the part "Uncle Johnny" and "Aunt Lula" played in the affair once again impressed the jury.

When Price was dismissed, Miller stood. "The plaintiff calls Sanford Hall," he announced in measured tones.

An excited ripple went through the crowd as Sanford made his way to the stand. He stared at the back wall of the room as he took the oath. Seated, he turned his attention to Mr. Miller. After some preliminary questions, Mr. Miller came to why Sanford Hall was here.

"Mr. Hall, please tell this jury if you are a member of the night riders."

Hall's eyes blinked but did not leave Miller's face. "Yes, I am." His voice was barely audible.

Miller turned to face the defendants. "Do you know these men?" he asked.

"Most of 'em."

"Are they also members of the night riders?"

"Yes. Ever' one of 'em." The defendants flinched at that reply.

Miller launched into a series of questions that exposed the very soul of the night rider movement. Hall told of meeting places, secret signals, the oath and passwords. He named names and places, and even revealed that they referred to themselves as "the Silent Brigade." They had few secrets left when Hall finished his tale.

"Now, then, Mr. Hall," Miller intoned. "Do you know if these defendants are guilty of the offense charged here?"

"Objection!" Mr. Headly shouted.

"Overruled!" The Judge's voice equaled Headly's volume.

"Yes sir, I do."

"How do you know?"

Sanford Hall hesitated momentarily, looking at Mr. Miller. "They told me so," he said.

"They told you so? Openly?"

"Yes sir. They bragged about it. They said they 'feared no judge or jury.'"

Miller circled the witness chair. "All of them?"

Hall shifted to face Miller. "All except George Brown — he denied it."

"Did you participate in the Hollowell whipping?"

"No sir," Hall answered quickly. "I was brought into the Silent Brigade after it happened."

"Why did you join?"

For the first time since he'd been on the stand, Hall's eyes moved to the defendants. "They said they'd kill me if I didn't join," he said calmly.

"Do you have any other evidence to give here?"

"Yes sir," Hall answered. "I know they're guilty because I attended a meeting at the Nabb school house when they met with these lawyers to plot their strategy for this case."

"When was this meeting?"

"It was in January." Hall seemed much less nervous now.

"This year, 1908?"

"Yes sir."

"Let the record show that this was before the suit was even filed," Miller said to the Judge. Evans simply nodded.

"And these attorneys representing the defendants here were present at this meeting?"

"Yes sir."

"Please tell the jury what transpired at this meeting."

Hall looked confused. "Huh?"

"Tell these gentlemen what happened."

"Oh. Well, the lawyers told each man that he'd have to come up with an alibi for the night of May 1. They said that ever'body better have a witness to come to a trial in Paducah to swear to where they were that night."

"So they were preparing a defense for a suit which had not yet been instituted?"

"That's as I understood it."

"How did they know an action was forthcoming?"

"They were in touch with some other lawyer — I think his name was Yost — who had passed the word."

Everyone in the room now understood the effort to arrest Hall before he got to the witness stand. The jury was clearly impressed. Sanford's story checked out in every detail, and I think every person in the room knew he was telling the truth. It appeared that this case was over.

"And all of these defendants were present at this meeting in January?"

"Yeah. Ever' one of 'em."

"Your witness," Miller announced, a note of triumph in his voice. He was right — he had 'em!

Headly and Laffoon just stared at each other in silence. You could have heard a pin drop onto a feather pillow. In a minute, Judge Evans said, "Mr. Headly, do you have questions for this witness?" I thought I caught a little satisfaction in the Judge's voice.

"Uh, yes sir," Headly said, standing. "Mr. Hall, you say you, too, are a night rider?" I thought his use of the word "too" was a slip.

"Well, I was," Sanford replied. "I doubt I'm in very good standing now."

"Yes, well. You say that you did not participate in the raid against the Hollowells?"

"If I had, I'd be asittin' out there rather than here," he said waving toward the defendants.

"Did you participate in any of the raids the night riders carried out against the towns?"

"Objection!"

"Sustained." Evans voice was firm.

"But, Your Honor ..." Headly was stuttering.

"The objection is sustained. Move on, counselor."

Headly looked toward the table where his partner, Mr. Laffoon, was drawing figures on a pad. Even I felt a little sympathy for him as he stumbled to find some crack in Sanford Hall's testimony. In the end he failed and gave up.

"The plaintiff rests," Miller said as Sanford Hall walked out of the court room in the company of two U. S. marshals. I hoped they planned to sleep with him — he'd be needing their protection 24 hours a day for the rest of his life.

Judge Evans stalled the proceedings long enough to allow Sanford a chance to clear out and then recessed for the day. What a day it had been!

* * * * *

The city of Paducah was buzzing with talk of the trial. Everyone was in agreement — Mary Lou Hollowell had beaten the night riders! It seemed senseless to point out that this case was on behalf of Bob. The defendants and their lawyers probably spent a restless night. I know I did. I could not see any way they could mount a defense against all what Sanford Hall had revealed, but who knows what kind of tricks they still had up their sleeves?

* * * * *

The answer to that question turned out to be "None." When court resumed on Tuesday morning, the defense jumped right into the same testimony they had previously presented. This time, though, in light of what had happened, it was a more obvious farce than before. Neither the lawyers nor the defendants seemed to have any enthusiasm for what they were saying and the jury appeared to be bored as the parade of witnesses told their lies.

Mr. Miller and Mr. Du Relle pounced on each defendant for cross-examination. As each denied that he had any part in the attack on the Hollowells, the attorney would ask if the witness could speak to the guilt of the other defendants. He said that he could not, except in the cases where one defendant was the alibi for another. Miller and Du

Relle worked like men possessed — they were determined to exhibit the guilt of each man, just as Judge Evans had directed. At length, the defense rested, having presented a very poor case.

Mr. Miller rose to give his closing argument. "Gentlemen of the jury," he began, "the facts of this case have become obvious. We have presented but a small amount of testimony on behalf of the plaintiff, but what damning testimony it is!

"On the other side, the defendants have presented alibi testimony to an excess. I would like to call your attention to the remarkable fact that in this farming community, during the strenuous season, when people work hard through the long days and use, and need to use, the short nights for sleep, people throughout the area should have happened to be awake at precisely the same late hour on that particular night; that seventy of them, a year afterward, many of them with nothing whatsoever to impress it on the mind, could tell just where they were and what they were doing even down to the most trivial particulars.

"Please take note, gentlemen, that each and every one of these defendants happened to be awake in the wee hours of May 1, 1907, and in the company of someone awake like himself, and is able to remember precisely enough to swear that he was not at the scene of the trouble.

"Yet, these people in every part of the neighborhood, on all roads and approaches, some distant and out of hearing of the tumult, others so near as to even hear the voices of the assailants and see the flashes of the firearms, and all wide awake, could tell nothing to show what direction the lawless band came or went. If these witnesses are to be believed, apparently a troop dropped from the sky or rose out of the earth, and with a force of arms and loud tumult destroyed a home, and then as suddenly and mysteriously disappeared, and, apart from the wrecked building and bruised, bleeding victims, left no mark or trace behind."

The defense attorneys struggled —unsuccessfully — to find some way to nullify Sanford Hall's testimony. Their closing argument was weak and pointless.

In his instructions to the jury, even Judge Evans got in on the act, commenting that, "such memory is remarkable and beyond my powers."

When the jury filed out, no one moved. Subdued conversation filled the room for the few minutes the jury deliberated. Silence descended on the room as the jury filed back in. When they'd settled in the box, Judge Evans asked the foreman if they'd reached a decision.

The foreman of the jury stood and faced the judge. "Yes sir, we have. We find for the plaintiff and award damages in the amount of $35,000."

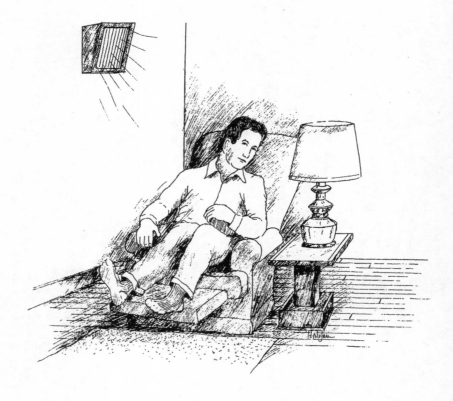

Chapter 25

Monday, April 26, 1965

If I had known I was going to live this long, I'd have taken better care of myself. I just celebrated passing age 75 a few days ago, causing me to reflect on how quickly the years slip away. Sitting here in a LA-Z-BOY in the air conditioned comfort of the suburbs makes those horse-and-buggy days of 1908 seem far, far away. The Black Patch war is just something a few folks read about in history books now. You know how people wonder about things in history books? One time I was talking to my little granddaughter about it when she asked me if it really happened. If she'd been there when the Silent Brigade caught me under that school house, she wouldn't ask such silly things!

I used the money from the Princeton store's insurance settlement to open what proved to be a quite successful chain of hardware stores here in Louisville. Those stores are providing a nice income for my daughter and son-in-law right to this very day. I guess that's one of the reasons they don't complain about me living with them.

All thoughts of the Black Patch war had been far from my mind until this morning when my granddaughter brought me the newspaper, as usual. At my age, reading the paper is one of the few activities I'm allowed. I've tried to tell these big city doctors that .... I digress, that's another story. Anyway, I happened to see an article announcing that Mary Lou Hollowell died yesterday in a Paducah rest home at age 95. She had not crossed my mind in some time and I was surprised, at first, to learn that she was still alive. It soon occurred to me, though, that she'd have to outlive all the others involved in the event just so she'd have the last laugh. And I'll bet she did, too. I'm satisfied that she went to heaven — the devil'll be afraid of her, no doubt.

Yeah, I know, you want to hear the end of the story. When you get to my age, you'll learn not to be in such an all-fired hurry. Well, all right. The perfect Hollywood ending would be to say that the Hollowell case put a stop to the night rider business, but that just ain't the way it happened. Here's what did happen:

Right after Bob got the judgment for $35,000, the boys filed an appeal, but made no real effort to press it. They knew they had no chance with the federal court — John Miller had done his job well and proved each defendant quite guilty — but they still thought they could avoid paying up. Pretty soon, it came to light that every single one of the defendants in that case was flat broke. A few weeks before the trial, they'd been the leading citizens of the county, but then, of a sudden, each one had a mortgage on all property he owned and was destitute. John Miller would have none of that. He sent the U. S. marshal, armed with arrest orders, to explain to them that the judgment did not involve any levy on property, but rather was an order for immediate payment. The marshal gave each one of them the choice of coming up with the money or imprisonment. That got their attention. Right away, their lawyers urgently requested that Miller meet with them in Princeton. He took a train over there and said that he sat in a man's office for a couple of hours while they ignored him — testing his eagerness to settle, he allowed. He hung around until he was fed up, then just went back to Paducah. Laughing, he told me that his telephone was ringing when he got back to the office. They offered to settle for $15,000. I guess Bob Hollowell was eager to get the thing done and the $15,000 was sufficient to pay his legal fees and purchase a better farm than the one he'd been run off of, so he pounced on that offer like a duck on a June bug. So much for his suit.

The actions for Price and Mary Lou were scheduled for the November 1908 term of the Paducah federal court. Before that time came, Governor Willson granted Mary Lou a pardon on the plant bed scraping indictment, killing any hopes the Silent Brigade had on that score, and the tobacco "farmers' friend", Congressman A. O. Stanley, managed to get a bill through Congress that removed a tax on processed tobacco, thus increasing the farmers' profit. With that, the basic purpose of the Silent Brigade was gone. Membership dwindled, most of the night rider violence stopped, and things settled down in the Black Patch. I guess Bob was happy with the settlement, so the other two suits never came to court. I'd love to know how he ever got Mary Lou to agree to that!

The Duke Trust took a mortal blow in November 1908 when the New York Appeals court ruled the American Tobacco Company in violation of the Sherman Anti-Trust Law and ordered that the company be broken up. Although it took a few years and a United States Supreme Court conformation of the ruling, the Black Patch farmers were — at last — out from under the heel of James B. Duke.

I said that the Hollowell case did not end the Silent Brigade, and all by itself, it didn't. But it did open the way for several other victims to follow suit, and they did just that. Over the next two or three years following the judgment for Bob, Doc Amoss and his cronies were up to their ears in court actions filed as a result of the various raids, whippings and such. They came out of the suits all right, but had to pay a bunch of judgments. All the money they had to pay, the breaking up of the Duke Trust, and higher tobacco prices caused most of the Black Patch residents to just lose interest. When they did, the Silent Brigade was dead. It's a comment on the sentiment of the times, though, that some counties in the area allocated tax money to help pay the judgments.

My old buddy Milt Oliver, Sanford Hall and Dr. David Amoss ended up linked together by fate. In March 1910, a Christian County grand jury indicted Doc Amoss and others for the Silent Brigade's raid on Hopkinsville. The indictment was based partially on testimony provided by Milt and Sanford. At the time, I wondered how they got it by Commonwealth Attorney Denny Smith, him being one of them. As the old saying goes, "politics makes strange bedfellows." It seems that Mr. Smith had decided to run for state office and he evidently thought that coming out against the Silent Brigade would help his chances for election, so he went along and decided to prosecute Amoss, the night rider "general."

For some reason, the trial was delayed until March 1911. In the interim, Sanford Hall and Milt Oilver laid low, but Milt didn't lay low enough. He was standing out in his yard one evening watching for Halley's comet (as some writer says, I am not making this up!) when a shotgun blast knocked him to the ground. Although seriously wounded, he survived. When he first became involved, Milt had refused militia protection — said he could look after himself. After he got shot, he changed his mind. From then until after Doc Amoss' trial, armed militiamen accompanied him everywhere he went.

The Silent Brigade looked high and low for Sanford Hall, and I'm satisfied that he'd have been dead within a minute if they'd found him. On the basis of a rumor that had him here in Louisville, a hundred or so of the boys came to the house where Hall was reportedly living. Not finding him, they returned to the Black Patch and took out their frustrations on his brother, Herbert. Some say that Herbert ended up at the bottom of a well with a stone tied around his neck, others say he was simply ambushed. Whichever way it was, they certainly got him. Later, a crude mail bomb was sent to Sanford via the Paducah post office. Fortunately for him, he did not pick it up, and it ended up in a postal warehouse where it was disarmed without mishap.

When the trial date rolled around in March 1911, both Oliver and Hall showed up to testify against the Silent Brigade and Doc Amoss. Each of these two, and others, told of their involvement in the night rider movement in general and the Hopkinsville raid in particular. Denny Smith made a pretty good case for the state, showing Amoss to be the organizer and leader, but Doc Amoss made a good case, too. Like I've told you, he was a smart man. The defense made out Milt and especially Sanford to be pretty shady characters, bringing up the bootlegging charges. It was interesting to note that the prosecution had witnesses of questionable character telling the truth while the defense had impeccable witnesses lying through their teeth. The jury went with the upstanding citizens — Doc Amoss was acquitted. With his followers all gone and him off the legal hook, the Black Patch War was officially over. So, by the way, was Denny Smith's political career, but that, too, is another story.

Some say that Sanford Hall lived out his days in Louisville. Miller said that he thought Sanford joined the U. S. Army under an assumed name. Whatever it was, he disappeared from the area. I don't know what ever became of Milt. The last time I was in Princeton, closing out my bank account, I happened to meet him on the street. He didn't look happy, but I guess he'd managed to retain a sense of humor. In response to my question about what he'd been doing, he said, "Plowin' corn for Mary Lou." I reckon most of the defendants were doing the same: it'd take a lot of corn to pay off the $15,000! I thought that comment was a tribute to her — it was Bob's judgment they were paying.

Yeah, I know. You want to know who wrote that letter telling Governor Willson the night rider story. John Miller said that he never did find out, but I don't believe him. Over the last fifty years, historians have analyzed the whole night rider situation to death and figured out about that letter. It seems as how on May 11, 1908 — the very day of Bob's second trial — Sanford Hall was indicted by a Lyon County grand jury on four counts of bootlegging. In August, Denny Smith announced that he was ready to prosecute Hall and scheduled a trial. On the given day, Sanford Hall was absent, so Smith asked that a warrant be issued for his arrest. At that point, the county attorney stepped up and handed the judge a pardon for Hall signed by Governor Augustus Willson. This makes it evident that Sanford Hall had agreed to betray his night rider oath, wrote the letter to Willson, and testified in Bob's and other trials, in exchange for the pardon for the Lyon County charges. That's the historical fact. You'll never convince me that even if someone didn't tell him, Miller wasn't savvy enough to have known about it.

I've spent a lot of time wondering about the cryptic signature "S. R." on that letter. Ideas like "Silent," "Sanford," and "Secret" come to mind for the "S," but "Rider" is about all I could ever come up with for the "R." I guess what the writer had in mind is one of those things we'll just never know.

Me? Well, I never did find out who burned down the store in Princeton. The state fire marshal investigated and found no trace of arson. What a surprise that was! It could well be that the Silent Brigade was trying to make sure that I didn't testify against them, or it could have been an accident. I prefer to think the latter. Anyway, in 1912, I married a pretty little girl named Jessica who was the bookkeeper for my stores. We only had the one daughter before Jessica died and after that, I didn't have much time for anything, what with a child to raise and the business and all. Like I said, all this was far from my mind until the article about Mary Lou in this morning's paper brought back a flood of memories; some happy, many painful. After I read it, I just sat in my chair for several hours, reliving old times. I guess I was half asleep and dreaming when I called out "Lorena."

"What is it?" my daughter answered from the kitchen. I hate all these new-fangled "conveniences," especially that damned intercom system.

BIBLIOGRAPHY

Campbell, Tracy *The Politics of Despair* Lexington: University
of Kentucky Press, 1993

Clark, Thomas D. *A history of Kentucky* Lexington: John
Bradford Press, 1950

Cunningham, Bill *On Bended Knees* Nashville: McClanahan
Publishers, 1983

Kroll, Harry H. *Riders in the Night* Philadelphia: University of
Pennsylvania Press, 1965

Miller, John G. *The Black Patch War* Chapel Hill: University
of North Carolina Press, 1936

Nall, James O. *The Tobacco Night Riders of Kentucky and
Tennessee* New York: The Standard Press, 1939

The Courier Journal, Louisville: Various issues from April 1906
through June 1908

The Paducah Sun. Paducah: Various issues from April 1906
through June 1908

United States vs. Hollowell, et al Trial transcript and records
from Civil Docket No 1877, Western District of
Kentucky, 1908

Wilson, Samuel M. *History of Kentucky*, Louisville: S.J.
Clarke Company, 1928

ABOUT THE ILLUSTRATOR

The beautiful illustrations in this book were produced by Mr. Harold W. McLaren of Stanford, Kentucky. A graduate of Eastern Kentucky University, Mr. McLaren has been an educator for more than thirty years and is currently assistant principal at Mercer County High School. Mr. McLaren's art works, many featuring historic locations, are prominently displayed throughout Central Kentucky. In addition to being a talented artist, he is an outstanding educator and administrator, community leader, husband father and friend.

Printed in the USA
CPSIA information can be obtained
at www.ICGtesting.com
JSHW022322140824
68134JS00019B/1249

9 781681 622279